STORM'S WRATH

AMELIA STORM SERIES: BOOK FIVE

MARY STONE
AMY WILSON

Copyright © 2021 by Mary Stone

All rights reserved.

No part of this book may be reproduced in any form or by any electronic or mechanical means, including information storage and retrieval systems, without written permission from the author, except for the use of brief quotations in a book review.

❦ Created with Vellum

Mary Stone
*To my readers, who are the best ever. You mean the world to me.
Thank you from the bottom of my grateful heart.*

Amy Wilson
*To my one and only, my husband and best friend, and the best boys
a mother could dream of, who all worked with me to make this
story possible.*

DESCRIPTION

Hell hath no wrath like a woman scorned...or determined to stop a killer.

Several weeks after being set up for a crime she didn't commit and almost being killed by a fellow FBI agent in the process, Amelia Storm is ready for a new assignment. But nothing could have prepared her for what lies ahead—a spate of brutal killings so unusual the Organized Crime agent and her partner have no choice but to team up with members of Violent Crimes.

When three dismembered bodies are discovered, all evidence points to a madman...especially when a nineteen-year-old goes missing. There's something more to the case, though. A father. A child. Scattered body parts.

Is a serial killer on the loose? Or something worse?

From the wickedly dark minds of Mary Stone and Amy Wilson comes Storm's Wrath, book five of the Amelia Storm Series. Be careful, though. You may never drive at night again.

1

Returning the fuel pump to its holder, Willow Nowland gave her midnight blue Honda Civic a pat. She and the car had been through more than their fair share of changes since she started college a year and a half earlier. This semester had been especially trying, but Willow pushed the thoughts from her mind. She was headed home for Thanksgiving break, and she had so much to be grateful for.

"Home." She'd even been able to leave campus earlier than expected. Instead of a few days, she'd be home for a full week. She smiled, twisting the Honda's gas cap shut, then jumped when the sound of a dog barking broke through the silence.

She glanced around. A black sedan was parked at a fuel pump catty-corner to her, but other than an employee's truck, there were no other vehicles present. Or humans. Or dogs that she could see.

Willow rubbed her upper arms to dispatch the unexplained sense of unease spreading across her nerves. She was just being silly. After spending the last few months on the perpetually active campus of Breely University in Peabody,

Illinois, the sight of such a sparsely populated gas station was unnerving.

She reminded herself this wasn't Peabody. She'd made a pit stop in Cedarwood, and she shouldn't expect a convenience store in a small town to be bustling at nine o'clock on a Sunday night.

And Willow would know. She'd grown up in Mendoza, Illinois, which boasted a population only slightly more than Cedarwood.

Creepy or not, the absence of other patrons was normal.

I'm just being paranoid.

Her car had been acting up lately, but she didn't trust the mechanics in her college town. She'd much rather take her beloved Civic to a shop whose owner she knew. And with a population of a little more than seven thousand, Mendoza was one of those places where everyone knew everyone else.

As much as Willow had hated the town's lack of entertainment during her high school years, and as much as her mother used to complain about the neighbors always knowing their family's business, there was a distinct comradery that came with being part of such a small community.

The mechanics in Peabody wouldn't hesitate to rip her off, but a similar shop in Mendoza? Since everyone knew each other, a mechanic in her town would go out of business as word traveled like lightning down an electrical wire that the mechanic was untrustworthy.

She cringed at the crack in her windshield. She'd only noticed the mark a week earlier. *One more thing to fix.* To her dismay, a year and a half's worth of engineering classes didn't mean she could fix her own car.

It's okay. I'll get you into George's shop tomorrow, and you'll be all fixed up before Thanksgiving. We just have to make it home. You can do it.

Satisfied with her mental reassurance to the car, Willow headed inside the well-lit convenience store, smiling at the "The closer you get, the slower I drive" bumper sticker on the back of the black sedan. She could imagine enraged tailgaters getting even angrier at the sight of the admonition.

Fishing her wallet from the kangaroo pocket of her hoodie, Willow shouldered open the glass doors. A rush of warm air and the faint scent of roasting hot dogs rushed up to greet her like an old friend and chased the remaining unease from her mind.

She was at a gas station in a small town less than an hour from home. The clerk behind the counter was a normal guy around Willow's age, not a greasy psychopath in faded clown makeup.

As she tucked her wallet under one arm, Willow picked out one of the coffee energy drinks she'd grown to love and rely on over the course of her third semester at Breely University.

She'd always had a knack for mathematics, but Breely's undergraduate program for industrial engineering was no joke. While most of her friends had enough free time to attend parties and other social gatherings, Willow was stuck in her dorm room with her nose in her laptop.

The hard work had paid off, though. Her grade point average was only a hair below a perfect four-point-oh, and she'd been on the Dean's List every semester. She'd completed her remaining assignments earlier that day, and she was free and clear to kick back and enjoy the holiday break with her parents and her three brothers.

Willow strolled absentmindedly to the front of the store to wait behind the man at the counter ahead of her. At his side, a girl no older than seven or eight fidgeted with the glittery skirt sticking out from beneath her puffy orange and pink coat. Her cheeks were smudged with the same silvery sparkles as her dress, and a matching headband held stray hair out of her face.

Willow barely kept herself from cooing at the adorable sight. As the only girl of four kids, Willow had always been defensive of her obsession with all things sparkly and glamorous. Any time she saw a younger girl decked out in a glitzy outfit, she was compelled to offer some form of encouragement—the same sense of positivity she'd lacked when she was a kid.

As the girl's large blue eyes shifted to her, Willow offered a wide smile.

"I like your dress." Willow patted her own cheeks. "And your sparkles. I *love* glitter."

The girl beamed. "Me too. I just got done with a dance." She paused for a quick twirl.

Willow's face ached from her grin, and her heart overflowed from the cuteness. "That sounds fun. I like to dance too. When I was little, I always wanted to be a ballerina."

The girl's attention perked up. "My mom and dad said I can start ballet next year. I have to be eight to take lessons. Mom says it's because we live in a small town, so there aren't very many teachers. Do you live in Cedarwood too?"

"No, I don't. I'm from Mendoza, which is about an hour away. I'm going there to visit my family for Thanksgiving."

"Oh, I love Thanksgiving!" She glanced up to her father as she tugged on the edge of his canvas jacket. "Dad, Dad, are we going to have apple pie for Thanksgiving?"

"We sure are, sweetie." Tucking a wallet into his back pocket, the girl's father scooped a couple candy bars off the counter.

A grin split the little girl's face, and Willow found her enthusiasm contagious. "Awesome! I love apple pie. I hope I get a whole pie to myself."

The father chuckled as he held out a hand to his daughter.

"Let's not get ahead of ourselves, kiddo. Come on. It's getting late, and I promised we'd go for a drive before we go home."

Willow set her chips and drink on the laminate counter before waving to the pair. The girl was sweet and reminded her of a time that seemed a lifetime ago. "Have a good night."

The girl's smile widened as she waved. "You too. Byyyy-eeeee." She dragged out the last word until the door closed off the sound.

After Willow paid for her items, made her way back to her treasured Honda, and fastened her seat belt, the child's cheery disposition still warmed Willow.

Willow patted the dashboard as she slid the key into the ignition. "Okay, just a little while longer. You can do this. We can do this."

The engine hummed to life without hesitation. She hadn't had any issues *starting* the car, but she'd noticed a spike in the normally stable temperature gauge, as well as sluggish acceleration over the past couple weeks.

All she could do now was hope the repairs wouldn't cost an arm and a leg.

Before merging onto the road, she pulled out her cell and texted her brother. *Just got gas and a drink. Headed out of Cedarwood now.*

Her family had expressed some concern at her driving all the way from Peabody alone, but in her typical fashion, Willow had dismissed their worries. She'd been living away from home for a year and a half. Besides, how else was she supposed to get her car to a hometown mechanic? It just made sense to drive home.

To appease their worry, she'd promised to stay off the interstate and stick to the state highways. With the issues her car had been having, she wasn't sure it would handle the higher speeds of the interstate. Besides, going slower on the interstate was probably more dangerous than driving the backroads home. She didn't need some trucker riding her bumper or blowing by her in a fit of impatience.

"We'll make it. Won't we, Car?" Though many of her friends had given their vehicles pet names, Willow hadn't yet found a title that seemed to fit the little Civic.

Maybe she could come up with one on the final leg of her trip north.

She chuckled to herself and cracked open the coffee drink. After a long swig, she placed the can in the cup holder and shifted the car into gear, easing it out onto the road for the remaining drive home.

One hour, maybe a little less, and I'll be sitting at the kitchen table eating my way through the pantry.

On cue, her stomach grumbled. Real food was a precious commodity for broke college kids, and she fully intended to stuff herself full of tasty treats over the next few days, waistline be damned. She could hit the gym when she was back in Peabody, but for now, she was on vacation.

Everyone knows the calories consumed on vacation don't count. Willow smirked at her flawed logic.

As the drum beat to the fourth song on the playlist pounded through the speakers, Willow caught a glimmer of light on the side of the road ahead. Willow recognized a pair of hazard lights when she saw them.

"Shit." Flicking off her high beams, she eased her foot off the gas.

It's a stranger in the middle of nowhere.

"Yeah, but they might need help." She felt stupid responding to herself. The speed limit was only fifty-five, and though she'd slowed down to below fifty already, she was approaching the stranded motorist quickly.

She ran through her options.

First, she could continue driving as if she hadn't seen a thing. She could cruise off into the moonless night, and no one would have the first clue she'd ignored a person in need of help.

Well, no one other than the driver of the other car…and herself.

Biting her bottom lip, Willow tightened her grip on the steering wheel.

Her second choice was to stop. On the side of a rural Illinois highway without even the light of the moon to accompany her…

Wasn't this how most horror movies started?

Probably. Naïve college kid pulls over to help a person in need, gets knocked unconscious and then dragged off to be used as a sacrifice in a ritual to summon a demon that fed on the souls of innocents.

"Don't be ridiculous," she chided herself.

She wasn't in a Wes Craven film. Freddy Krueger wasn't driving the car on the side of the highway, and no one was waiting for the blood of a nineteen-year-old woman to unleash the fires of hell.

She groaned at the indecision. Her parents had raised her to be decent and well-mannered. What would her mother say if Willow told her she'd ignored a person in need of help just because she was paranoid?

Not to mention the karmic aspect of the decision to abandon the driver. Willow's Honda was on the fritz, and it would be just her luck to pass by the stranded motorist only to have her own car break down a few miles later. She'd always been a firm believer that what "comes around goes around," and that those who remained willfully ignorant of the plight of others would get what was headed their way.

Guilt sawed at Willow's heart.

"Fine."

In a different part of the country, she could have justified continuing down the highway. But she'd been born and raised in a small town less than forty-five minutes north of here.

One of her high school friends had moved to Cedarwood after graduation, and Willow had driven the route to and from Mendoza to visit her whenever she could. She might not have been in Mendoza yet, but she *was* home.

As a sense of renewed confidence pulsed through her veins, Willow sat a little straighter and tapped the brake pedal. She double-checked the rearview mirror to ensure there were no surprise vehicles at her back, and the Honda's headlights gradually drifted over to the bumper of a black car.

She blinked in surprise. "The closer you get, the slower I drive."

The man and his glittery daughter.

Willow pictured the girl's big smile, and she worried about her being stranded on the side of the road when she should be home in bed with her comfy pajamas and a beloved stuffed animal by her side.

She'd be fine. And maybe, just *maybe*, karma would smile on her, and she wouldn't be stuck paying for a costly car repair of her own.

Slowly, Willow rolled to a stop behind the car, its flashing hazard lights making her squint.

She patted the dashboard. "Sorry, Car. We've got to help these folks out, then we'll be on the home stretch for real."

Before killing the engine, Willow retrieved her phone and composed a short text to advise her brother that she'd stopped to help a man and his daughter.

If she hadn't added the "and his daughter" to the text, she'd likely have received an angry call within minutes. Her brothers were all protective of their sister.

Willow tucked the phone in her pocket and eased open

the driver's side door. At the same time, the man stepped out into the night.

Chilly November air greeted her, and Willow clenched her jaw to keep her teeth from chattering at the sudden drop in temperature.

Forcing a smile to her lips, she waved to the man before she took her first few steps. "Hello again. Car trouble?"

He raked a hand through his gray-tinged hair and groaned, exasperation mixed with embarrassment. "Yeah. Wouldn't have figured with a car this dang new, but then again, I've never really been a car guy."

Willow laughed. The faint hint of anxiety in his voice reassured her that he was a real person and not some deranged sociopath. "I'm not much of a car gal myself, but I'm sure we can put our heads together."

"I sure hope so. I think it's just the battery. I pulled over to take a call from my wife." He scratched the back of his neck. "My, um, my brother got in an accident and almost died a few years ago. The other driver was talking on the phone and wasn't paying attention to the road, so ever since then, I've always pulled over when I need to take a call."

"That's totally understandable." Willow's voice sobered a notch. "I'm Willow, by the way."

The man's mouth quirked into a smile, and he extended a hand. "Nice to meet you, Willow. And thank you for stopping. I'm Dan."

As she closed the distance between them, Willow caught a glimpse of the little girl in the back seat. With her head propped against the doorframe, the glitter-coated child was fast asleep.

Willow accepted Dan's handshake. "Well, like I said, I'm no expert, but we can give the battery a shot of juice." She jerked a thumb over her shoulder. "Let me grab my cables, and you can start hooking them up while I pull around?"

He rubbed his hands together and blew on them for warmth. "Sounds good. I'll pop the hood."

Judging by how he shifted his weight from one foot to the other, Dan was just as eager to get off the side of the highway as Willow. They had a common goal, and fortunately, Willow had experience jump-starting cars.

She pulled open the driver's side door and leaned across the seat to press the trunk button on the key fob.

Nothing.

Pressing her lips together, she hit the button a second time and then a third. Nothing, and then…nothing.

"Dammit," she muttered to herself. The trunk release lever next to the driver's door had been broken since she'd bought the Honda.

With a sigh, she pulled the key from the ignition and straightened. The batteries in the fob had begun to run low, and she hadn't yet remembered to search for a replacement.

Add that to the list of car stuff I have to deal with this week.

Whatever. She'd replace a hundred fob batteries if it meant she didn't have to worry about major car repairs.

Gravel crunched beneath her Converse as she circled around to the back of the Honda. Humming quietly to herself, she jabbed her keys into the trunk's lock.

Crack.

She whirled at the faint sound on her right, peering down the steep, grassy slope that ended in a half-frozen ravine dotted with cattails and weeds. Not that she could see the vegetation, but she knew the plants were there.

Only now, something else was there too.

A deer? Raccoon? Or a coyote? Or is it…

"Stop it," she scolded herself and faced the trunk again, finished turning the key.

Crack.

Her mouth lost all moisture as a snippet of information

she'd learned from a crime show she'd binged popped into her mind. She didn't remember all the technicalities, but she'd basically learned that a person's peripheral vision had adapted through evolution to allow it to sense danger.

Danger? Here?

She was sure she was overreacting. She *had* to be overreacting. Chances were the scuffle in the weeds was just a deer or even a smaller animal like a raccoon or a cat.

But still…

The hazard lights of her and Dan's cars were virtually the only source of illumination, and they were pointed in the wrong direction. No matter how hard she strained to see movement from the corner of her eye, she couldn't bring herself to face the intruder. Fear had rooted her to the spot.

All she caught was more of the night's ubiquitous darkness.

You're not worried about an animal. You know what you're worried about. You're worried that man is going to try to sneak up on you—

She silenced the paranoid musing.

If she didn't fish out those jumper cables and head back to Dan's car, the man would start to wonder if *she* was the psychopath.

Still…something was wrong. The churning bile had knotted her stomach, and she suspected the unsettling sensation was there to stay. The clamor of her heart against her ribs was like the persistent knock of a door-to-door salesman desperate to meet his daily commission quota.

Crack.

Refusing to be afraid this time, she turned to face the direction where the disturbance had originated. Just in time to meet the yellowish glow of a pair of iridescent eyes.

With a yelp of surprise, Willow jumped back a step. Resting a hand over her pounding heart, she bit off a slew of four-letter words as the grass rustled and the eyes disappeared.

Based on the chatter that followed the movement, she'd just been scared to the point of a coronary event by a raccoon.

Little bastard.

As she blew out a sigh and reached for her cell, a shoe scuffed against the concrete.

Had she not just emptied her entire adrenaline reserve on a relatively harmless woodland critter, she'd have damn near leapt out of her skin at the newest noise.

Willow pivoted to face the sound of the man's footsteps.

"Is everything okay?"

She was right. Dan *had* come over to her.

Laughing at herself, Willow nearly slumped against her trunk in relief…until she looked into his face.

Evil.

It was the only word her stricken mind could think of.

As the man arched one arm back, the eerie golden glow of the hazard lights caught the stainless-steel bar in his grasp.

A tire iron.

Willow had only a fraction of a second to react, and all she could do was open her mouth.

The building scream never left her lips.

With another kind of *crack*, the tool collided with the side of her head, and pain exploded outward from the site of the blow.

No!

Though she wanted to run, her knees buckled, and her head slammed into something just as hard as the tire iron just before her world went dark.

※

Cold concrete and the faint scent of mildew greeted Willow as she drifted back to the world of the waking. At least, she thought she was awake. But when she blinked to clear the film from her vision, all she could make out was more darkness and a throbbing pain in her head.

A surge of panic pulsed through her veins. Why couldn't she see? Why wouldn't her damn eyes work?

Taking in a sharp breath, she finally noticed the vague outline of her confines. She wasn't blind. She was in the dark.

Her head was filled with cobwebs, and her mouth felt like it'd been stuffed with dirty cotton balls. The taste on her tongue was foul, and though she wanted to try to spit out the bitterness, she couldn't summon so much as a semblance of moisture to her lips.

What the hell had happened? Where was she? How did she get here?

All she could remember was the blink of the Honda's hazard lights, that damned raccoon, and…

The tire iron.

No. That wasn't real. She'd pulled over to help a stranded father and his daughter. She'd introduced herself, and the man had told her his name was Dan. She must have smacked her head somewhere else and had imagined the surprise attack, hadn't she?

Squeezing her eyes closed, she started to lift a hand to touch the source of the pronounced ache above her temple. As she moved, metal clinked against the floor, but she wasn't sure why. Not until the edge of a shackle dug into her wrist.

The chains rattled as she sucked in a sharp breath and sat bolt upright.

Chains. She was *chained*. To what? She couldn't see anything in this…room. This cell. This…wherever in the hell she was.

Willow swallowed the sting of bile threatening to climb up the back of her throat. She couldn't be sick now. She needed to *think*.

The kind father of the glittery little girl had snuck up behind her while she was busy retrieving cables from the trunk of her car, and he'd hit her on the side of the head with a tire iron...once? Twice? Her head ached all over, so it was hard to tell.

The series of events was blurry, but she could still recall the glint of that heavy tool with crystal clarity. Almost as if her subconscious had realized the significance of the item and had highlighted it before her conscious mind could place the danger.

Biting down on her lower lip to stifle a whimper, Willow again lifted a trembling hand to touch her temple. She half-expected to be greeted with the sticky warmth of blood, but she noticed no such wound. Just a lump.

As she pressed on the injury, pain lanced through her skull. Tears burned at the corners of her eyes, and she used every ounce of mental fortitude to keep the display of weakness at bay.

No wonder she was confused. More than likely, she'd sustained a concussion.

Along the back of her scalp, though, her fingers touched something sticky. Blood.

I don't have time to coddle myself. I need to think.

Dan had hit her, and then...he must have taken her. Where? And...how? How had no one driven by to see him loading her unconscious body into his car?

She knew the answer. No one had seen him because no one had passed their stopped vehicles.

Not that the "how" or the "why" mattered now.

Focus.

Heart thundering in her chest as if it sought its own freedom, Willow patted her Breely University hoodie and then her jeans.

Nothing. He'd even taken the spare key she'd tucked in her back pocket.

Like the gaping maw of a house-sized beast, another wave of helplessness threatened to swallow her whole. As she pulled both knees to her chest, she almost gave herself over to the bout of panic.

No. Stop it. You might have a concussion. You need to stay on track.

Fighting against the chains restraining her hands, she awkwardly wiped at the corners of her eyes and sniffled. In the event she was in an accident or became lost in a wooded area, her father had always told her the most important first step was to get her bearings. There wasn't much she could do to get to safety if she didn't know where the hell she was.

Replaying her father's words in her head gave her a renewed sense of purpose. Find out what's happening and go from there.

She brushed her fingertips along the sturdy length of chain that bound the shackle of her wrists together. Her vision had adjusted as much as she could expect, but even so, she could hardly make out the shape of her own damn hands.

As she tugged on the heavy-duty chain, she followed the length to its point of origin.

A cement wall—rougher than the smooth concrete of the floor but still well-constructed. Wherever she was, the place wasn't old or decrepit, though the musty scent made her think that she might be underground.

As she started to grope along the solid wall, a quiet click echoed throughout the space. Willow ripped her attention away from the wall as a new rush of ice-cold fear surged through her tired body.

The sliver of light that fell through the crack in the door

was muted, but she might as well have been staring at an exploding star. With a creak, the slat of illumination grew until she was forced to block the hellish glow with an upraised hand.

This is it. The door is open. Do *something.*

She licked her dry lips. She had no earthly idea what could have lingered on the outside of this abysmal pit, but the prospect wasn't any worse than the idea of rotting in the dark.

"I know you're about to scream for help."

Dan's voice had been normal, even warm when she'd encountered him and his daughter at the gas station. Now, his words were as cold as the vacuum of space. The hairs on her neck spiked like the quills on a porcupine.

From beyond her hand, Willow noted a faint movement as Dan flicked a switch to bathe the space in harsh fluorescence. "You can scream if you want. If you think it'll make you feel better. But I can tell you right now that—"

"Help!" She belted out the word with as much force as she could muster, and she dragged one syllable out for six. Though the overhead light stung Willow's retinas like a thousand tiny needles, she forced aside the discomfort as she blinked repeatedly. "Please, can anyone hear me? Help! I've been kidnapped, please! Someone! Anyone!"

She scooted a little closer to the doorway, though she'd still not risen to her feet. With the monster so close, she suspected she was better off on the floor and out of his immediate grasp.

As she finally opened her eyes enough to make out the shape of the man, he crossed his arms, his stare flat. "Like I was saying. You can scream if it'll make you feel better, but *no one* will ever hear you. You're under eight feet of dirt and a solid nine inches of concrete."

Willow opened and closed her mouth in disbelief, but the

only sound that left her lips was a pitiable squeak. How could this man remain so calm and composed?

She considered shouting for help again, but Dan's stony countenance dissuaded her.

"Who are you?" she croaked out instead. Her head ached worse than before, and she fought to stay conscious.

"Are you done screaming?" A flicker of annoyance crossed his face—a normal face. The face of a parent, a neighbor, a friend...

A father.

Willow squared her jaw, planted both hands on the smooth concrete floor, and prepared to stand. Dan towered over her seated position, and she wanted to at least rid herself of one symbol of her powerlessness.

He raised a hand. "I don't know if you should do that, Willow."

White-hot anger burned to life, momentarily dwarfing her fright. "Thanks, *Dan*, but you're not my fucking dad."

Rather than exasperation, Dan's mouth twitched with... amusement. "Suit yourself."

This was all a sick game to him. Watching her struggle. Watching her yell in vain for help. All of it.

Willow harnessed the rage as fuel. With one hand on the cool, rough wall for balance, she ground her teeth together as she forced unsteady legs to hold her weight.

By the time she was upright, her breathing came in labored gasps. She would swear she'd just climbed a mountain and not simply risen to stand. Her head throbbed with each beat of her heart, and even as nausea rocked her stomach, she mentally avowed to show no sign of weakness.

Brushing the matted strands of golden blonde hair from her face, Willow took in a steadying breath.

She didn't have a chance to exhale before Dan took two steps forward to close the meager distance between them.

His fingers clamped down on her chin with the same strength of the metal binding her wrists.

Willow tried to jump backward and out of his reach, but her shoulders only met the cold roughness of the wall.

Despite the movement, Dan's hold didn't loosen. His malevolent gaze flicked from one side of Willow's face to the other as he lifted her chin. "Natural blonde, good. Blue eyes, also good. Healthy skin tone, maybe a little on the paler side. But it *is* November, and we're in Illinois. I doubt he'll care too much about that, anyway."

He snapped up his other hand and tugged at Willow's bottom lip, then the top lip. To her dismay, she didn't think to try to bite him until he'd dropped both arms back to his sides and stepped away.

With an approving nod, he stroked the side of his face. "Teeth are a little crooked, but you've obviously got good oral hygiene. That's important. I think he'll appreciate that. Although..." He looked upward as he appeared to fall into a moment of deep thought.

"What?" Willow was struggling to keep up with what had just transpired.

Had the man just examined her like she was livestock? And who in the hell was the *he* the bastard kept mentioning?

As if he could sense her thoughts, his dead eyes shifted back to her. "He's not the one who likes pulling out teeth, anyway. It'll be fine."

Willow's anger had already begun to wear thin, and the casual mention of someone who enjoyed *pulling out teeth* pushed the remainder of the sentiment to the wayside. All that was left in the wake of her ire was dread.

"W-what are you talking about? *Who* a-are you talking about?"

Dan's lips parted in a smile, and Willow immediately

wished he'd go back to the emotionless stone expression he'd worn upon his entrance.

"Willow Nowland, you're going to make someone very happy. Soon. Very soon."

The room was bathed in darkness as Dan flicked off the lights, plunging Willow into despair as his words echoed around her concrete tomb.

2

As Amelia waited for the elevator to reach her floor in the FBI parking garage, she double-checked her reflection in the silver doors. Her retro-inspired eye makeup was in place, and no wayward hairs stood out from her neat ponytail. The look, coupled with her silky off-white dress shirt and charcoal slacks, lent her a stylish air of professionalism. She was confident no one meeting her for the first time would guess she'd spent ten years in the military.

Well, not until she referred to a meal as "chow" or offered a salute in lieu of a wave goodbye.

With a cheery ding, the elevator door slid open to reveal an empty car. Good. Hopefully, she wouldn't be forced to make conversation with someone before she could down her first cup of coffee. Stepping inside, Amelia tapped the button for her floor and waited.

A week after Glenn Kantowski almost killed her outside Newark, Illinois, Amelia had moved out of her old apartment. She'd made use of her stockpile of personal time, splurged on hiring movers, and had her new place set up less than forty-eight hours after leaving the old apartment.

She'd been at the new place for a week now, and she and Hup, her adopted cat, had both adjusted to the change. Part of her still missed staying with Zane, especially since she hadn't spoken to him outside of work since she'd taken the time off. They exchanged the occasional text message, but after the conversation in her hospital room, their relationship had shifted.

When she'd blurted the question about whether he thought she might be a wolf in sheep's clothing like Glenn had been, she'd wanted to clear the air. For a beat, she'd even considered coming clean about her ties to the D'Amato crime family.

Now, more than two weeks later, she was glad she hadn't. If Zane had distanced himself from her based on her question alone, she didn't want to find out how he'd react if he learned about Alex Passarelli.

Maybe she'd compromised his trust when she'd deferred answering his questions.

As the counter ticked to her floor, she made a valiant effort to push aside the thought. The Leóne Family RICO case had officially been shelved, and with the aftermath of the Storey investigation finished, they were due for a new assignment.

That might be what it is. Maybe we just need to get back to normal. Something to get our minds off what Glenn did. About all the deceit we uncovered during the Storey case.

Amelia straightened her back as the elevator came to a halt. They'd been moved out of the repurposed chair graveyard, much to her chagrin. She would have preferred to have a locked door between her and Joseph Larson whenever possible.

As Amelia neared her desk, she spotted Zane's black peacoat draped over the back of his seat, but the man was nowhere to be found. Swallowing a sigh, Amelia set her handbag beside the keyboard and shrugged off her jacket.

"Agent Storm, there you are."

Amelia spun to face the Special Agent in Charge as her heart rate spiked. "SAC Keaton, I'm sorry. You startled me."

Jasmine's expression softened. She was well aware of what Amelia had experienced over the past month. "I'm sorry for that. I should have let you know when I saw you instead of running up on you like this."

Dammit. She prolonged the word in her head. *Get a grip. You can't act like a frightened child in front of your boss. Pull it together, ya wuss, and show her how strong you are.*

"That's all right." Amelia made her best effort at a smile. "What can I help you with?"

"A briefing. I'm pairing you and Agent Palmer with a couple agents from Violent Crimes. We've got a case southwest of here. It's in a rural county, and the sheriff's department isn't equipped to deal with it properly."

Eager to get back to work, Amelia stashed her purse in her desk. "Is it urgent?"

SAC Keaton beckoned for Amelia to follow. "It is. What the local authorities suspected was a serial killer seems to have turned into something…worse."

"Worse than a serial killer?" Amelia wrinkled her nose as she fell in beside the SAC.

"Human traffickers."

Oh, hell.

With those two words, Amelia felt like a kid who'd just stumbled off the tilt-a-whirl at a carnival, and Jasmine was the best friend coaxing her back for another spin.

Here we go again.

3

As Special Agent Amelia Storm stepped through the doorway to the sixth-floor conference room, eagerness to dismantle a human trafficking ring steeled her resolve. Two unfamiliar faces turned in tandem to regard her arrival, as well as a much more familiar set of slate-gray eyes.

Two agents, both of whom Amelia assumed were the Violent Crimes personnel the SAC had mentioned, were seated on one side of the oval table. Special Agent Zane Palmer, on the other hand, had taken a spot on a cushioned leather bench positioned against the wall.

Amelia pulled her focus away from Zane before the first shards of uncertainty could pierce her confidence. At least they'd be working together again. Zane had a way of calming her down in tense situations and sorting through the BS of a case. She'd never had a better partner than him since joining the FBI.

Dropping down to sit at the other end of the bench, she looked to the man and woman at the table. She could vaguely recall seeing the woman around the office, but since Violent

Crimes and Organized Crime were on different floors of the building, she didn't run into her often.

Her wavy, ash blonde bob only just brushed the shoulders of her crisp black blazer, and a pair of kind, albeit astute hazel eyes briefly met Amelia's as she smiled and lifted one slender hand in greeting.

The man, however, was someone Amelia had never come across before today. She was sure she'd remember a pair of sapphire eyes as vivid as his.

His whiskey brown hair was brushed straight back from his forehead, leaving only a few stray strands to touch his eyebrows. As she noticed the lack of a wedding band on his left hand, she couldn't help but wonder how many pretty women had been mesmerized by those eyes.

Despite a chiseled jawline that made him seem like he might have just strolled off a Hollywood set, Amelia noted his navy tie was slightly askew. Coupled with the faint shadows beneath his eyes and the equally faint laugh lines on his clean-shaven face, she was able to establish that he was, in fact, a human being.

"Morning, Storm." Zane's voice snapped her gaze to the side. Despite his eight months in the Chicago FBI office, his words were still tinged with a hint of his native Jersey accent.

Oh, thank god.

After an entire weekend with a grand total of three text messages exchanged between the two of them, when normally there was a constant stream of communication, Amelia had feared Zane was distancing himself from their friendship.

She fought to suppress the broad smile threatening to burst forth, barely winning the battle. "Morning. Happy Monday."

He tilted his stainless-steel thermos at her before taking a long drink. His sandy colored hair was roughly parted on one side, and the strands were swept forward in a style that was both professional and fashionable. Though Amelia and her cat had stayed with Zane for almost two weeks while Amelia had laid low to evade a hitman—er, hit*woman*—there were no signs of Hup's fur on the tall man's tailored suit.

She didn't know how he did it. How he came across as so poised, professional, and *suave* at any given time of day. Even when Amelia had occupied his spare bedroom, she was sure she'd never caught a glimpse of him that he hadn't wanted her to see.

His perpetually flawless appearance—aside from the stubble that graced his cheeks, though the unshaven look lent him a handsome, rugged aesthetic—fit his personality.

Polished.

Guarded.

Amelia had been so sure that he wore his true state of being on his sleeve, but she realized now how naïve the assumption was.

As much as she loathed the idea of naivety, she almost wished she could return to that not-so-distant past. Her pulse still picked up when she thought about how close she'd come to being able to run her hands along the lean, muscular frame Zane hid beneath his expensive suits.

How close she'd come to…

Nope. Stop it.

Suddenly self-conscious, Amelia glanced down at her silky button-down and charcoal slacks.

Though the stitches had been removed from her side a few days earlier, she still wasn't quite comfortable enough to wear form-fitting clothes over the site of the gunshot wound. The off-white, designer blouse was fancier than her typical attire, but when she was beside a man whose appearance was always impeccable, she figured she was right at home.

Just don't get used to this. Once I'm fully healed, the fancy stuff moves to the back of the closet again.

Amelia shook off the thought. The hour was early, but it was time for her to focus.

When she'd arrived at the Chicago FBI field office that morning, she hadn't expected SAC Keaton to approach her with an urgent new human trafficking case with elements of a serial killer.

Strange though the dichotomy might have appeared to an outside observer, serial killers set Amelia on edge far more than the prospect of a human trafficking ring. She was used to the mob, but serial killers…they were a different breed.

The motive of ninety-nine percent of traffickers was simple. They wanted money, and they wanted power.

Easy, clean-cut, and predictable. To be sure, traffickers were the scum of the earth as far as Amelia was concerned, but they weren't difficult to understand.

Serial killers, on the other hand…

In the nearly two years she'd spent with the Organized Crime Division of the FBI—fifteen months in the Boston field office, and now eight in her home city of Chicago—Amelia had heard plenty of horror stories about the country's various serial murderers.

She'd been told about men who'd peel off a woman's face just so they could dress up and pretend for a fleeting moment that they'd taken on the deceased's identity. Then, back in Boston, there had been one man who'd scooped out his victims' eyes and pureed them in a blender so he could use them as a new color of paint.

No one *paid* those psychopaths for what they did. It was just the way they were. There was scientific evidence to suggest that the average psychopath—if any such person could even be considered average—possessed a brain that was physically different from a normal, empathetic person.

Some psychopaths and sociopaths functioned on a higher level than their peers. They'd seek out high-octane jobs like piloting aircrafts, performing surgery, or running a Fortune 500 business. And then, some psychopaths painted satanic symbols with pureed eyeballs.

How in the hell was a civilized society supposed to deal with *them*?

She wasn't sure, but part of her was curious. Maybe Violent Crimes was the next stepping-stone in Amelia's FBI career. The thought had occurred to her before, but until recently, she'd never given the idea any real consideration.

After having lived through the betrayal by a fellow agent, and after being chased and almost killed by the same woman, Amelia had begun to view her job in a different light. In her current position in the Bureau's Organized Crime Division, every crime was connected to an operation larger than itself.

A misdeed as seemingly innocuous as a spree of nonviolent thefts could lead back to a well-entrenched crime family who'd descended from Al Capone himself. In the span of a day, Amelia could go from investigating stolen computers to taking cover from the gunshots of an overeager hitman.

She'd spent the first ten years of her adult life as a sniper in the United States Army, and in that time, she'd worked alongside some of the country's most elite specialized warfare factions. Though the FBI had been enthused by the prospect of adding a person with her lengthy military history to their roster, Amelia still hadn't quite figured out how a decade in the Army was supposed to translate to an investigative entity like the Bureau.

But she'd keep trying. If nothing else than for the memory of her older brother.

As she pictured Trevor's easy grin and the perpetual, youthful sparkle in his eyes, a phantom hand clamped down around her heart. Trevor had kept secrets from her. More secrets than even she knew existed, she was sure, but she still missed him.

In the years leading up to him being shot in a Chicago side street, he'd worked with the D'Amato Crime family. A detail that her high school boyfriend and current D'Amato capo, Alex Passarelli, had neglected to mention to her for god only knew how long.

When did my life turn into such a mess?

She heaved a mental sigh. Or, at least, she thought the sigh was in her head.

As the two unfamiliar agents, along with SAC Keaton and Zane Palmer, all turned in tandem to regard her, a flush heated Amelia's cheeks.

She straightened her back and crossed her legs in a vain attempt to regain her shattered professionalism. "Sorry. I, um…I haven't had any coffee yet."

The statement was true. She'd pounded an energy drink on her drive into the office, but she hadn't drunk any *coffee*.

The male agent seated at the oval table lifted a noncommittal shoulder. "That's fair." He inclined his chin at the woman beside him. "Agent Cowen sees me bright and early often enough to know that I sigh at least seven-hundred times before noon."

Amelia pressed her lips together to stifle a definitively unprofessional snort of laughter. To her relief, she was able to ward off the unflattering sound.

Agent Cowen's chair creaked as she leaned back heavily. "Steelman's right. He's some kind of sighing machine until he has at least a hundred milligrams of caffeine."

With an exaggerated wink in Amelia's direction, Agent Steelman scooped a paper cup of coffee from the table.

Now, it was Zane's turn to snicker.

The sound was music to Amelia's ears. A sound she hadn't heard in close to a week, far too long for the good-spirited agent. Now, a different sort of flush threatened to expose her.

Clasping both hands in her lap, Amelia stole a quick glance at her friend. A ghost of amusement still lingered on his handsome face. It wasn't much, but she'd take it.

Amelia liked Agent Steelman already, with his sarcastic gestures and dry wit. They'd get along just fine.

As Jasmine Keaton took her spot at the end of the oval table, her shrewd gaze swept over the little gathering. "Well, I'm glad you're all getting along well at seven-thirty in the morning. I've got a meeting at eight, and we've got a lot to go over, so I'll make this as fast as I can." The SAC waved at Steelman and Cowen. "Agent Dean Steelman, Agent Sherry Cowen, you'll be working with Agents Amelia Storm and Zane Palmer from Organized Crime. Indefinitely, until this case is closed, or the potential for human trafficking has been completely eliminated."

A stern visage replaced Dean Steelman's joviality. "This is about the dark web activity, yeah?" His words were laden with a Southern accent, but Amelia was out of her depth when it came to linguistics to place the precise location.

SAC Keaton scooped up a remote to turn on the overhead projector, and then she fished a tablet from the leather laptop bag beside her chair. "That's part of the reason. Here, I'm sending you all the files from the Massey County Sheriff's Department."

Zane's eyebrows knitted together as he pushed open his matte silver laptop. "Massey County? That's a few hours south of here, isn't it?"

"Two and a half, or thereabouts." Sherry Cowen produced a ballpoint pen from her handbag. "It's a good-sized county, but it has a pretty low population."

Amelia wanted to pull out a notepad to at least appear as if she was being productive, but she'd left all her belongings at her desk. Tightening her hands together in her lap, she was reminded of the times she'd shown up to her high school classes unprepared.

An inauspicious start to the work week and a heck of a first impression.

At the gentle nudge of an elbow against her upper arm, Amelia jerked her head around to Zane's expectant gaze. As if he'd read her mind, he scooted next to her and moved the laptop until they each had a clear view of Jasmine Keaton's email.

A wave of tentative relief loosened the grasp of uncertainty that had clawed at her mind.

Before Amelia had been forcefully sedated and loaded into the trunk of a black mustang owned by an accomplice to Agent Glenn Kantowski, Amelia had opened her laptop in front of Zane right after she'd done a lengthy search on Luca Passarelli.

Naturally, Zane had been curious about why she'd pulled up information on the prominent D'Amato Capo.

Amelia had been faced with a split-second decision to come clean to Zane or to lie.

At the time, the FBI had been in the midst of an investigation into the person who'd killed City Councilman Ben Storey and tried to frame Amelia for the crime. If Amelia had told Zane the truth, that Luca Passarelli was the father of a boy she'd dated for almost four years in high school and that the boy was now a mafia capo himself, her entire ugly past would have undoubtedly wound up on display for all the Federal Bureau of Investigation.

But she hadn't been able to bring herself to lie to Zane. They had forged a level of trust she was unwilling to shatter with the utterance of an easy lie. She'd deflected instead.

She'd explained there were things she wasn't ready to share

with him yet, and he seemed to accept that. And while she'd worried holding back might tarnish their friendship, he'd still come to visit her in the hospital with a stuffed calico to serve as a substitute for her cat Hup. Even in the hospital, she'd tried to explain that not knowing everything about her didn't mean she had a dark side. They'd even shared an embrace.

Amelia blinked away the thoughts and peered down at the laptop screen. Straight into the bright green eyes of a girl clad in a black gown and matching graduation cap.

"Larissa Umber." SAC Keaton scrolled down on the screen of her tablet, and the image projected on the whiteboard moved as well. "Twenty-five, born and raised in Chicago. Her last known address was with her mother, Pamela Umber, in North Lawndale. She worked as a server in the restaurant at the Sheraton Hotel downtown. A coworker reported her missing about two weeks ago when Larissa missed her third shift in a row."

The SAC's grave tone sliced through the fog in Amelia's head, and thoughts of her secrets faded into the background. As a photo of Larissa's ashen face appeared on Zane's laptop, Amelia's spirits sank a little lower. Even after all her time in the military and her near-two years in the FBI, the news of an innocent person's death still struck a pang of sympathy in her heart.

After losing her mother to cancer when she was ten years old, and then her brother more than fifteen years later, Amelia was intimately familiar with loss.

SAC Keaton zoomed in on the text beside the picture of Larissa's lifeless face. "Her body, or what was left of it, was found just outside Cedarwood, Illinois. Cedarwood is right on the Illinois River, and it's the seat of Massey County. Population of about fifty-five-hundred according to the latest census."

One of Zane's eyebrows quirked up. "How much of her body was found?"

"Not much." SAC Keaton pointed at the whiteboard. "Only what you see there, Agents. Larissa's severed head was found wrapped in a garbage bag on the bank of Fox Creek, just a couple miles northeast of Cedarwood. The authorities in Massey County have been advised to send Larissa's remains to the Cook County Medical Examiner ASAP, and the garbage bag they found was sent to our lab for further analysis. Massey County did their best, but they don't have half the resources the Bureau does."

Amelia leaned in and scanned the report. With each new detail, the unease in her stomach churned.

Nineteen days earlier, Larissa was reported missing by her friend and coworker, Julie Breyer. According to Julie, Larissa was a dutiful employee, and she'd never missed a shift.

However, Larissa's past was another story entirely.

Not long after the girl's nineteenth birthday, she was caught aiding a drug trafficking ring by attempting to smuggle pain pills through the airport with the help of her then-boyfriend. Fortunately, prosecutors had recognized Larissa as the young, naïve girl she was.

Hhmmm, swap the pills for heroin, and it starts to sound like Lainey, except for the naïve part...

Amelia quickly dismissed the thoughts of her younger sister, who was facing jail time in Milwaukee after trying to smuggle heroin through the airport. She turned her attention back to the SAC's briefing.

Though Larissa was charged with a Class E felony, her prison sentence was markedly shorter than her thirty-five-year-old "boyfriend's." As part of the criminal booking process, she'd provided both fingerprint and DNA samples to the national database.

And now, the conviction was the only reason they knew who she was. The Massey County M.E. hadn't been able to identify her with the remains they'd found, so DNA had been submitted for analysis to make a positive ID.

The night before, the results had finally come through. Due to Larissa's prior federal charge, the FBI had been alerted to the crime.

Larissa had clearly been troubled, but what struck Amelia more than anything was that the poor girl had gone through rehab, completed her subsequent parole, and seemed to have been on track for a better life. She'd even started classes at a local community college.

All her plans, her hopes for brighter days, her dreams, and her ambitions had been snuffed out when she was murdered, decapitated, and left to rot in the middle of nowhere.

Amelia felt sick when she reached the reason why DNA had been used as a means to identify the young woman. The other agents must have hit the same point in the case report because the air in the conference room grew somber.

"Based on those looks, you've all read why we had to use DNA to identify Larissa." SAC Keaton's jaw tightened as she fought to keep the anger from her face. "Her eyes were both gone, and according to the Massey County M.E., at least one of them was removed antemortem. In addition, all her teeth were pulled. The M.E. couldn't say if any of that had been done post-mortem, but we ought to get a clearer picture in the next few days."

Dean Steelman shifted in place. "She was tortured." He jerked a thumb at Amelia and Zane. "And these two are here because we think it might have something to do with that charge she was popped with six years ago? Some kinda mob retaliation?"

Silently, Zane lifted his index finger to point at a line of text on the screen of his laptop.

Amelia followed the motion, and her blood turned cold.

"Shit." The word slipped out before she could stop herself.

The two agents from Violent Crimes turned their curious stares to Amelia.

She ignored the sudden scrutiny. "Third paragraph, second sentence. A few months before Larissa was arrested for possession, she was taken in by the CPD for suspected solicitation. They let her go without charging her, but according to this report, she was working for a Leóne prostitution ring."

When Sherry and Dean's expressions changed little, Amelia had to remind herself that the two VC agents hadn't chased after Leóne human trafficking rings for the better part of half a year.

The pair might have been aware of the Leóne family's influence, but they didn't truly understand how deep that particular rabbit hole went.

Lucky bastards.

"Larissa did work in a Leóne prostitution ring, but I'm afraid this isn't quite that straightforward either." SAC Keaton tapped her tablet, and the image of a weathered human skull appeared on the whiteboard. To its side was a headshot of a woman who couldn't have been much older than Larissa. "Four years ago, the skull of Heather Breysacher was found in Massey County. It wasn't found in the same spot as Larissa's, but it *was* found near Fox Creek, north of Cedarwood."

Amelia wondered what the odds were that two unrelated decapitations could have occurred in the same rural Illinois county. Slim to none, if she had to guess.

The SAC swiped, and the picture changed to a much whiter, less-worn leg bone. "This is a human femur. Of course, just a femur doesn't prove that this person is dead, but..." SAC Keaton pressed her lips together, "most amputations are performed in a hospital. So, the likelihood that the person who lost this leg to the Illinois wilderness is doing just fine seems a little asinine to me."

"Jane Doe, found a little over a year ago. She hasn't been identified." Zane enlarged the image on his screen. "But the forensic anthropologist who examined the bone *was* confident that it belonged to a woman. And the M.E. confirmed the leg was severed neatly. Whoever did it knew how to pull on the limb, so they'd only be cutting through cartilage as opposed to trying to saw through bone."

"Correct, Agent Palmer." SAC Keaton's finger hovered above the touchscreen as she scanned the four agents. "The next picture is more graphic than the other three, just so you're all aware."

After spending years of her life in a combat zone, Amelia doubted there were any gory pictures in existence that could scar her.

But the photo of a dismembered, partly decomposed torso came close.

The body belonged to a female, but both breasts had been severed, and only rotting tissue remained in their place. Both arms, legs, and of course, the head were all gone.

"This is Jane Doe Two. She was found a day after Larissa, about half a mile downstream in the Fox Creek. Just like Larissa, Heather, and Jane Doe One, she was wrapped in a plain, black garbage bag. I've already had Massey County send that to our lab as well. But based on the lack of evidence found on the bags in the two older cases, we aren't optimistic." SAC Keaton finally leaned back in her seat. "Questions?"

Sherry tapped a yellow legal pad with the end of her pen. "The two most recent victims, Jane Doe Two and Larissa Umber, their TODs are both within a few days or weeks of one another, aren't they?"

SAC Keaton dipped her chin. "Correct. We've been called in to help on this case not just because of Larissa Umber's past conviction, but because the Massey County authorities think that whoever this killer is, trafficker or serial killer, he's escalating."

4

I blew on my steaming mug of coffee as my gaze wandered to the shadowy doorway on the other side of the room. The door opened to a hallway with two locked doors on the left belonging to a pair of holding cells, each of which was constructed of solid concrete—walls, floor, ceiling, everything. On the right was another pair of doors. One was to the "suite," as I'd deemed it, and another to my best rendition of a morgue.

Willow Nowland was in the farther of the two cells on the left, and I took a moment to thank whatever deity might be listening that the girl had stopped her incessant screaming.

I'd *told* her.

I always told them that they could yell for help, but no one would ever hear them. My intent wasn't intimidation, though I enjoyed the sheer horror the statement brought to their faces.

My goal was to save them the trouble and save myself the headache. *Literally.*

When I'd tried to offer Willow a meal earlier, she'd kicked

the food aside and spat at my feet. I needed the little shit to eat. My client was paying me for a slender blonde, but he didn't want a malnourished skeleton.

The Russian, as I liked to call him, was a fan of women who were less than half his size. Not that the man was overweight—far from. The brutal son of a bitch was six feet, seven inches of solid muscle.

But he was specific that the women be in good shape, preferably with an hourglass figure.

I set the mug back on the polished black desk and massaged my temples. I'd been awake for more than twenty-four hours, and I still had at least twelve more to go before I'd find any respite.

The decision to take Willow had been impulsive. I could recognize that much. My damn *kid* had been asleep in the back seat of the car.

What would I do if I found out she'd *seen* Willow?

No, I couldn't think like that.

I already knew how I'd explain the situation, and I knew damn good and well that my daughter hadn't actually seen me land the blow on the side of Willow's head. I'd made sure she had no clear line of sight.

If she had seen Willow, I'd tell her the young woman didn't have jumper cables, and we'd gotten lucky, and I'd started the car without them.

I was her father. She'd believe me.

I leaned back in the office chair and allowed my head to fall back to face the drab gray ceiling.

I'd carved out a workspace for myself in the front section of the underground addition I'd made to my lakeside cabin. I couldn't quite call the place a basement since it was in the backyard and was only connected to the surface dwelling with a subterranean hallway.

Was I in a bunker?

Ridiculous.

Calling it a bunker made me feel like one of those survivalist nuts my wife watched on the Discovery Channel. Sure, I had some food tucked away, some bottled water, and a couple rifles. But I didn't have any damn C-rations.

Shaking my head, I pushed open a sleek laptop. There my mind went again, wandering off to parts unknown. Christ, I needed a nap.

After I'd driven my daughter home with an unconscious Willow in the trunk, I'd come back out to the cabin to secure my newest prize.

My heart had pounded in my chest the entire time, and I didn't achieve any semblance of relief until I'd moved her car to a more remote area. From there, I'd walked another six miles to my own vehicle, and then I'd swung by the cabin on my way home.

Though I'd been sure to temper my strength when I'd struck Willow with the tire iron, I hadn't expected her head to hit a rock when she fell. After the double whammy, I'd been compelled to check to see if she'd regained consciousness.

She had, of course. I'd covered all my bases.

Taking the girl had been rash, but I was still confident I'd made the right decision.

The second I saw her, I'd known I had to have her. She was perfect. I swore I'd come across her golden hair and those pale blue eyes in a dream. That flawless skin…

I couldn't wait to cut open her flat, toned stomach.

They were almost always dead when I got to them, but in truth, that was how I preferred them. If they were dead, they couldn't fight back, and they couldn't scream for help when the scalpel sliced through skin, muscle, and delicate tissue.

My heart raced at the possibility, but I shut out the thoughts.

The hardest portion of my endeavor—obtaining and securing the subject—was finished. Now, I just had to make sure my client was aware that I'd acquired a perfect match to his specifications.

Straightening in my seat, I typed in a few passwords and launched an anonymous web browser. The software filtered any of my online queries through multiple layers of encryption to make tracking my location or identity virtually impossible. Commonly referred to as an onion network, the digital infrastructure was utilized to access otherwise unseen parts of the internet.

In layman's terms, the dark web.

The software itself wasn't illegal. In fact, my wife, who'd been a law-abiding citizen for her entire life, made use of the network to avoid her personal information falling into the hands of advertisers. She'd even persuaded a few of her friends to do the same.

My intent, however, was much different.

I located the private message thread between me and my client and did a quick run-through of the photos I'd taken of Willow before she'd regained consciousness.

I licked my lips at the memory. I'd stripped her buck naked, and she hadn't even noticed. Maybe she *did* have a concussion.

After selecting the highest quality photos to give The Russian an idea of what he was paying me for, I typed out a succinct message to ask when I could expect his visit.

Between my lack of sleep and the headache that had only just begun to recede, I was especially grateful to be dealing with an established client. The Russian knew my rules, and he knew the drill.

He'd provided me with a list of specifications, and I'd been given a two-month span to fulfill the order, or he'd move on to a different source to procure his playthings. He was too good a client to lose. But Willow had been gifted to me, and I could now proceed with the pattern The Russian and I had established.

Once a matching individual was in captivity, I allotted a period of five to twelve days for the client to come to me. If they didn't show, then I killed the subject myself.

They always showed, though. The hefty bitcoin deposit they made beforehand all but ensured their obedience.

Though I'd been hesitant to snatch another girl so soon after Larissa and Faith, I couldn't refuse my Russian friend. The man was his own brand of fucked up, and I loved nothing more than watching him take out his pent-up rage on a pretty, college-aged girl.

As my pulse picked up, I licked my lips again.

Yes, taking Willow had been the right choice. I was going to enjoy her.

5
———

Zane and Amelia were only a few blocks away from the FBI field office when Zane started to regret his decision to drive. He hated Chicago's traffic.

Steelman and Cowen will probably make it to Cedarwood before we even get to North Lawndale to talk to Pamela Umber.

As he braked to a stop behind a line of cars leading up to a red light, he looked over to Amelia.

Her forest green eyes were fixed on the glowing screen of a tablet, and she twirled a lock of blonde-tipped hair around her index finger as she read. The golden hue melded into her natural dark brown in what he'd learned was called a *balayage*. Or a color melt. He couldn't recall which, and he didn't honestly know what either term meant.

Zane hadn't yet met Amelia's hair stylist sister-in-law, but Amelia was always quick to tell him all about Joanna Storm's latest piece of fashion advice. After spending ten years in the military, Amelia seemed to have soaked up all Joanna's wisdom like a stylish sponge.

He didn't realize his eyes were still on Amelia until her curious stare flicked up to meet his. Even as he jerked his attention back to the road, he was well aware that the effort was too little and too late.

"What?" Amelia flicked the piece of hair back over her shoulder. "Do I have something on my face? Did I spill coffee on myself?"

Rubbing his neck as if the motion would chase away the flush that crept up to his cheeks, he shook his head. "No. You don't. I was just…you look nice. That's all."

You look nice?

He mentally punched himself in the face. Was that really the best line he could come up with? Why in the hell did his suave persona fly out the window whenever he *wanted* to be smooth around Amelia?

From the corner of his eye, he watched as she drew her sculpted eyebrows together in confusion. "Um. Okay. Thanks. You, uh, you look nice too." She brushed something from his sleeve. "But I'm sure you already knew that."

Her puzzled expression transferred to Zane as the distant light turned green. Sure, he put effort into his appearance, but most adults around his and Amelia's age range tried to look good. "I'm…not sure what you mean by that. But thank you? I think?"

She cradled the tablet in both hands and shifted in her seat. "You're welcome, I guess. You're sure there's nothing on my face, though, right?"

Good lord. Since when did our dialogue become so strained and awkward?

Perhaps they'd mentally reverted to teenagers, at least as far as their interactions with one another were concerned.

He managed a glance at her. "No. Nothing on your face. Promise."

A glimmer of skepticism remained, but otherwise, she seemed to accept the reassurance. "Okay. I'm…I'm sorry. I didn't mean to make that weird."

"Not weird." It was weird, but *he* was the one responsible. Time to focus on work. "Not at all. We haven't been gone for very long, but have you found anything in those documents SAC Keaton sent us?"

Amelia seemed to perk up at the mention of their case. "Not much. Mostly just repeats of what we went over in the briefing. I was looking at Larissa's old drug charge, trying to see if I could find anything that might indicate that she'd…" She spun a finger in the air.

"Pissed off the León family?" he finished for her.

"Yes. I was trying to figure out a more eloquent term, but that's exactly right."

Eloquence wasn't exactly Zane's strong suit that morning, in more ways than one. He pushed past the lingering embarrassment. "Were you able to find anything?"

Amelia's shoulders rose and fell as she heaved out a long breath. "Not yet. The prosecutor was under the impression that the León family might have had something to do with supplying the drugs that Larissa and her 'boyfriend' were caught with. But according to Larissa's statement, she'd gotten the pills from some street gang called The Central Crew."

To the best of Zane's knowledge, most of Chicago's street gangs could be traced back to the larger syndicates—such as the San Luis Cartel, the León family, or the Russians.

Problem was, even the guys who ran the gangs were scared shitless of the mob and the cartels. The cases where a gang member had been willing to testify against an established syndicate were exceedingly rare and often resulted in the witness's death.

Zane scrolled through his mental rolodex and came up empty. "The Central Crew? Never heard of them."

Amelia let out a sound that resembled a groan. "That's because they don't exist anymore. It was a small outfit that operated in East and West Garfield Park until about five years ago. The CPD busted a bunch of them, but they never rolled on their suppliers. The CPD *suspected* that they'd been pushing drugs for the Leónes, but they were never able to confirm."

By the time Zane brought the car to a stop again, they were still behind the same damn light.

Well, at least they had plenty of time to discuss the case before they reached Pamela Umber's apartment. "So, in other words, there aren't any gangsters left out there who'd even possibly have an ax to grind with Larissa?"

Amelia tapped her thumb on her tablet. "Exactly. I mean, it's possible that she did something to get on the Leónes' bad side, though. Maybe one of their capos came to her to try to get her to work the streets again, and she said no?"

Zane flattened his palms against the wheel. "Maybe. I guess we can't rule it out, can we?"

"I guess not." She rested the tablet on her lap and slumped down in her seat. "There wasn't much else there, though. No recent citations or anything. As far as I can tell, she was on the up-and-up."

Which was part of what made the entire situation even more heartbreaking.

"What kind of crazy son of a bitch chops up people and...*disperses* their body parts around the rural countryside?" Though the query was rhetorical, part of Zane still hadn't quite wrapped his head around the concept.

After a decade of working as a covert operative for the Central Intelligence Agency, Zane had come across just about all manner of criminal. He'd spent the majority of his tenure with the CIA deep within the ranks of the Russian mafia, and by proxy, the Russian government.

But even there, the motivations of the most ruthless contract killer were straightforward.

Money. Loyalty. Power.

He made a mental note to pick the brain of one of the FBI's Behavioral Analysis agents when he had a chance.

"We still haven't ruled out traffickers." Amelia stretched her legs. "This could be how they're disposing of the bodies of the people they've abducted."

"I'm not sure. Traffickers usually sell people when they're still alive."

Amelia held up a finger. "Usually. This one could be doing something different."

Zane fought the urge to rub his tired eyes. "Could be, or they could be a fucking serial killer."

She propped an elbow on the doorframe. "Also true."

For the rest of the drive to North Lawndale, Amelia went back to her diligent research on the tablet, though Zane suspected she was merely perusing the same case files they'd already read.

Larissa hadn't been dating anyone, and Pamela had effectively been ruled out as a suspect from the get-go. With no driver's license and no car of her own, there was little to no chance Pamela could have made the trip all the way down to Massey County. In addition, there were no reports of bad blood between Pamela and her daughter.

Otherwise, the only news Amelia relayed back to him was that Larissa's social media usage was limited to sharing inspirational quotes on a couple platforms.

The poor woman really had been trying to rebuild her life. Which begged the question…if the Leóne family was involved, why would they target her now?

As Zane stepped onto the cracked asphalt in front of a gray stone apartment building, he pulled on the collar of his wool jacket in an effort to ward off the wind's chill. He'd dropped a fair chunk of change on the garment. Though he hadn't expected a formal black frock to provide any real comfort or warmth, the coat had exceeded his expectations over the past three years.

On the other side of the car, Amelia tucked the tablet into her handbag and cinched the waistband of her knee-length trench coat.

Turning to the side, he covered his mouth to stifle a quiet snort of laughter. They couldn't have looked more like a couple Feds if they'd tried.

A sidewalk in the same state of disrepair as the street and two flights of creaky stairs brought them face-to-face with apartment 303.

Zane steeled himself.

Aside from the detectives who'd established the initial missing persons report, no law enforcement agents had visited Pamela Umber since her daughter had disappeared. The task to deliver news of the girl's death fell to Zane and Amelia.

Tucking one hand in his jacket, Zane rapped his knuckles against the worn wooden surface. Four solid thuds. The *cop knock*, as he'd referred to it in his younger years.

"Just a second." The woman's muffled voice came almost immediately. Pamela Umber had been laid off from her office job a month earlier, but Zane was still relieved to hear that he and Amelia hadn't wasted their time traveling to an empty apartment.

A chain rattled as the door creaked inward, and a pair of inquisitive eyes peeked through the narrow opening. "Can I help you?"

Zane flipped open his badge, followed in short order by Amelia.

Pamela Umber's face fell immediately. Without speaking, she unhooked the brass chain and pulled open the door.

"Mrs. Umber, I'm Special Agent Zane Palmer, and this is Special Agent Amelia Storm. We're with the Federal Bureau of Investigation, and we're here to talk to you about your daughter."

He always kept these types of conversations as professional as humanly possible. If he didn't, he suspected he'd stray much too far from the boundary of professionalism. Zane never got used to the heart-wrenching dialogue when he broke the bad news to families. He likely never would.

Pamela's sweater-knit slippers scuffed the linoleum as she stepped to the side. "Come in, Agents."

"Thank you, Mrs. Umber." Zane followed the woman's lead, Amelia close on his heels.

"Please call me Pam."

A short hall led to a living area that was open to the dining room. The dark brown couch and love seat weren't top of the line, but the furnishings and décor were comfortable and orderly. Despite the stale scent of cigarette smoke and empty beer cans that had followed them up to the third floor, the only scent he caught in Pamela Umber's apartment was cinnamon and nutmeg.

Rubbing beneath her nose, Pam dropped down to sit on the love seat before she gestured to the sofa that rested beneath a wide window. "Have a seat. Please tell me what you know about Larissa."

Aside from another sniffle, the petite woman was calm, her movements devoid of any tremor. Clearly, Pam Umber already had a familiarity with federal law enforcement.

Better to break the news right away than leave the woman hanging.

Zane took his spot on the center cushion. "Mrs...." He cleared his throat. "Pam. I'm afraid we have some bad news about Larissa." He waited while the woman braced herself. "A week ago, remains were found on the bank of Fox Creek outside Cedarwood, and subsequent tests have revealed them to belong to your daughter. So far, the evidence indicates that there was foul play involved. We believe your daughter was murdered."

He used the term "remains" because he wasn't keen on offering Pam all the grisly details right out of the gate. If she requested the specifics, he would provide her as many as he was allowed, but not a moment sooner.

Pam's eyes became glassy as she tugged at one of the drawstrings of her hooded sweatshirt. The muscles of her jaw tightened, and she swallowed repeatedly before finally covering her face with both hands.

As the first sob wracked her thin body, Zane's throat tightened in sympathy.

After losing his younger sister to a drunk-driving accident when he was a kid, Zane Palmer was no stranger to loss. A voice in his head suggested he could provide Pam comfort by relating to her pain, but he swatted the idea away.

That was precisely the boundary he didn't want to broach. He'd made that mistake once already in his career, and he wouldn't make it again.

Amelia leaned forward to inch a box of tissues closer to the grieving mother. "I'm so sorry for your loss, Mrs. Umber. We're committed to finding who's responsible for her death. We'll do everything we can."

With a trembling hand, Pam swiped at her cheeks and reached for a tissue. As she blotted her bloodshot eyes, she bit her lower lip.

"For six years, I've tried to prepare myself for this exact conversation. Any time she'd come home late, or any time she'd just up and disappear for days, sometimes even *weeks* on end, I'd try to imagine this." She gestured to Amelia and Zane before placing her splayed hand on her chest. "I'd try to picture it in my head. I wouldn't eat, and I barely slept because I was so busy trying to prepare myself. I thought it'd help, but I shouldn't have bothered."

Zane managed a quick look at Amelia. Though her features were calm and collected, he didn't miss how the blood had drained from her knuckles as she clasped her hands together.

Lainey Storm, Amelia's younger sister, was a heroin addict who'd recently been charged with possession of a Schedule 1 controlled substance. Lainey and Larissa were even close to the same age. It was no small surprise that the case hit close to home for Zane's dear friend.

Last Zane knew, Lainey was facing one year of jail time, potentially even less if she displayed good behavior, which she had not yet managed according to the Milwaukee DEA agent. Her probation would last another two years afterward, during which time she'd be expected to submit regularly for drug tests.

For Amelia's sake, Zane hoped the mandated rehabilitation served its intended purpose.

Zane pulled himself from the solipsism. The slow whirl of a ceiling fan pushed another wave of cinnamon and nutmeg over from the candle burning in the dining area.

I should get some candles. Maybe one that smells like pumpkin pie.

He clung to the inane thought like a life raft. The interview was far from over, and though the worst was finished, they still had plenty more trying subject matter to slog through.

Clearing his throat, Zane produced a little notepad from his jacket. "We just have a few routine questions to ask, so please don't take any of them personally."

Pam snatched another tissue and blew her nose. "I understand. Go ahead."

He clicked open a pen. Though he could take the same notes by typing on a tablet or on his phone, he always thought that such a device would make him come across as an aloof asshole. At least with a pen and paper, the witnesses he spoke with knew that he was doing his damn job and not dicking around on Reddit.

"First of all, could you tell us a little bit about your daughter? Did she have any friends who came to visit, maybe someone from one of her college classes?"

Pam shook her head. "No, not really. She was friends with a girl named Julie from where she worked at the restaurant. At the Sheraton. They'd get coffee on occasion, and I met her a couple times. She's a nice kid. I always thought she was a good influence on Larissa, and Larissa *loved* Julie's little girl."

Zane scrawled out a few notes. "Julie Breyer, correct?"

"Yeah, that's her."

"Julie reported Larissa missing when she didn't show up for her third shift in a row." Zane met Pam's gaze. "Could you tell me why you didn't report Larissa missing yourself?"

A flicker of indignation passed over the woman's tired face, but the anger was short-lived.

"Honestly, I thought she'd…relapsed. I was angry, hurt, but I wasn't really surprised." Her voice cracked, and she pressed the tissue to her nose. "Jesus, that makes me sound like such a horrible mother. I should've known something was wrong. Larissa was so happy…she was doing so well. But I just thought…" She left the sentiment unfinished and hung her head.

"I understand." Amelia's words were soft, each syllable tinged with sadness. "Addiction is complicated. My…my sister is an addict too."

Pam's shoulders slumped, but when she brushed strands of hair from her forehead, there was a hint of relief in her countenance. "So, you know, don't you? How much you blame yourself, and how much you think about where you messed up, where you could've changed something that would've kept all this from happening."

Amelia's grasp on her hands visibly loosened. "Yes. I've been there."

As Pam wiped the newest round of tears from her cheeks, Zane mentally commended Amelia's effort.

But at the same time, he felt like a wimp.

He hadn't been willing to share his own struggle because he didn't want to become mired down by emotion, but Amelia hadn't hesitated.

Then again, that was the give and take in their friendship.

He knew about her father's seventeen-year spree of alcoholism, her sister's spiral into heroin addiction, her brother's death in the line of duty as a CPD detective. Moreover, he knew how those events had affected and shaped her.

But Amelia knew nothing about him. Sure, he'd regaled plenty of stories about his embarrassing middle school incidents, but right around age thirteen was where the openness stopped.

Wasn't that the way he wanted it? He wanted every detail about her, but he provided only breadcrumbs in response.

Dammit, Palmer. Focus. You can dwell on this shit later.

He gave the pen a couple clicks. "Did Larissa have any connection to Cedarwood or to Massey County? Any friends, family members, anyone like that?"

Pam's eyebrows knitted together. "Massey County? I don't think Larissa's ever been there. Money was tight when I was raising her. I don't think we ever left Chicago except for maybe once or twice when my parents were still alive. It was always just me and her, and I wasn't the best role model, you know?" She pushed up the sleeve of her sweatshirt to point to a handful of scars near the inside of her elbow. Track marks. "My baby girl came by her problems honestly. I've been clean for more than ten years, but, well..." Her face crumpled again, and the woman sobbed for several long moments before excusing herself and heading to the bathroom.

When Pam returned, looking a little better after a hard cry, Zane and Amelia went through the remainder of the questions they'd planned to ask, but there was no indication that Larissa maintained any connection to her troubled past. In the year that Larissa had been clean, she and her mother had even attended counseling sessions together. The therapy was courtesy of the insurance from Larissa's job, and the recommendation had come from her friend, Julie.

According to Pam, Larissa wanted to pursue a career as a drug and alcohol abuse counselor. When Larissa had disappeared, she'd been coming up on her first significant set of exams for the semester. All her courses had been online in order to allow her to continue her job as a server at the Sheraton. She'd experienced some stress, as expected, but she was also excited.

Less than four hours after they'd been assigned the case, Zane already had a low-burning hatred for the person who'd killed Larissa.

The girl had fought hard to dig herself out of the hole of addiction only to end up abused in a very different way.

Life just wasn't fair.

For good measure and to ensure all their bases were covered, Amelia went through a handful of photos with Pam before they left. A few of the mugshots were men from the now-defunct Central Crew, and the remainder were known Leóne henchmen.

Pam hadn't recognized a single one of them.

Settling back into the driver's seat of the black, work-issued sedan, Zane waited until Amelia had taken her spot before he started the engine.

He drummed his fingers against the steering wheel.

"Everything so far seems like it's telling us that Larissa wasn't on the mob's radar anymore."

Amelia fastened her seat belt before she turned to him. "But we can't rule it out unless…"

"Unless we hear it from the source. You thinking what I'm thinking?"

Her expression turned thoughtful. "Emilio Leóne's still in MCC Chicago. He's trying to appeal his conviction."

"Good." The wheels chirped on the pavement as he pulled away a little too fast. "We've got to go downtown to the Sheraton, so we might as well stop by to pay that jackass a visit while we're there."

❆

A HARSH BUZZ overhead was followed by the metallic click of a magnetic lock disengaging. Leaning against the mesh grate that covered a wall-spanning panel of durable plexiglass, Zane turned his head to the entrance of the prison interview room. At his side, Amelia uncrossed her legs and straightened in her rickety plastic chair.

With its cement floor, concrete walls, and reinforced windows, the space was the epitome of drab and uninviting.

The musclebound corrections officer prodded Emilio Leóne toward a rectangular table bolted to the floor. When the Leóne capo's hateful gaze fell on Zane and Amelia, Zane offered a demure wave as a self-satisfied smirk made its way to his face.

Interviewing Emilio would be a damn sight easier than breaking the news of Larissa's murder to her mother.

Once Emilio's shackles were affixed to the table, the guard took his leave. Though corrections officers typically waited outside the door, Zane had dismissed the man after informing the officer that their discussion with Leóne regarded sensitive information that was crucial to an ongoing FBI investigation.

After another MCC guard, a man named Russel Ulmer had facilitated the murder of a federal witness who'd been in custody at the facility, Zane trusted the prison personnel as far as he could throw them. With a man like Emilio—a man whose pockets and influence both ran deep—there was always the distinct possibility that the guards had been paid for their loyalty.

Zane crossed his arms and flashed Emilio one of his trademark grins. "Mr. Leóne. It's been a while. You look… well, not good, but not terrible. How's prison life treating you?"

A vein protruded from Emilio's forehead as he clenched his jaw in obvious anger. "What do you people want?"

Leaning slightly to one side in her chair so she could reach into the back pocket of her gray slacks, Amelia produced a folded picture of Larissa. In a swift movement, she slapped the printout atop the table and shoved it toward the prisoner.

Emilio jumped, and Zane almost laughed aloud. The big bad mob boss was still afraid of Amelia.

Zane didn't blame him.

Amelia sat up straight in her chair. "Do you know who she is?"

The capo's dark eyes flicked to the picture, but only for a split second. "No. Is that it?"

Though Zane wanted to spit out a litany of colorful insults, he swallowed the bout of anger. He'd dealt with enough men like Emilio during his tenure with the CIA and the FBI. He knew that open displays of rage wouldn't get him anywhere.

Indifference was the key. Amusement, even. Anything to throw them off-kilter.

Zane flashed Emilio another sarcastic smile. "Tell you what, Emilio. I figured you'd pull some shit like this, and I came prepared with a counteroffer. Want to hear it?"

A muscle in Emilio's scruffy jaw ticked. "Is this the sort of counteroffer I should have my lawyer present for?"

Zane's phony grin widened. If Emilio decided not to cooperate, he'd enjoy throwing the shithead's life into chaos. Maybe he'd make the practice a regular hobby. "No. Not yet."

In the silence that followed, Zane could swear he heard Emilio's teeth grind together. "What the hell do you want, Fed?"

Before Zane could answer, Amelia waved a hand at Larissa's picture. "I want you to stop being an obstinate little shit and look at that damn picture. After that, I want you to tell me if you recognize her."

Despite the practiced calm on Emilio's scruffy face, his eyes were ablaze with fury. "Why should I help you?"

Blowing out a sigh, Zane uncrossed his arms and straightened. "Because if you don't, my partner and I are going to make a side trip to your cell before we leave today. The two of us will *personally* rip the entire thing apart." He lifted his eyebrows to fix the capo with an expectant stare. "You know, just in case you're paying off anyone in here to ignore all that contraband you've got stashed up there."

Trepidation settled in beside Emilio's anger, and he shook his head. "You can't do that. Not without a war—"

Zane threw back his head and laughed. "A warrant? Please, Emilio. You're not a private citizen anymore. You're a felon, and you're a *prisoner*. We don't need a warrant to look for contraband."

Amelia held up a finger in feigned enlightenment. "Not to mention, I'm on good terms with the warden." Fear crossed the prisoner's features, and Amelia laughed. "And based on that look, our friend here knows that Mr. Gillem isn't in his family's pocket. I'm sure Gillem would be happy to toss you in solitary for a few weeks to make an example out of you."

Rubbing his hands together, Zane pushed away from the wall and inched toward the door. "What do you suppose we'll find? You don't look like you're high on anything, but I'm willing to bet you've got a shiv or two for protection. Probably a phone—"

As well as he could manage, Emilio threw up his restrained hands. "Okay! I'll look at the damn picture."

With the tips of his fingers, he dragged the paper closer. For a several moments, he studied the image of Larissa in her graduation robe and cap.

Anticipation mixed with disgust as Zane stared at the man's features. Emilio León had been responsible for overseeing the León family's prostitution ring for years. The man had no misgivings about sending underaged girls out to work the streets if their suffering meant he'd line his pockets.

If Larissa had any noteworthy dealings with the Leónes during her time as a working girl, then she would have crossed paths with Emilio at some point.

Nodding his head slightly, Emilio used the tips of his fingers to slide the picture across the table. "She looks familiar, like I might've seen her somewhere before." He lifted a shoulder as if the statement didn't matter. "But I don't know her."

Amelia's eyebrow arched sharply. "You sure about that, slick?"

A flicker of annoyance passed over Emilio's face at the condescending pet name. "Yes. I'm sure."

For a long, drawn-out moment of silence, Zane pinned Emilio with a scrutinizing stare. He searched for anxiety or fear, any indication the man was lying.

There were no signs of deception. As far as Zane could tell, the León capo had told them the truth.

However, Emilio's honesty begged one question. If the man barely recognized Larissa, barely even cared about her existence, then why would the Leónes have wanted her dead?

Zane's stomach sank.

Maybe they were dealing with a serial killer after all.

6
―――

The manager's office of the restaurant in the Sheraton Hotel was the size of a broom closet. As Amelia glanced from an OSHA printout to a clipboard that held the employees' schedules, her shoulder brushed against Zane's. The length of the desk—if that's what the countertop built into the wall could even be called—at their backs was barely enough for the two of them to stand side by side.

If the broad-shouldered Dean Steelman had taken Amelia's place, she suspected he would have had to take a seat on the file cabinet beside the door.

Amelia had been employed at a movie theater for a spell while she was in high school, and she couldn't say she was surprised by the cramped space. Management offices in customer-facing jobs like restaurants, retail stores, and movie theaters were usually bare bones.

The cramped space closed in on Amelia like the memories rushing back from her past. Larissa was right around the same age as Amelia's sister. If Larissa had been from Englewood instead of North Lawndale, she and Lainey might have even gone to school together.

The two young women had grown up poor, in rough neighborhoods, and had fallen into the same sinkhole of addiction. Where Larissa's drug of choice had been prescription pain pills, Lainey's was heroin.

Unlike Amelia's sister, however, Larissa had pulled herself out of the miasma.

Some days, Amelia wondered if Lainey was too far gone to ever return to some semblance of a normal life.

Less than a month earlier, Amelia's sister had been booked for a flight that would have taken her from Milwaukee to Chicago. Amelia had paid to reserve a room for Lainey at a renowned rehabilitation center in the city, and she'd been so damn sure that Lainey finally intended to go through with her promised attempt to get clean.

She'd assured herself that this time would be different. That Lainey wasn't trying to swindle her out of a chunk of cash to feed her addiction. After all, what in the hell could Lainey even do with a one-way plane ticket to Chicago? She couldn't change the passenger name, and the TSA would laugh in the face of anyone who tried to board in her place. Right before they arrested the person for attempted fraud.

But just like Lainey had done so many times before, she'd proven Amelia's flash of optimism wrong.

At the security checkpoint of the Milwaukee airport, Lainey had been caught with a baggie of heroin. The DEA agent who'd arrested her had called Amelia shortly afterward.

Apparently, Lainey had thought to use her sister's position as an FBI agent to seek some sort of leniency with the Drug Enforcement Agency.

Amelia had wasted no time shattering her younger sister's delusion. She'd advised Agent Pablo Menendez to treat Lainey the same way he'd treat any other suspect, which was exactly what the DEA agent had done. Lainey had pled to a

Class E felony, much like Larissa Umber had done when she was nineteen.

Though Amelia wanted to tell herself that her little sister could follow the same path as Larissa, she couldn't take any more false hope.

Lainey was on her own.

As a slender woman with a strawberry-blonde bob and silver nametag approached the open doorway, Amelia straightened and pulled her focus back to the restaurant. Dwelling on her sister's betrayal wouldn't get her anywhere.

The scent of frying burgers wafted into the cramped office, and Amelia's stomach grumbled.

"Sorry to keep you waiting. I, um, just had to help one of my servers with a refund issue." The woman, an assistant manager named Amy, stopped just inside the doorway. Her large blue eyes shifted between the agents, looking like her nerves might jump through her skin.

Zane offered one of his patented reassuring smiles. "Not a problem. I know how customers can get."

Did he? Amelia couldn't recall if he'd ever told her about his employment history before he'd joined the FBI.

The manager took one last look at the storage area behind her before she squeezed the rest of the way into the room. Had the door not opened from the outside, Amelia doubted they'd have had enough room to close the damn thing.

By the time Amy turned to face them, Amelia had retrieved a small notepad from the inside pocket of her coat.

Taking his cue, Zane cleared his throat. "Ms. Dern, we're here today to follow up on Larissa Umber."

Amy's face fell, and sadness seemed to weigh down her shoulders. "Larissa was such a sweet kid, and she was a great employee."

One of Zane's eyebrows quirked up. "Was? You've heard what happened to her?"

Wringing both hands, Amy dipped her chin. "Yes. Julie Breyer told me a little while ago. She and Larissa were good friends."

Amelia scribbled a few notes to keep herself anchored in the present. Her heart was broken for Larissa's mother and friends, but the sentiment was fuel for her growing determination. "The notes from the missing persons investigation say you were the manager on shift the night Larissa was last seen. Is that correct?"

"Yes, I was. Julie and I were both working with Larissa that night. Julie was off a couple hours before Larissa."

"Did you notice anything peculiar that night? Any specific person or table who might've had an...unusual interest in Larissa?"

Amy rubbed her cheek as she considered Zane's question. "No, not that I noticed. The officers asked me the same thing when they were doing the missing persons investigation, and I've thought about it a lot since then. But nothing sticks out. We were really busy that night, so all my servers had a lot of tables."

Before Amelia posed her follow-up question, she mentally acknowledged that she was going out on a limb. "Were there any unruly customers that night? Anyone who seemed angry or upset with the service?"

"Not any more than usual, and no one that jumps out at me."

Zane leaned back against the edge of the desk, his gaze fixed on Amy. "Did Larissa have trouble with any of your other employees? Any ongoing feuds, or maybe any men who'd tried to get her to go out with them?"

Amy sighed, and Amelia didn't miss the resignation in her expression.

The woman *wanted* to be helpful, but she knew she was just rehashing the same information she'd given the Chicago PD. "No. Larissa was one of those employees who got along with everyone."

Amelia slowed her writing. After the fat lot of nothing in the CPD's missing persons case, including interviews from employees at the Sheraton's restaurant, her expectations had been low. Still, as Zane went over another handful of questions, Amelia was struck by a twinge of disappointment.

According to Amy, Larissa had left alone that night, much the same as any other day of the week. Larissa didn't have a license or a car, so she would take the L home. The walk to the nearest stop was only eight blocks.

She'd left the restaurant like she always did, but somewhere in that eight-block trip, a killer had laid in wait. Larissa had never used her pass for the L.

Once Amelia and Zane had finished talking to Amy, they interviewed all the remaining employees on shift.

Sixteen people, and not a shred of new information.

As a cook named Monty left the office and eased the door closed behind himself, Amelia finally heaved a sigh that had been building throughout the afternoon.

With a low groan in his throat, Zane rubbed his eyes. "My thoughts exactly. What's our next stop? Security cameras?"

Stretching as well as she was able in the cramped space, Amelia shook off the mental cobwebs. "Yeah, I think so. The cameras from the restaurant and from the exterior of the hotel. See if anyone intercepted Larissa while she was on her way out of the building."

"I guess the CPD didn't go that far for a missing persons report, did they?"

Amelia scoffed quietly. "Not for a recovering addict with a rap sheet. I'm surprised they even came in here and talked to Larissa's coworkers. After no one knew anything, they probably just wrote it off as a relapse and went on with their lives."

Though Amelia always strove to go above and beyond the call of duty in her career, she wasn't under the illusion that everyone who was a part of the criminal justice system held the same philosophy. In fact, she'd *never* been under that illusion.

That was why she'd become a part of the system. To do better, and to demand that those around her do better.

"All right." Zane's voice pulled her from her ruminating. He stifled a yawn with the back of one hand. "Let's get some caffeine and a quick bite to eat, then hit the security office here. I've heard your stomach growling for quite some time, Storm." A smile played at his lips. "After that, we can walk to the L on the same route that Larissa would have taken. See if there are any more cameras that might've caught something."

Amelia tried to fight the compulsion to yawn, but she was unsuccessful. "Right. There was a transaction on her card for a gas station close to the L. We can check that out too. And my stomach hasn't been the only one talking." Amelia was grateful for the ease that had returned to their banter.

Zane rubbed his hands together and flashed her an expectant glance. "Let's get to it."

❅

Gripping the back of Zane's chair, Amelia dropped the other hand to her hip as she leaned in over her friend's shoulder to peer at a computer monitor. The office used by management at the chain gas station was more spacious than the cramped room at the Sheraton, but not by much.

A bald man with a gut that made him look seven months pregnant stood beside a closed door, both hairy arms crossed over his chest. Doug's name tag proclaimed that he was the general manager, and he'd refused to leave Amelia and Zane's side since their arrival.

Amelia still hadn't determined if the man was making a misguided effort to be helpful, or if he was just an overbearing prick.

She tried to ignore Doug's presence and studied the black and white image on the screen instead. "Is that her?"

"Yeah, that's her heading inside." Zane tapped the screen. "The transaction took place two minutes and thirty-seven seconds later."

Pressing her lips together, Amelia watched the slow-motion replay.

Larissa's dark hair was pinned atop her head in a messy bun, and the edge of her name tag peeked out from beneath her zip-up hoodie. She exuded exhaustion, which wasn't surprising for someone who worked on her feet waiting on people all day, but Amelia didn't note any indication of fear or worry. If the young woman had crossed paths with her killer by this point, she wasn't aware of the encounter.

After selecting a bottle of soda from the cooler, Larissa went straight to the cashier. The clerk added a pack of cigarettes to the order, and Larissa paid without incident.

Amelia gestured to the monitor. "Pam said she asked Larissa to get her some smokes on the way home."

"Seems like she fully intended to return home. She looks good. Steady. Safe to assume she wasn't going back to the lifestyle. Which means..." Zane shook his head and glanced at the manager.

Amelia nodded, reading her partner's mind. With Doug listening to their every word, they needed to be careful. The term "serial killer" was more than enough to send the average person's mind spiraling with outlandish theories and urban myths.

A couple clicks of the mouse switched the feed to a

camera mounted just outside the entrance of the gas station. The lens gave a clear view of the four fuel pumps as well as the parking stalls in front of the building.

Larissa dropped the cigarettes in her handbag and tucked both hands in her pockets. At the edge of the sidewalk, she stopped, her head swinging to a disturbance that Amelia and Zane couldn't see.

Amelia could almost hear Zane's teeth grind together as he flipped to the second outdoor camera.

Nothing.

The new view gave them a vantage point of the street, but not Larissa.

Zane changed back to the first recording. "Something caught her attention." His head swiveled to the general manager. "This doesn't have sound? At all?"

The man ran a hand over his shiny head. "No. Just video."

Amelia wanted to spit out a series of four-letter words, but she swallowed the expletives before they could leave her lips.

Uttering a few sentences they couldn't hear, Larissa strode off in the direction of whatever had piqued her interest. A grainy shadow appeared at the edge of the screen, but the figure might as well have been a damn ghost.

Click.

Zane brought his finger down on the spacebar to freeze the image. "Another person. Looks like a man. Probably half a foot taller than Larissa."

"Shit." Amelia dragged the word out for a full six syllables. Tentative optimism loosened the grasp of the phantom hand that had squeezed at her heart on and off throughout the day.

As Zane pressed play, Amelia made her best effort to channel all her willpower into the shadowy figure a few feet away from Larissa.

Just take a couple steps forward. Into the light. Come on, just a little closer, you piece of shit.

Amelia slowed her breathing and focused all her attention just at the edge of the camera's field of vision. She stared, and stared, and stared. But no matter how she squinted or how much closer to the screen she leaned, the man didn't advance.

Finally, after what could have been thirty seconds or thirty hours, the figure walked backward and out of view.

Larissa followed, and neither of them reappeared.

A tomb-like silence descended over the room as Amelia and Zane kept their diligent stares on the video.

Watching. Hoping.

The seconds ticked away in the timestamp on the bottom left-hand corner of the feed. A full five minutes passed before Amelia gave up and straightened to her full height.

She and Zane had stopped to request footage from each security camera they'd spotted on their short trek to the gas station. Though a couple cameras had caught Larissa as she'd walked by, none had shown a second person on her tail.

There were still more places to check before they reached the L, but Amelia's gut said the search would be pointless.

Shaking off the moment of despair, she turned to the manager. "We need the names of anyone who was on shift when this footage was taken, and if they're here right now, we'll need to speak with them." Her stare turned frosty. "Alone."

The bald man opened his mouth as if he thought to protest, but as soon as he caught her expression, he clamped his jaw shut. "Okay. I'll get those for you."

Their search for a needle in a stack of needles continued.

At this rate, Amelia wondered if they'd ever make it to Cedarwood.

7

As Dean Steelman watched the greasy black liquid pool in the bottom of a coffee pot circa the seventies, his hope that the brew was superior to what the FBI provided in its Chicago office was dashed. With a sigh, he leaned against the drywall beside a tall window and crossed his arms.

The main breakroom at the Massey County Sheriff's Department was simple but functional. A stainless-steel refrigerator stood at the end of the laminate counter that spanned the length of one wall. All the basic necessities of a home kitchen were present—a toaster, microwave, sink, and coffee maker. Everything aside from the range and oven.

Dean held back another sigh. Based on the hotel rooms he and Sherry had checked into earlier, the kitchenette at the sheriff's department was the closest he was going to get to a real kitchen while he was in Cedarwood. God, he hoped there was a decent coffee shop somewhere in this damn town.

While Dean had spent the first eighteen years of his life in a little shithole in the hills of West Virginia, he'd grown accustomed to the luxuries of larger cities. *Especially* the options for coffee.

The more frou-frou the latte, the better. Dean had always hated the taste of black coffee, and he wouldn't hesitate to conceal the bitterness with whatever was handy. He'd never live down his preference if he was back in his hometown, but god willing, he'd never have to go back there.

His musings were cut short as a pair of deputies strolled through the wide doorway.

Rubbing his forehead, Dean glanced to the coffee pot. The ancient appliance hadn't even filled the carafe to the halfway point. Apparently, he should have plopped down on the leather couch to take a nap while he waited for the damn thing.

Dean exchanged a wordless greeting with the two men before they went about pulling their respective lunches from the giant fridge.

The taller of the two, a lanky fellow with close-cropped blond and silver hair, turned to his partner as he started the microwave. "Man, when I took this job and moved to Cedarwood from Peabody, I thought I was leaving the frantic parents behind, you know?"

His friend nodded.

Oh, you don't even know the half of it.

Turning to the coffee pot, Dean kept the thought to himself. He was pointedly aware that the deputies viewed him as an outsider. The last thing he needed was to act smug and give the deputies another reason to be wary of him.

Twelve years of experience in law enforcement, ten of which had been spent in the FBI, had taught him how to behave if he wanted cooperation from the locals.

The first deputy held up both hands in a gesture of innocence. "Don't get me wrong, I feel bad for the lady. Drove all the way down here from Mendoza looking for her daughter.

Canvassed Highway 26 up and down, trying to find the kid's car, but no luck. Her daughter's cell sent calls to voicemail, she doesn't respond to text messages, all that."

A hint of sympathy flashed over the shorter man's features, reminding Dean that small-town cops tended to form a stronger bond with the communities they served. No one in Chicago would think twice about a frantic mother searching for her kid, but the two men in the breakroom were both visibly concerned.

Then again, if the cops in Chicago became emotionally invested in every case that came across their desks, they'd be dead from the stress by the time they hit age twenty-two.

Dean checked the coffee again. Two-thirds full. There was probably enough for him and Sherry, but he was intrigued by the deputies' conversation.

"Damn." The shorter man took his spot at the microwave, and Dean's stomach grumbled as he caught a whiff of garlic and butter. "I'd probably freak out if one of mine went missing too. Even if they were adults." He frowned. "How old was the missing girl? Nineteen?"

"Yeah, nineteen. She was headed home from college for Thanksgiving break. Stopped at Oliver's to get gas, then sent her brother a text saying she was stopping to help some stranded driver." The tall deputy's face grew solemn. "That was the last they heard from her, and she never made it home. The mother said she had one of those apps that lets you find all the phones on your plan, but she couldn't find her daughter's."

"You think she got in an accident?"

With a sigh, the tall man sank onto a seat at the end of the couch. "I don't know. Even if that's what happened...no one's heard from her. It doesn't look good, you know?"

The man had a point.

Curiosity piqued, Dean cleared his throat to get the men's

attention. Both sets of eyes shifted to him. "How often do people go missing 'round here? Massey County, I mean."

The tall deputy shrugged as he and his friend exchanged contemplative glances. "People disappearing without a trace? Not often. The county's population is just over eleven thousand." He tilted his chin at Dean. "You're one of the Feds who's in town for that severed head they pulled out of Fox Creek, aren't you?"

"Sure am." Dean pulled open a cabinet door and retrieved a pair of mugs. By now, Sherry probably thought he'd given up on the breakroom and had gone in search of real coffee. When he turned back to the deputies, their faces had become inquisitive.

As the microwave beeped, the shorter man pulled out his food. "Do you think this girl might be part of that whole mess?"

Dean ignored the new rumble in his stomach. "Hard to say, but I've never been much for coincidences. What's the missing girl's name?"

"Willow Nowland. Student at Breely University in Peabody, on her way home to Mendoza."

After he'd filled the pair of mugs with the dark sludge and doctored his with as much sweetener and powdered coffee creamer as he could rustle up, Dean thanked the deputies and made his way back to the mostly empty conference room that had become their base of operations.

Like the break area, the space was relatively unadorned but functional. And considering that the next door down the hall led to an unoccupied office, Dean figured the Massey County Sheriff's Department must have had more room in their building than they did people to fill it.

As he elbowed open the door, Sherry's head jerked up from where she'd been engrossed in her laptop.

"There you are." She stifled a yawn for emphasis.

"Thought you'd gone on a field trip to try to find a café or something."

Dean snorted. He'd worked with Sherry Cowen for a little more than a year, and by now, they'd each become familiar with one another's quirks.

He set his steaming mug on the rectangular table and started for the whiteboard. "I thought about it, but I'm too damn tired after that drive."

Sherry tossed him a look of feigned indignation. "You didn't even drive."

With a sarcastic smile, Dean scooped up a dry-erase marker and pointed to her. "Exactly. For two and a half hours, I was in some kinda nap limbo, you know? Tried falling asleep but never quite got there." He hated when he got sidetracked and focused back on what he'd just learned. "Whatever. That's not important. I heard a couple deputies talkin' about a girl who went missing yesterday."

Propping both elbows atop the table, Sherry scooted forward. Curiosity shone in her brown and green eyes. "Missing girl? In Massey County?"

"Willow Nowland." Dean pronounced the girl's name as he scrawled it along the top left-hand corner of a spacious whiteboard. "Nineteen, college student. Mom said she couldn't trace her cell, and all her calls were going straight to voicemail. It's possible she was in an accident, but the deputies haven't found her car."

Sherry cupped her chin in one hand, a common gesture when she was thinking. "Probably a good idea to keep her in mind. Better safe than sorry."

"My thoughts exactly." Dean dropped the marker back to the metal tray at the base of the board. "Any word from our friends in Organized Crime?"

When he and Sherry had been introduced to Agents Palmer and Storm earlier in the day, Dean hadn't been quite sure what to make of the duo. He prided himself on being a good judge of character, and though he had no reason to think poorly of the agents, they were…curious.

Then again, if Dean had to deal with human traffickers on a regular basis, he'd be "curious" too.

Traffickers were the worst of the worst, the scum of the earth and the bottom of the barrel. He'd rather deal with a brutal serial killer than a ring of traffickers any day of the week.

Despite the disdain, he could admit that part of him was intrigued by the pair.

Palmer and Storm had come with a reputation. Over the course of the summer, they'd taken down two separate mob-run trafficking operations. One in Chicago, and the second on a farm in Kankakee County.

The details of both operations were still fuzzy to Dean since Organized Crime operated on a "need to know" basis. All he knew for certain was what he'd seen in the Bureau's press conferences.

Most recently, and more interestingly, word around the office had it that Amelia Storm had been kidnapped and almost killed by *another agent*. Rubbing his temple, Dean tucked the piece of information away. He made a mental note to ask Agent Storm if the story was true.

The door creaked open to reveal a familiar deputy. Heath McCannon was an inch or two under six-foot, but what he lacked in height, he made up for with his broad shoulders and a barrel chest.

With his fiery red hair and pale green eyes, the guy embodied the popular media's depiction of an Irishman. Dean had six inches on McCannon, but he figured the deputy could bench press him without breaking a sweat.

"Agents, thanks for waiting on me." McCannon produced a rolled-up paper as the door swung closed behind him. "I've got a topographic map of the area around Fox Creek, marked with the locations where we found the victims' remains."

Dean finished a long sip of still-hot coffee and offered the deputy a grateful smile. "Perfect. Let's take a look."

McCannon walked over to the whiteboard, clearly eager to make headway on their case. "I've got a handful of guys who're rotating shifts looking through one of the areas we think Larissa's remains might've come from. I'd ask the sheriff to put more guys on it, but we don't have a ton of manpower to go around as it is."

"Which is why we're here now." Returning the mug to the table, Dean stood behind the chair next to Sherry and watched McCannon unfurl the map.

Heath McCannon had been a driving force behind the county's decision to call in aid from the FBI. Asking for help wasn't always easy, especially with the peculiar sense of pride that was so prevalent among law enforcement circles.

As far as Dean was concerned, McCannon's adamancy that they bring in the FBI had taken guts.

The county often went years without a single homicide. In most reports, Massey County could count its violent crimes on one hand. Put bluntly, Massey County was ill-equipped to deal with a serial killer or a human trafficker.

Once all four corners of the paper were held in place by magnets, McCannon stepped to the side. Sherry rose from her seat, and she and Dean joined the deputy at the front of the room to study the map.

Along Fox Creek, each victim's remains were marked with a red X. The killer *had* to have buried them near the banks, but the better question was *where*? Fox Creek originated more than ten miles north, near a lake just off the Illinois River.

Had the remains found their way into Fox Creek *from* the Illinois River? Dean held back a groan. God, he hoped not.

McCannon tapped a section of land approximately one hundred yards upstream from where Larissa's severed head had been discovered, and Dean turned his attention to where the detective's finger pointed. "This is where we're searching right now. We think that with the recent rain, the vic's body...her *head* could've been washed out from where she was buried. Since her TOD is within the last couple weeks, the gravesite would be new, so it's more likely that it could be disturbed."

"What about here?" Sherry pointed to a space a little farther north. "The banks of the creek get a little steeper up here, but this part slopes down before it drops off."

Rubbing his chin, McCannon appeared thoughtful for a beat before he spoke. Insightfulness must have been one of the deputy's strong suits. "Could be, yeah. Definitely worth checking out since our guys and their dogs haven't found anything where they're at now."

Dean merely nodded his agreement. He wasn't quite ready to share his bleak realization with Sherry and McCannon. Plus, the actual likelihood that the individual body parts of four different women who'd been murdered in similar ways had just so happened to find their way into the same creek were astronomical.

At least, that's what Dean would continue to tell himself.

8
———

When Amelia and Zane finally reached Cedarwood, the sun had dipped down to touch the horizon. The sight of the small town was almost foreign to Amelia. She'd spent the first eighteen years of her life in the inner city of Chicago, and until she'd met Alex Passarelli, she'd hardly ventured outside the city.

As Zane steered them past the town square—a *literal* square, to Amelia's bemusement—she was taken aback by the sheer lack of…anyone. A restaurant, the craft store to its side, and a used clothing store all sported neon "closed" signs. The heart of the town was desolate, and the sun hadn't even set.

Maybe the people who live here heard there might be a serial killer in the area.

Amelia could admit the prospect would be enough to keep her indoors if she were a civilian.

A few blocks north of Cedarwood's heart was the sheriff's department. The single-story building was wide, but its gray cement exterior was unremarkable. In truth, the place was more akin to what she'd expect from a call center, not the hub of an entire county's law enforcement operations.

She thought about making a sarcastic observation to Zane, but her own exhaustion prevented it. Amelia was grateful the awkwardness between them seemed to have eased. Of course, she couldn't speak for her partner, but it certainly felt like they were falling back into their comfortable rhythm. The long car ride down had been filled with easy banter and casual conversation.

Zane's friendship was too important to her, and the thought of losing it sent tingling anxiety down the back of her neck.

Amelia was relieved they had not needed to dive into some heavy dialogue to salvage their bond. She was no good at emotionally charged conversations. Hell, she didn't think she'd ever been good at such delicate discussions. But so many years of walling herself off from her family and friends had taken a toll akin to cutting off circulation to a limb for an extended period of time. Returning feeling to nerve endings that had been dead for so long was a painful process, and there was no guarantee of success.

As the hum of the engine ceased, Amelia jerked herself back to the present. Sliding a tablet into her handbag, she unfastened her seat belt and cast an expectant glance to Zane. "Ready?"

He tapped a finger on his lower lip. "Should we do this first, or should we check into that hotel? We're just leaving all our shit in the trunk out here, unattended."

Laughter bubbled up in Amelia's throat, and she clapped a hand over her mouth to stop it.

Zane shot her a look of feigned exasperation. "What?"

She waved away the question. "No, nothing. It's just that…we're in a town of fewer than sixty-five-hundred people, and we're parked in front of the sheriff's station. I *really* don't think anyone's going to come creeping along out here to break into the trunk of an FBI vehicle so they can steal…what, exactly? Our clothes? My little TSA approved bottle of conditioner?"

His smile had grown wide by the time she finished the explanation. "I'll have you know that I have a pretty impressive pog collection, Agent Storm."

Amelia blinked at him, making no move to hide her confusion. "I don't even know what a pog *is* or why you would have brought them with you. Are you expecting lots of downtime, Agent?" Amelia couldn't restrain her smirk.

Laughing, he shoved open his door. "No, my dear clueless friend, I did not bring my prized collection with me. I forget you're five years younger than I am. At twenty-nine years old, you missed out on the joy of collecting pogs as a kid."

As she stepped out into the golden sunlight, Amelia turned to him and planted both hands on her hips. "Thirty now. Thank you very much."

He drew his eyebrows together. His obvious befuddlement took the place of his good humor. "What? You turned thirty? When? Why didn't you say anything?"

Amelia's heartbeat picked up, her mouth suddenly dry. Butterflies frolicked in her gut at her friend's worry over her forgotten birthday. She cleared her throat for fear her voice would betray her. "Um…the seventh. It was right in the middle of when Glenn was trying to kill me and right after she'd killed Ben Storey. Didn't seem like an optimal time to jump up and say, 'Hey, guys, it's my birthday!' You know?"

His shoulders drooped, and he shook his head. "Yeah, I guess that's true, huh? Well," he blew out a long breath as he stretched both arms above his head, "to be fair, it really isn't your responsibility to tell your friends that it's your birthday, is it? I *know* you've told me before, but I didn't remember. I'd say it was because of the Storey case, but that'd be a lie. I'm sorry I missed it."

Amelia offered him a grin as they stepped over the curb. "It's okay. I don't remember your birthday either."

He snickered, and Amelia hated the way her stomach fluttered again.

A sheriff's deputy with a head full of salt and pepper hair greeted them. With a polite smile, the man directed them toward a hall just past the collection of desks dotting the open space.

Part of Amelia was surprised that, in addition to the man who'd greeted them, she only spotted two additional deputies. But like she'd told Zane, they were in a town of fewer than seven thousand residents. The sheriff's department wasn't a constant hive of activity like the police precincts in Chicago.

Amelia knocked on the door marked "Conference Room B," but she didn't wait for a response before she let herself and Zane inside.

As the three occupants of the minimally decorated space turned to them, the deputy pushed to his feet. Skirting around the edge of the table, he extended a hand first to Amelia and then Zane. "Agents, it's nice to meet you. I'm Deputy Heath McCannon."

She and Zane introduced themselves before they greeted Agents Steelman and Cowen.

Amelia hoped the two agents and Deputy McCannon had a more productive day than she and Zane.

As Agent Steelman approached the whiteboard, his vivid blue gaze lingered on Amelia for a beat longer than normal. Amelia wondered at first if the man was checking her out, but his attention didn't drift away from her face, and his curiosity wasn't consistent with the lewd intent of someone like Joseph Larson.

Goose bumps tickled her arms as a sudden wave of self-consciousness washed over her. Unshouldering her handbag,

Amelia pulled out a chair and slumped down to sit. She wanted to make herself at home *beneath* the table so no one could see her, but she'd have to settle for the hard plastic chair for the time being.

First, Joseph Larson's attempt to blackmail her into screwing him—no, his attempt to *rape* her—and then Glenn. At least no one other than Zane knew about Larson, but she was sure the rumor mill had been working overtime after Glenn had tried to kill her.

Wasn't the FBI office supposed to be a secure location? A safe place?

Put a group of people together, and human nature takes over. Sigh.

How in the seven hells had she wound up working side by side with a rapist *and* a murderer?

Amelia had personal experience with the Bureau's extensive background checks. It was a small miracle they hadn't uncovered her high school relationship with Alex Passarelli.

Then again, the D'Amato crime family wasn't exactly public about their personal lives. She and Alex hadn't shared pictures of themselves on social media, and their little circle of friends knew better than to try to take pictures and post statuses about the son of a D'Amato capo.

But more than anything else, social media simply hadn't been as pervasive.

The scrape of a chair's legs against the tiled floor jerked her from her reminiscing as Zane took a spot at her side.

Amelia forced an amiable expression. She hoped her friend hadn't noticed the sinkhole into which she'd briefly fallen, but she doubted she'd be so lucky. Zane Palmer was like a damn mind reader.

"Looks like you guys had a productive day." Zane inclined his head at the whiteboard, and Amelia's gaze followed.

Sure enough, four different names, a map marked with

the location of each victim's remains, and a handful of dates and locations had been scrawled across the board.

Moving closer to the whiteboard, Dean Steelman tapped a capped marker next to the first name, Heather Breysacher. "Yeah, somethin' like that. I don't know if I'd call this 'productive.' Organized, maybe. Productive? Not so much. Best I can say is we got this all together so we can send it to the BAU before we go to bed tonight."

The FBI's Behavioral Analysis Unit had always piqued Amelia's curiosity, but her lingering sense of embarrassment from Agent Steelman's stare kept her from asking any questions.

"It is productive." From her spot at the other end of the table, Sherry Cowen stood. "We didn't find any new leads, but we need to know all this information if we're going to get anywhere."

In the silence that followed, Amelia took stock of the whiteboard.

Heather Breysacher, twenty-four when she was killed, worked as a middle-school science teacher in Bloomington, Illinois. Next was Jane Doe One, but there was little elaboration, only that her leg had been found about a year earlier. Jane Doe Two's slot was similarly empty. Her torso had been discovered, and the medical examiner established she'd been tortured.

And then, of course, there was Larissa.

Agent Cowen tapped her finger beside Heather's neatly printed name. "Heather's head was found by a woman who was hiking with her dog. Deputies combed the area after, and they found an arm that also belonged to Heather. Both the head and the arm had been neatly severed with precise cuts. The speculation was that the killer has some medical background since he or she knew to pull on the arm in such a way that allowed them to cut through cartilage and not bone. They never found anything else, though."

Amelia raised a finger. "And that was four years ago?"

Cowen nodded. "Yes. Heather was eventually identified via dental records, and we think that's why the killer pulled out Larissa's teeth. Serial killers tend to follow news about their crimes, and this one would have heard that Heather had been identified using her old dental records. A serial killer's obsession with their own news coverage varies a little from one killer to the next, but experience says most will pay attention to the news."

Deputy McCannon crossed his muscular arms, his attention fixed on the two agents from Violent Crimes. "Killing is like a ritual for them, right?"

"Right." Sherry's attention stayed on the whiteboard. "The more they kill, the more they hone their 'method.' It's unusual for them to break out of that routine, at least by much. They might gradually add certain elements to their repertoire, but not all at once. It's a…process."

Though Agent Cowen was addressing the deputy, Amelia's ears had perked up at the explanation. She knew more than the average citizen about serial killers, they all did, but Cowen and Steelman had a far deeper understanding.

Maybe I could ask for their opinion on the guy who made paint out of eyeballs.

She silently groaned. The story had been relayed to her by an agent in the Violent Crimes division in Boston. After more than thirty years with the Bureau, the man had seen it all. He and Amelia used to wind up in the cafeteria at the same time for their lunch break, and she'd pick his brain for the most bizarre, gruesome stories he was willing to regale.

Agent Kenny Ingram had been her first friend in the

Boston field office, and she hoped he was enjoying his retirement.

As Dean Steelman's scrutinizing stare settled on Amelia and Zane, Amelia fought the urge to sink even lower in her seat. "What'd y'all find on Larissa Umber? Any signs the mob might've been involved?"

To Amelia's relief, Zane jumped in to relay the potential leads they'd followed that afternoon. He went over how they'd spent the time chasing after security camera footage that, aside from what they'd found at the gas station, was useless. They had learned Larissa hadn't been seen after her stop to buy cigarettes and soda. Zane also briefly summarized their conversation with Pamela Umber, and last but not least, their short interview with Emilio Leóne.

Though the subtle gesture might have been in Amelia's imagination, she could have sworn Dean Steelman silently acknowledged the mention of the prominent Leóne capo.

Considering that neither he nor Agent Cowen had known much about the Leónes earlier in the day, the man must have done his homework.

As Zane concluded his rundown, the name in the top left-hand corner of the whiteboard caught Amelia's attention. "Willow Nowland?" She flashed the two VC agents a puzzled glance. "Did you find another victim? Who's that?"

In tandem, Sherry Cowen and Dean Steelman turned to the girl's name. Rubbing his cheek, Steelman and his partner exchanged contemplative looks.

Are they hiding something? We're supposed to be working together.

The first tendrils of anger flashed in the back of Amelia's mind, and she curled her hand into a fist to avoid smacking the table like she so often did in interrogations.

Sherry Cowen held both arms out at her sides. "Well, we aren't really sure if she's involved yet. Steelman overheard a couple deputies talking about how her frantic mother had shown up at the department earlier to report her missing. The circumstances are…"

"Unusual," Steelman finished for her. "Especially in a place like Massey County. Last her family heard from her, she texted to say she was stopping to help a stranded motorist. Considering she had updated her family twice while en route and that her car was nowhere to be found on the only highway that leads out of Cedarwood to her hometown of Mendoza, it looks suspicious as hell. And since we've reason to believe our killer is escalating, we can't rule out that this might be related."

Deputy McCannon seemed to soak up all the information like a sponge. "So, we've got a killer who tortures his victims and then cuts up their bodies and buries the pieces in different locations. And who also might have ties to human trafficking. That about right?"

One of Steelman's eyebrows arched sharply. "You think he's *both*?"

The deputy held up his hands. "I'm proposing it as a possibility. Last I knew, trafficker and serial killer weren't mutually exclusive, you know?"

His proclamation seemed to drain any semblance of warmth from the room.

Dammit.

The deputy was right.

It was a theory Amelia had been thinking about herself, and it twisted her stomach in knots to know she wasn't alone in that belief.

A human trafficker who moonlighted as a serial killer.

If Willow Nowland *was* involved, the clock was ticking.

9

Zane reached for another pillow to prop his back against the headboard of the queen-sized bed. Though not quite as luxurious or polished as the Sheraton he and Amelia had visited earlier in the day, the hotel was comfortable enough. No free breakfast, but Zane would survive. He couldn't expect much more from the small town. A miniature fridge, thirty-two-inch television, iron, hair dryer, and coffee maker were the only appliances provided.

Good enough for a few days. Provided this case only *lasted* a few days. He hadn't brought many wardrobe changes, and he preferred the comfort of his own bed. Besides, Thanksgiving was in a few days. He hated working cases over holidays.

Who wouldn't?

The town seemed nice enough, but Zane was accustomed to city life, having been born and raised in Jersey City. He'd spent some time in Russia's more rural areas, but there was no comparison between the subarctic and the wooded countryside of Illinois.

To say he was out of his comfort zone was an understatement. Small Town, U.S.A. wasn't his forte.

Serial killers weren't his forte.

What in the hell were he and Amelia doing here, anyway?

His fingernails scraped against his scalp as he raked a hand through his hair. Agents Steelman and Cowen had the serial killer angle locked down, so perhaps he and Amelia needed to view the killings from the perspective of a human trafficker.

Wiggling the wireless mouse to keep the laptop's screen saver from launching, Zane glanced to his side as the door that separated his and Amelia's rooms creaked open.

Her damp hair hung over her shoulders in ropy strands, and a droplet of water rolled from the edge of one to plop on the carpet at her stocking feet. She'd washed away most traces of her makeup, but dark smudges remained beneath her lower lids.

As if she could sense his scrutiny, Amelia rubbed beneath one eye and then the other. "Find anything while I was in the shower?"

He scooted over and gestured to the comforter beside him. "Not much, but I think I had a…not a revelation, but something a notch under that."

She bit her bottom lip, and he could tell she was suppressing a smile. A rush of her strawberry-coconut-scented conditioner wafted past him as she took her seat. "An idea, you mean?"

"You know what." He gave her shoulder a playful shove. "I don't need this kind of abuse, okay? I'm doing my best over here."

"Okay, you're right. I'm sorry." She patted his forearm and sat up a little straighter. "What was your notch under a revelation?" She concealed a smile by biting her bottom lip.

As she crossed her legs, he was disappointed to see that

she'd opted for black track pants instead of the running shorts she'd worn on her first night as his temporary roommate.

Before his imagination could run amok, he forced himself to focus on the photo of the missing girl on his computer screen. Willow's smiling face was more than enough to chase away any tempting thoughts about Amelia's bare legs.

He angled the laptop to face Amelia. "Well, first I was trying to figure out what Larissa and Heather had in common, and I wasn't seeing anything. Other than both of them being from outside Massey County, there was nothing. Larissa grew up in the inner city, and Heather was raised on her grandparents' farm north of Springfield. She was a straight-A student, and Larissa was, well…"

"Larissa had a hard life, and Heather was like the all-American girl. Like that Tom Petty song."

Zane didn't hide his surprise. Having grown up in Englewood, Chicago, Amelia's music preference trended toward rap and hip-hop. "Since when do you listen to Tom Petty?"

She let out a matter-of-fact huff. "Tom Petty is timeless, okay?"

"You're not wrong. And, yes, that's an accurate comparison. Larissa got dealt a shitty hand, and Heather didn't. One thing I thought was really interesting was this." He pulled up Heather Breysacher's case file. "Here, look. Her text message history. She'd just texted her friend and said that she was stopping to help someone with their car."

Amelia's eyes went wide. "There's no way that's a coincidence. Statistically speaking, what're the odds that it's a coincidence?"

He lifted a shoulder. "Slim, but it *is* possible. And, honestly, when you consider Larissa, Heather, and Willow together, it's even more difficult to find some common thread between the three women. Our two friends from VC are looking at these murders like they're the work of a serial killer."

"Right. That seems to be their wheelhouse."

"So, my 'notch under a revelation' says maybe we stick to ours. Come at this like we're dealing with a trafficker."

"That makes sense." She paused to wave a pack of Starburst at the screen. "So, the first question is what kind of trafficker kills the people he's selling?"

Though Zane wanted to express excitement at the sight of the fruity candy, the good humor drained from his body before he had a chance. "I'm not sure. Not the kind we're used to dealing with."

She fiddled with the wrapper, but he suspected the gesture was just to keep her hands busy. "What if he's not the trafficker? What if he's the one buying people?"

"Maybe." He was still considering other scenarios. "But why would they all go missing from different places in Illinois? Well, *all* of them meaning Willow, Larissa, and Heather. Willow was from LaSalle County, Larissa was from Cook County, and Heather was from Peabody County."

With a quiet rip, Amelia opened the candy. "That's a good point. Maybe it was something he requested? By varying where the targets were from, it wouldn't raise as many red flags. Reduce the possibility of getting the Bureau involved, you know?"

"That's true." Zane rubbed his chin. "Either way, whether he's buying or selling, it's good to keep trafficking activity in mind. The dark web activity that Cyber Crimes spotted around this area could just be some dumb kid trying to buy an eight ball online, or it could be a trafficker hunting for his next victim."

"Could be. There are other ways for traffickers to find buyers and sellers. Word of mouth, in-person meetings, coded messages, and phone calls, that sort of thing." Amelia shook two Starbursts into her palm.

She handed him the yellow one. "You remembered my favorite kind."

She threw him an exaggerated wink. "Because you're the only person on the face of the planet who prefers the yellow ones."

He waved a scolding finger at her. "You're one to talk. You like the orange ones. Besides, they wouldn't make the yellow if people didn't love them."

Silence descended over them like a shroud, and with each passing heartbeat, the air grew more somber. Here they were, joking about Starbursts while Larissa's mother was likely crying herself to sleep. While Willow Nowland was... God only knew where.

The same realization seemed to have dawned on Amelia. The forlorn sympathy was clear in her eyes. "If Willow is involved, and if she was taken by the same person, she might still be alive. If they're a trafficker, at least."

Absentmindedly, he reached over and brushed a piece of hair from her shoulder. "What're you thinking?"

"We don't really have much to lose by looking into Willow Nowland, do we? I mean, we need to find who's responsible for killing Heather, Larissa, and those two other women, but none of them are coming back. But Willow could still be alive. And if we just ignored her disappearance because it didn't fit into this neat little box, we might be signing her death warrant."

An icy barb of dread raised the hairs on the back of Zane's neck. "You're right. Might piss off the sheriff since he was the one who had to put in the formal request to the FBI, but I think I can live with that."

"Even if she was just in a car accident, she could still be lost out there somewhere, maybe even injured." Amelia folded the little orange wrapper. "I can go to her last-known location, then check around the area to see if I can find any sign of her or of where she might've gone."

"That's a good idea. I can stay behind to cover for you, or at least explain why you're out cruising."

Zane was sure the flash of disappointment on her face was just his wishful thinking. Deep down, he knew the proposition was a subconscious way of pushing her out to arm's length.

Amelia closed her hand and crumpled the wrapper. "Yeah, that's a good plan. You can let Cowen and Steelman know what I'm following up on."

His reassuring smile never quite made it to his mouth as he tried not to dwell on spending a whole day apart from his friend.

10

As I replaced my toothbrush in the decorative holder beside one of the bathroom's double sinks, I scooped my phone from the marble vanity. Leaning against the counter, I did a rapid inventory of all my online history on the device. Though I tried to refrain from using the anonymous onion network on my cell, it was better than having to drive all the way out to the cabin to reply to my client.

I didn't care to bring my work home with me, but when I'd received a message from The Russian earlier in the night, I'd been overcome with relief. In three days, I'd have a front-row seat to watch him tear Willow Nowland apart.

My pulse picked up at the thought. The Russian loved when they fought back, and I knew Willow would fight. She'd be a sight to behold.

And the aftermath...my cock twitched at the mental image of cutting into her toned body with surgical precision. Watching her blood rush down the drain in the stainless-steel table.

Beautiful.

I'd always wanted to be a surgeon, but I'd only made it

partially through medical school before I realized it wasn't the path for me.

I wanted to tear people apart, not put them together. Oh sure, I could have been a coroner. Even briefly considered it, but that profession had no flare. No panache. What I did with these girls was art. The fools who worked in the coroner's office didn't have the medical expertise that I possessed. Ignorant elected officials. Not even the best of them could reconstruct what I so masterfully *de*constructed.

I took in a long breath and rubbed my eyes. I was at home, and I couldn't lose myself in those thoughts here.

Here, I was someone else.

Here, I was a husband, father, and medical supply salesman. And a damn good one on all counts.

My day job really was perfect. My travels helped me search for the perfect subjects for my buyers. And the fact that I could work remotely when I wasn't traveling allowed me to tend to those locked away in my fortress. While the pay was good, it wasn't as good as what the buyers paid me...

Focus.

After a recent storm had unearthed a couple of the body parts I'd buried, I wasn't keen on hanging on to Willow any longer than absolutely necessary. Not to mention, I was going to have to find a new location to dump her remains.

I stifled a yawn. I'd do that tomorrow.

Satisfied that there was no trace of the communication trail between me and The Russian, I locked the screen and reached beneath the vanity for my mouthwash. Dental hygiene had always been a top priority for me, ever since I'd been stuck with braces for three years during high school. But as a result of that period of humiliation, my teeth were perfectly straight.

More than I could say for the classmates who'd teased me for having the dental appliance. Methamphetamine had rotted the teeth out of a couple of their heads, and bar fights had ruined the smiles of a few more.

Rubes.

Deep down, I'd always known that I was better than them. I'd only had to wait for time to prove me right.

Over the years, I'd entertained the idea of handing one of my former classmates over to a client—provided one of those sorry saps met the specifications—but the opportunity had never arisen.

Their children were getting older, though. Some of my classmates had started their families much earlier than I, and their spawn would be the right age in a year or two.

The mirror showcased just how much I liked that idea.

Wouldn't that just be perfect?

Chuckling quietly to myself, I took a swig of mouthwash and rinsed for sixty seconds. I ran the faucet for a moment to wash down the blue liquid clinging to the sides of the sink. Patting the corners of my mouth dry with a hand towel, I switched off the light.

I entered the master bedroom, and my wife glanced up from the book in her hands. The corners of her caramel brown eyes crinkled as she smiled. "Ready for bed?"

In response, I flopped onto my side of the plush mattress, much to her amusement. Although my wife had never wronged me and was great with our daughters, a part of me hated that she was a nurse. She didn't have the same vision I had.

Like the rest of her profession, she toiled away trying to repair broken people. To no avail. Oh sure, she might help someone get well enough to leave the hospital, but all such fixes were temporary. My work was lasting. Permanent.

"I'll take that as a yes." She giggled and set the hardcover novel on her nightstand, snapping me back to the present.

I returned her smile as I slid beneath the blankets, then leaned over to kiss my devoted, clueless wife.

Even though Larissa and Faith had been found, today had still been a good day. The Russian's message meant I'd soon spend glorious hours dismantling Willow's firm flesh.

I patronized my wife with a token, "I love you," before rolling onto my side away from her.

I was confident the sheriff's department would chase their tails in circles during their investigation. Massey County wasn't equipped to handle a murder with so few clues. They'd give it a shot, get frustrated, and the case would go cold.

Just like it had for Heather Breysacher four years ago, and just like it had for Dakota Tamlin last year.

As I closed my eyes to drift off to sleep, all tension flowed out of my body.

They could try their best, but they'd never find me.

11

Tightening her grasp on the steering wheel, Amelia squinted at the dried grass and weeds that grew in the divot beside the shoulder of the highway. Since the speedometer told her she was driving at twenty below the speed limit, she alternated her focus between the rearview mirror, the road before her, and the ditch.

For once, she was well-rested, though the act of falling asleep after her and Zane's conversation had proven somewhat difficult. Ultimately, Amelia had reminded herself that she wouldn't do Willow any good if she was a walking zombie. There were scarcely any clues to examine in the girl's abrupt disappearance, and Amelia needed her wits about her if she wanted to make any progress.

Fortunately, the Massey County Sheriff's Department had been more than willing to hand over Willow Nowland's missing persons report when Amelia had posed the request that morning. The sheriff hadn't yet shown up, so she figured she'd dodged a bullet.

Willow's parents had eagerly granted permission for a

GPS trace on the last-known location of the girl's phone. The coordinates pointed to a spot along Highway 26, not far before an intersection that gave the option to continue north or turn east.

Though Amelia assumed a midnight blue Honda Civic on the side of the road would have caught the attention of a sheriff's deputy or a state patrolman, she kept a vigilant watch for the car. As Amelia crept along, the navigation system in the center console advised her that her destination was soon arriving, but there wasn't so much as a hint of the vehicle.

After double-checking that no one was behind her, Amelia scanned along the road in search of any sign of an accident. But the grass and the cattails were undisturbed. All vegetation was brittle and dry, and she was confident she'd have noticed if a car had plowed through the brush.

With an exasperated sigh, Amelia sped up until she reached the upcoming intersection.

GPS isn't terribly precise. Maybe Willow was on the other side of the road.

She nodded to herself. If the motorist she'd stopped to help had been traveling south, then Willow might have pulled onto the opposite shoulder.

Amelia clung to her cautious optimism as she scanned the southbound ditch.

Nothing, nothing, and more nothing.

Why in the hell couldn't they be somewhere with security cameras?

Spitting out a colorful slew of four-letter words, she drove along for a couple more fruitless miles. All that was left to do was to pull over for a closer view of the shoulder and the ditch.

Based on the silence of her phone, the sheriff hadn't even

noticed Amelia's absence. Not that he controlled where the FBI directed its resources, but she didn't want to risk the man calling SAC Keaton to bitch about how her agents had decided to run amok.

Not that Amelia was running amok. She knew exactly what she was doing, but SAC Keaton and the Massey County sheriff might not share her opinion.

She brushed aside the twinge of anxiety and refocused on the road. A quick U-turn brought her back into the northbound lane, and she eased the car to a stop about a hundred yards south of Willow's last-known location.

Stepping out into the abundant sunshine, Amelia blinked repeatedly and straightened her zip-up hoodie. She was so accustomed to dressing well at the FBI office that the skinny jeans, Vans sneakers, and hoodie almost tricked her into thinking she'd made a wardrobe mistake.

There's nothing wrong with being practical. These clothes make perfect sense for someone who might need to walk through ditches or overgrown brush.

As far as she knew, the killer they sought could drive by at any moment. They'd kept their presence in Cedarwood low-key so far, but all their efforts would be for naught if one of the citizens discovered the FBI was in town.

The small-town grapevine would kick in, and the entire town would be abuzz with rumors about why the Bureau had rolled into their quaint little village.

The quaint village with a ringside seat to the dumping ground of at least four women who had been brutally tortured and murdered.

Amelia scoffed at the thought. Most of the men and women in Cedarwood were undoubtedly appalled by Chicago's criminal activity. Meanwhile, at least one citizen quite literally had a serial killer as a neighbor.

Was the killer the town creeper, or did he blend in with his neighbors? Dennis Rader, also known as the BTK killer, had been married with two kids. Rader had been active in his church, and he'd coached at least one children's sport.

Did Cedarwood have a BTK or a more reclusive Jeffrey Dahmer?

As Amelia picked her way along the side of the road, she was careful where she placed each foot. If there *was* evidence in the gravel, she didn't want to try to explain why she'd stepped on it.

Her thoughts kept threatening to wander, but she hurled a mental lasso to rein her attention back to the present.

Gravel. Dead grass. More gravel. A patch of exposed dirt.

Just as she was about to curse her luck, she noticed a dark splotch at the edge of the shoulder. Stopping short, she crouched to get a closer glimpse.

Whatever the substance was, it had long since dried into a deep, rust-tinged brown. A casual onlooker might have thought the stain was coffee or soda, but Amelia knew better.

She'd seen the color of dried blood on concrete.

Could be roadkill.

Could be, but where was the rest of the animal? Save a deer, any small critters who got hit or even clipped by a car would limp into the brush to lick their wounds. But as Amelia squinted at the grass next to the blood, she noted no trace of a trail. The splotch started and ended in a single spot.

This isn't roadkill.

Shadows lightened as a puffy white cloud moved away from its position in front of the sun. Amelia was about to pull the sunglasses off her head, but a faint, golden shimmer near the edge of the stain caught her attention.

Inching closer, but not too close, Amelia peered down at a fist-sized rock.

As the breeze moved again, Amelia inhaled sharply.

The rock was stained with dried blood, and a few strands of hair clung to the edge of the stone.

Golden blonde hair, just like Willow Nowland's.

Amelia retrieved her cell phone and dialed the Massey County Sheriff's Department. She needed a crime scene specialist...now.

12

As the Cook County Medical Examiner appeared on the screen of his laptop, Dean half-expected her to be standing in a morgue with a corpse at her back. Instead, she sat in a leather office chair—far more comfortable than the hard plastic seats he and Zane Palmer were stuck with for their morning video call—with a neatly organized bookshelf visible over her shoulder. Her silvery blonde hair was pulled away from her fair face in a neat ponytail. The corners of her pale blue eyes crinkled as she spotted Dean.

He could have sworn Zane's eyebrow raised at the woman's kind expression. Almost like the subtle look was enough to tell Palmer about the flirty smiles and longer-than-normal glances Dean had shared with Sabrina Ackerly.

Hell, maybe it was. Maybe Palmer was a mind-reading android.

Clearing his throat, Dean pushed the laptop until the built-in webcam image included the man from Organized Crime. "Mornin', Dr. Ackerly. It's just me and Agent Palmer right now. Our deputy friend's out lookin' for body parts with some of his guys, and Agent Cowen's helping them."

Palmer offered the medical examiner a cheery smile. "Hello, Doctor. Agent Storm's following up on a potential lead."

Right. Forgot about Storm.

Dean ignored the slip-up and turned the camera back to himself. Palmer was barely visible in the corner of the lens, but Dean didn't feel the need to crowd closer to the man to ensure they were both in the shot.

"You've got news for us?" he asked.

Sabrina straightened, her face turning from friendly to focused. "More like an update. I've finished a more in-depth exam of Larissa Umber and Jane Doe Two. The forensic anthropologist is meeting with me a bit later today so we can conduct a more detailed review of Heather Breysacher and Jane Doe One, but we aren't sure how much we'll find that hasn't already been noted."

Well, if anyone *would* catch a clue that had previously been missed, that person would be Sabrina Ackerly. The woman was brilliant, as evidenced by the fact that she'd become the chief medical examiner of Cook County before she'd even hit thirty-five.

For the life of him, Dean couldn't figure out why he was always drawn to women who were light years out of his league.

He shoved the thought aside and reached for his mug of breakroom sludge. "What have you found?"

"Well, I've more or less confirmed what the Massey County M.E. suspected. All Ms. Umber's teeth had been pulled, but..." she rubbed her temple and looked down, presumably to her notes, "only about half of that was done post-mortem. The rest were pulled antemortem."

Dean couldn't be sure if the pit in his stomach was the result of low-quality coffee or the confirmation that Larissa Umber's teeth had been ripped out of her head while she was still alive. While she was begging for her life and crying out in pain.

"She was tortured?" Palmer's question was more a statement than a genuine query.

"Yes. Not just the tooth extraction, either. Her…eyes were gone. One had clearly been removed post-mortem, but the other…" She left the sentiment unfinished as her gaze shifted back to her notes.

"Antemortem." Zane Palmer leaned back in his chair and crossed his arms. Though his expression was grim, he gave away no semblance of shock.

Like he dealt with such brutality on a routine basis.

"That's correct, Agent Palmer." As Sabrina lifted her chin, she squared her shoulders. "Time of death for Ms. Umber was a little more difficult to calculate since she'd been found in cold water. But based on the state of decomposition, taking into consideration the weather recently, I'd put the TOD at approximately two weeks ago."

"Two weeks?" Dean echoed.

To his side, Palmer rubbed his chin. "She went missing a little over three weeks ago. Which means…"

"She was alive for a week before they killed her." Dean's attention drifted back to Sabrina. "Which is consistent with extensive torture."

Resting an arm on the laminate table, Palmer leaned forward in his seat. "What about the Jane Does? What can you tell us about them?"

"Decomposition of Jane Doe Two's remains was more advanced than Ms. Umber's, but not by much. The longer a victim has been dead, the more difficult it becomes to pinpoint a precise time of death. But that being said, Jane Doe Two's TOD is at least a week earlier than Ms. Umber's."

Dean kept his face carefully blank. "Signs of torture?"

"Yes." Sabrina looked down, and the faint shuffle of

papers came over the speakers. "Her breasts had been severed, but that was done post-mortem. In addition, there was a Y-incision that had been stitched. The...*quality* of the sutures was consistent with what I'd expect from a person who's been trained in a medical field. Someone with experience. It's safe to say that they used the proper equipment, and not just a needle and thread."

The news learned during an ad hoc autopsy was disconcerting, but it didn't bring on the same sense of dread as the rundown of Larissa Umber's final hours.

Until Sabrina spoke again. "Agents, Jane Doe Two's organs were missing."

"What the fuck?" The utterance of disbelief slipped from Dean's mouth before he could stop himself. "I'm sorry. You said her *organs* were missing?"

"Surgically removed, yes."

"What the fuck indeed," Palmer muttered.

With the truly disconcerting revelations out of the way, the rest of Sabrina's report was more in line with what Dean had come to expect from his position in Violent Crimes. Though the lack of trace evidence was unfortunate, the cleanliness of the two bodies was another indicator that the murders were connected.

Once the video call had ended, Dean rubbed his eyes and pushed to his feet. "So, we're dealing with a killer who has some amount of medical expertise and who scrubs down the victims' bodies before he hacks them apart."

Palmer drummed his fingers against the table. "Why remove the organs? Was he worried about a pacemaker or some other medical device leading back to Jane Doe Two?"

Dean started to pace back and forth in front of a wide window. "Well, there's nothing in the medical records for Larissa or Heather that indicates they had something like that. But maybe Jane Doe did, and that's why he removed them and her breasts. It could be that he knows enough about the victims to know if he needs to remove everything." Dean stopped pacing and stared out the window. "My guess is this guy has a ritual. Every serial killer has one, big or small. We just need to pinpoint what it is. Could be the clue we need."

The sky was a crystal-clear shade of blue, dotted with white clouds that looked as if they could be plucked from the air like balls of cotton. But as Dean mentally ran through the medical examiner's report, he wished the weather would match their bleak case.

"What're the odds we're dealing with more than one killer?" As Dean turned to face him, Palmer held up both hands. "I know, there's a lot that ties these victims' remains together. I'm just posing a hypothetical question. What if we're looking at two separate killers who've both decided to use Massey County as a dumping ground?"

Running his fingers through his hair, Dean shook his head. The question seemed like it should have only set his nerves more on edge, but as he mulled over the thought, Palmer's words had the opposite effect.

"Sherry's the math wizard, not me. She's always telling me about statistics when we're working cases. If I had to calculate those odds, though?" He quietly snorted. "Probably less than the chance of being struck by lightning in the middle of Chicago. There's a lot of unoccupied land in Massey County. Four victims who just so happened to wash up in the same creek bed? Unlikely."

Palmer tapped out a rapid beat, and a crease formed between his brows. "Plus, each vic's body was surgically dismembered."

"So, if these murders *aren't* connected, we'd be looking for..." Dean counted off four fingers. "Four different killers who all have the medical knowledge to make those cuts."

"Exactly. Doesn't seem likely to me. Now, I want your honest opinion." Palmer's slate gray eyes drifted over to Dean. "Do you think this is a standard serial killer? Is Organized Crime just wasting our time chasing the trafficking angle?"

Dean made no effort to conceal the amusement. He expected Palmer to take offense to the reaction, but the man grinned instead. "If you had the answer to that, we wouldn't be here, right?"

The muscle in Palmer's jaw popped in rapid succession. "Right."

Dean leveled an appreciative finger at Palmer. "Nailed it. Honestly, Palmer, I've got no idea what the hell we're dealing with. My gut says serial killer, but we can't ignore the dark web activity that Cyber Crimes noticed around this area. It's a small town, and as someone who grew up in a small town, I can say that folks in places like Cedarwood aren't always the most technologically advanced."

"And it's not exactly prime real estate for the mob." Palmer pressed his lips together. "Not the mob, but it'd be easier for a solo trafficker to operate in a place like this than it would be in Chicago."

"Easier to hold people captive, you mean."

"More or less, yeah."

Like a match had been struck, a sudden thought burned to life in the back of Dean's mind. "Hold on." He raised a hand. "What if we're dealing with a serial killer who...for lack of a better term, *shares* his victims with his buddies. You've heard of the Toy Box Killer, yeah?"

Palmer's demeanor remained impassive, though his attentiveness indicated curiosity. "Heard of? Sure. Do I know anything about him? Not as sure."

"He was this sick bastard who'd kidnap girls, and then he'd bring them back to hold them captive. He and his girlfriend were both in on it, and they'd just rape and torture these girls for days, even weeks. Sometimes, their friends would visit, and they'd parade these girls out like they were livestock. They'd let 'em do whatever they wanted, as long as they didn't kill them."

A crease formed between Palmer's eyebrows. "It's like a lite version of trafficking."

Dean held both arms out to his sides. "What if that's what we're dealin' with? A little bit of both?"

"Shit." Palmer spat the word like it had been a foul taste on his tongue. "If that's what we're dealing with, then we need to find Willow Nowland. We need to make sure she wasn't taken by this guy."

"Yeah." Dean's tone had become somber.

In truth, he hoped his hunch was wrong.

Better for Willow to be dead than in the hands of such a deranged monster.

13

With all the strength she could muster, Willow pressed her fingertips down on the edge of the hexagonal bolt. Hoping, praying that she'd feel the damn thing move. She could make out only vague shapes and shadows in the darkness, but she *knew* she'd made progress since she started working on one of two bolts that attached her shackles to the concrete wall.

She had no idea how long she'd been twisting and pushing. Day and night blended together in this abysmal dungeon. All she had to gauge the passage of time was her captor's short visits to bring her food and water. Even then, she knew she was underground, and she couldn't tell if he showed up in the middle of the day or at four in the morning.

Though Willow was quick to gulp down the bottled water he provided her, she had yet to eat any of the food. One of the meals looked as if it had been purchased at a restaurant, but she'd kicked the Styrofoam container across the room.

Her stomach ached, and the gurgles and grumbles had

grown louder. Fatigue threatened to overwhelm her, but she wasn't ready to throw in the proverbial towel.

The bolt moved.

A rush of cautious hope lightened the heaviness in her tired limbs. For a beautiful moment, Willow wasn't bothered by the cramp in her stomach or the dull ache in her head. Her fingers were bruised and bloody, but the thing had *moved*.

Gritting her teeth against the throbbing ache in her fingertips, she leaned her weight into the movement as she pressed on the bolt's edge.

As her finger slipped, she barely kept herself from pitching face-first onto the floor.

Not that she cared. Her efforts had been rewarded with another slight shift.

Heart thundering in her chest, Willow straightened herself, wiped her hands on the front of her hoodie, and prepared for another round.

Just as she followed the chain back to where it was fastened to the wall, a metallic *click* ripped her away from the cautious optimism.

He was coming.

Bile tore at the back of her throat, and she spun around to face the direction of the noise. A slat of light pierced through the slight gap between the door and the ground.

Shit.

She'd been so preoccupied with the bolt that she hadn't even noticed the light. The illumination was a telltale sign that he was here and that he'd soon pay her a visit.

Otherwise, she was left with nothing but shadows.

As much as she'd come to hate the constant darkness, she hated the light more. Better she was left alone in the veritable abyss than forced to greet her captor. She'd been conditioned to know the light meant the arrival of her jailer. The sentiment was naïve, but she'd allowed herself to hope that he'd forgotten about her.

Not that he would. Her logical mind knew he'd snatched her off the side of the road for a reason. Willow just didn't want to know what that reason was.

Swallowing the acidic burn on her tongue, she dropped down to sit in front of the shackles. She didn't want him to know she'd been standing or that she'd exerted herself in any way. Jaw clenched, she stuffed both hands in her pocket and waited.

The hinges of the heavy door creaked as it swung inward. Willow squinted against the sudden brightness, and for several panicked moments, all she could make out was the silhouette of a man.

Dan—if that was even his name—had made frequent references to another man. A nameless man.

The man he assured her she'd make happy.

Willow didn't know much about human trafficking, only what she'd learned from the news, the crime shows she enjoyed, and a handful of online searches. The practice was more common than the average person knew, and Willow had told herself over and over that she'd do more in-depth research about the subject.

Was Dan a trafficker? Was he holding her just so he could sell her to a creep who'd ship her off to a distant country she'd never heard of?

Icy dread stabbed at her heart.

No, she wouldn't let him. She'd rather die than become a sex slave to some wealthy pervert.

Gradually, the tiny flashes in her eyes receded, and she looked up to realize her visitor was Dan. In one hand, he held a container of food, and in the other, a plastic spork.

She allowed herself to take in a calming breath. The idea that she'd be relieved to see the same man who'd knocked her unconscious and kidnapped her was bizarre, to say the least. But she'd rather deal with the known than the unknown.

As Dan's flat, listless stare settled on her, his expression was unreadable. When Willow was left alone with her thoughts, she often found herself wondering if he was even capable of emotion. Sure, he'd seemed pleased the first time he'd visited her cell, but chances were good the sentiment had been feigned.

The pastel blue polo, coupled with a pair of neatly pressed khakis, gave him the air of a little-league coach or a soccer dad.

An image of the little girl who'd been covered in glitter, supposedly Dan's daughter, flashed in Willow's mind.

Had he kidnapped her too? Had he taken her when she was a baby so he could maintain the outward appearance of an innocent man?

Willow licked her dry lips, pressing her back to the wall as Dan stepped closer.

"You need to eat."

She'd heard the same words uttered by her mother, father, even her friends. But there was always love and concern in their voices.

In Dan's, there was nothing. His request was as dead as his eyes.

Willow swallowed against a sudden bout of fear. "I'm not hungry." She'd wanted the retort to come across as defiant or confident. Instead, she'd sounded like a cross between a frog and a mouse.

True to form, Dan's face was an expressionless mask. "I don't believe you."

As he hunched down, Willow's heart leapt into her throat.

She dug her heels into the floor and pushed herself backward until the bolts bit through her sweatshirt and into the back of her neck.

Though she half-expected Dan to leap at her and rip out her throat like a wild animal, he merely set down the food. He waved the spork in front of his face. "If you don't eat of your own volition, I'm going to have to *make* you eat. And believe me." He pinned her with an ominous stare. "Neither of us wants that."

Willow's mouth felt as if it had been stuffed full of cotton like a bottle of over-the-counter pills. Her heart clamored in her chest with enough force to break free.

How would he make her eat?

The better question is, do you want to find out?

Tears burned at the corners of her eyes, but she blinked them away. He'd drugged the food, hadn't he? He wanted her docile, so he'd crushed up a fistful of tranquilizers and mixed them into the…the…what was that? Beans and rice?

Her stomach growled as she caught a whiff of garlic, and Dan's mouth curved into an eerie smile.

"See? I knew you were hungry." He jabbed a finger at the plastic container. "Eat, or I'll have to get creative."

Get creative? What in the hell did that mean?

She didn't want to know. She'd exerted so much effort to loosen the bolt that bound her shackles to the wall, and she'd need even more strength if she hoped to escape.

To build up strength, she had to eat.

While keeping a watchful eye on Dan, she used her foot to scoot the food container closer. She couldn't risk him seeing the progress she'd made on the bolt. Dan eyed her curiously as she shoveled the first few bites into her mouth, barely tasting the food.

He pressed one hand on each knee and pushed himself to

stand. The man had to be in his late thirties or early forties, but his movements were fluid and effortless.

All the more reason for Willow to maintain her health.

She needed every possible advantage if she wanted a shot at getting out of this crypt.

14

Zane almost leapt out of his seat when he received a texted update from Amelia. He and Dean were still seated at the rectangular table in the conference room, though all their peers were busy with fieldwork. Meanwhile, he and Dean had been left to sift through personal records and old case files.

As much as Zane wanted to find an excuse to leave behind the tedious work, he reminded himself that the research needed to be done.

Still staring at the succinct message from Amelia, Zane felt Dean's intent stare on the side of his head. Apparently, he'd done a poor job concealing the sudden rush of anticipation.

He held up the smartphone as if the device would vindicate him. "Storm found something. On the shoulder of Highway 26, the same spot where Willow Nowland's GPS went offline."

Dean Steelman's face lit up, his attention rapt. "What'd she find?"

Zane glanced to the screen to ensure he'd read it

correctly. "Blood. Dried blood and a few blonde hairs. She said a CSU analyst is on their way out there to test and see if it's human."

The other agent rocked back in his chair until only two legs touched the floor. "Shit. If it's human, and if it's *hers*, then that's big, Palmer. That's *huge*."

Hearing the number of "ifs" spoken aloud stole some of Zane's bluster. He set down the phone and massaged his temples. Though he was sure Amelia wouldn't send him such a confident message if she was unsure, a shadow of doubt nagged at the corner of his mind.

Before he could muse about whether or not the damn room was stealing his sanity, the door flew open. The pane of glass rattled with the force of the movement.

Face flushed, a vaguely familiar man in the brown and gold uniform of the sheriff's department swept into the room. He swiveled his glare back and forth between Zane and Dean before he crossed his arms. "What the hell do you people think you're doing, sending my crime scene techs out to run tests on some blood on the side of the road?"

At the heated question, posed with an air of authority, recognition dawned on Zane.

The sheriff.

The night before, he'd told Amelia he would stay behind to cover for her while she researched Willow's last-known location.

A half-million of Amelia's cheesy dad jokes whipped through Zane's head.

Looks like the sheriff's back in town.

He swallowed a groan and rose to stand. "Sheriff Thompson. I'm Special Agent Palmer, and this is—"

"Special Agent Steelman, I know." A flush crept up the man's thick neck, and Zane fully expected steam to shoot from his ears at any moment. "The Bureau was supposed to send the two of you here to help Deputy McCannon with the dead girls we've found out at Fox Creek. Not to waste my department's resources on a wild goose chase!"

A surge of anger threatened Zane's perpetually composed demeanor. He'd seen the genuine concern in Amelia's face when she'd suggested that Willow Nowland might be in danger.

Amelia was following up on a potential lead and putting forth her best effort to find a missing girl.

And now, here was the man in charge of running the entire Massey County Sheriff's Department, pissed off because the FBI was supposedly wasting his department's resources.

Why couldn't the sheriff see the big picture?

If the agent searching for Willow was anyone other than Amelia, Zane doubted he'd have felt the burn of ire beside his heart. But the agent *was* Amelia, and he was ready to jump-slide across the table to give the balding man an earful.

Before Zane could act, Dean Steelman snapped up a hand and shot him a knowing look. One that said *calm the fuck down, I'll handle this*.

"Sheriff, I'm sorry about that." Steelman walked around the end of the table instead of the action-movie-inspired jump Zane had envisioned for himself. "Sounds like we've got ourselves a misunderstanding."

Steelman's Southern accent seemed more prevalent as he addressed the sheriff, but Zane didn't have to stop to wonder if he imagined the change.

Dean Steelman had broken out his Southern charm.

"A misunderstanding?" the sheriff repeated. "What kind of misunderstanding is this? My department asked you guys for help finding a *killer*. Not a girl who hasn't even been missing for forty-eight hours! You know how many murders happen in this county each year? Zero! The people here in town are losing their minds, locking their doors, staying inside."

Not a bad idea when there's a serial killer running loose somewhere nearby.

Zane kept the remark to himself.

"I know, Sheriff. I understand." Dean tapped himself on the chest. "I'm from a town even smaller'n this one. I get where you're comin' from. But, we've got reason to believe that Willow Nowland disappearing like she did might have something to do with the killer we're huntin'."

The sheriff's anger visibly faded. "What evidence do you have to support that theory, Agent?"

With a slight shake of his head, Dean blew a raspberry. "That's the problem, ain't it? We've got *no* evidence. A few severed limbs and a medical examiner's report. That's what we've got. Now, Agent Cowen is out in the field helping a few of your deputies search for the rest of these women's bodies, and me and Palmer here just finished a video call with the Cook County M.E. a little bit ago. Agent Storm's following a lead, Sheriff."

Zane's calm had returned. "We wouldn't have much to gain by keeping Agent Storm here with us. And if Willow Nowland *is* connected to our other victims, then her life's in danger."

The mention of Willow's safety drove away the sheriff's remaining bluster.

Heaving a sigh, he rubbed the bridge of his nose and dipped his chin. "All right. When you put it like that, it makes a lot more sense. Sorry for losing my temper there for a minute, Agents. It's just, these murders, this isn't the type of thing that happens in Cedarwood, you know? There've been at least eight people who've physically stopped in the department today because they were scared."

"We're doing everything we can, and we'll keep looking

until we find something." Dean's assurance was so confident that, for a beat, Zane didn't doubt him.

They'd do their best. But with nothing more than a few remains, a blurry still shot from a gas station security camera, and a handful of disjointed clues, he wasn't sure how good their best would be.

As much as Zane hated to admit it, the site of Willow's disappearance was their most promising lead. He'd never been keen on the idea of waiting on additional victims to solve a crime. To him, the prospect was indicative of failure.

However, like so many other aspects of this job, the rules for a successful investigation weren't written in black and white.

The fact remained that Willow *had* disappeared, and if her vanishing was their only gateway to new evidence, then so be it. They'd do what they had to do.

Once the sheriff disappeared into the hallway with the reassurance that Zane, Dean, and the rest of the FBI team would update him regarding any new leads they elected to pursue, Zane slumped back down into his chair.

As Dean returned to his seat, Zane felt the man's scrutiny on the side of his head. Rather than turn to face the other agent, he gave the wireless mouse a shove and typed in his password to unlock the laptop, the screen of which he'd been staring at for the better part of the day.

For good measure, he'd re-reviewed all the security camera footage he and Amelia had collected the day before. He'd sent the footage back to the Bureau for enhancement, but he'd also tried to enhance it himself. He'd cranked up the contrast, zoomed in on different portions of the footage, and even inverted the color scheme, all to no avail. Nothing he tried made the shadow of the man at the gas station any clearer, and no matter how he squinted, he could find no one following Larissa as she'd departed the Sheraton.

Before Zane could get too carried away in the heaping pile of nothingness, Dean's voice cut through his thoughts. "You're protective of Agent Storm, huh?"

Zane blinked a few times before he spared Agent Steelman a glance. The question had caught him by surprise, but he kept his expression blank. "What does that mean, exactly?"

Steelman held up both hands in a gesture of innocence. "Doesn't mean anything. Just an observation. I mean, I'd probably be protective of my partner too if she'd just been kidnapped and almost killed by a rogue FBI agent."

A pang of guilt pushed aside Zane's knee-jerk defensiveness, and he fought to keep the emotion off his face. "Yeah… that." He couldn't hold back a resigned sigh. "I'm guessing the whole damn world knows about that by now?"

"I don't know about the *whole* world." If Dean's intent was to be reassuring, he'd failed.

No matter how hard Zane worked to suppress it, he knew at least a portion of his simmering anger had broached the surface.

Sensing the shift in Zane's demeanor, Dean patted the air with one hand like he was putting out a small fire. "Look, I didn't mean to step on any toes or ruffle feathers by bringing it up. But, I mean, I'd be lying if I said I wasn't curious how in the hell that happened, y'know?"

Yeah, you and me both, Steelman.

Thoughts of Amelia's near-death experience with Glenn Kantowski still came with a wave of guilt, no matter how many times Amelia had told him he'd done nothing wrong. Hell, when he reflected on the Storey investigation, he wasn't sure he'd done anything right.

First, he'd let a string of fake text messages—messages that Cyber Crimes had definitively proven weren't associated with Amelia or Ben—convince him, though briefly, that Amelia had been screwing around with a married man.

In that whirlwind of anger and jealousy, he'd almost bought into the lie Glenn had tried to sell to the entire Federal Bureau of Investigation.

The lie that Amelia, and not Glenn, had killed Ben Storey.

Then, when Zane had noticed Amelia snooping around the background of a D'Amato family capo, Luca Passarelli, the same unfounded suspicions poured into his head all over again.

Amelia had asked him to trust that she'd tell him more at another time and assured him any interest in the capo didn't define her.

Shouldn't he trust her by now? Or was he projecting?

Taking in a long, even breath, he shook off the rumination. Whenever the topic on his mind was Amelia, all he did was think himself in circles.

Zane kept his empty stare fixed on the laptop screen. "Glenn Kantowski was a traitor." The word rolled off his tongue with ease. Maybe Glenn hadn't plotted against the United States, but the woman *was* a traitor. "She had a personal vendetta with Ben Storey, and she tried to use Agent Storm as a scapegoat when she enacted her revenge. There's not much more to it than that."

Dean scratched his chin. "No, I suppose not, huh?"

In truth, Zane wasn't convinced Kantowski's motives had been so simple. The murder of a controversial figure like Ben Storey, a man who'd pissed off the powerful Leóne family *and* a sitting United States Senator, was never straightforward.

Part of Zane was still certain Storey had been assassinated, not killed in an act of passion or vengeance. However, he wasn't keen on throwing himself down that razor lined rabbit hole.

Not yet. Maybe not ever.

The short buzz of Zane's cell against the laminate table came as a welcome distraction. He scooped up the phone, and relief shot through him. "It's Agent Storm again. The CSU just did a field test on the stain that she found on the shoulder of Highway 26."

"What'd they find?"

"It's blood, and it's human."

15

As Amelia stepped onto the curb in front of the sheriff's department, the sun's rays had turned a darker shade of gold. A search for Willow Nowland's car had been unsuccessful, and though Amelia was reluctant to throw in the towel with several hours of daylight left, she was glad to be back at the somewhat familiar building.

Specifically, she couldn't wait until she was back in the presence of other FBI agents.

Holy hell, the Massey County crime scene tech liked to talk.

Amelia estimated that a cumulative total of thirty seconds of silence had elapsed since the young man had arrived on the shoulder of the highway. Zack Anders was twenty-six, had recently completed his master's degree, and was from Springfield, Illinois. Currently, he was the only Native American person employed at the Massey County Sheriff's Department, at least as far as he knew.

His interests included hiking, baseball, and video games. Amelia knew of an FBI agent who enjoyed two of those same pastimes, and she couldn't wait to introduce the two of them.

Zane had always been better at social interactions than Amelia, anyway.

Smiling and nodding at Zack's most recent story, Amelia held the door for him and the armful of evidence he'd collected. She could barely hear herself think as they went through the process of logging the items.

Zack was nice, and his observational skills were second to none. She could tell he was glad to be able to finally put his exemplary knowledge to use in a meaningful way, but Amelia wasn't in the mood for comradery.

But the case was Zack's first interaction with the FBI, and she didn't want to sour his outlook on the Bureau. So, she swallowed her exasperation and answered his six thousand questions. He might have been chatty, but he was polite, and all his queries were work-related and professional.

Without bothering to knock, Amelia shoved open the door to the conference room they'd claimed for their investigation.

She didn't bother to hide her surprise that Dean Steelman and Zane were the only two occupants. "Where is everyone?"

Steelman gave a hapless shrug as he looked from her to Zack. "Agent Cowen's out in the field with Deputy McCannon. They've got a couple other deputies and two cadaver dogs. They're tryin' to see if they can find the rest of our vics." He tilted his head at Zack. "Who's this? CSU?"

Amelia ushered Zack the rest of the way into the room. "Yes. This is Zack Anders, the crime scene tech that the sheriff sent out to help me."

Zack seemed to slog through a moment of uncertainty, but the bright smile returned to his face in short order. "Hello, Agents."

As Amelia dragged a hard plastic chair to the table, she made a point to keep her gaze away from Zane.

Somewhere along the line, her feelings for this man had

gone beyond platonic. If all she was worried about was their friendship, she'd have already found the mental fortitude to bring up the topic and clear the air. She wouldn't worry what he might think of her. She'd just act.

Later. I'll deal with this later. I wanted to know if working on a case together would get us back to normal, and it has. But right now, we have a missing girl to find.

Thoughts of Willow Nowland brought back Amelia's sense of purpose and determination. She was confident they'd made a breakthrough on the side of Highway 26, but there was still plenty of follow-up work to be done. The fact that she'd found human blood in almost the exact spot where Willow's cell had gone dark couldn't have been a coincidence.

According to Zack, the last rain to pass through the area had occurred two days before Willow's disappearance. The odds of another person pulling over to bleed in the same spot during that narrow timeframe were astronomical.

But it *was* possible. If Amelia wanted to bolster her theory that Willow was connected to the person who'd killed Larissa and the other women, she had to know for certain. She needed a DNA analysis, and she needed the results sooner rather than later.

Zack estimated that the county's lab could have expedited results within two to three days, but Amelia needed the test completed sooner. Fortunately, a faster alternative was only a two-and-a-half-hour drive north of Cedarwood.

Folding her hands, she painted an agreeable look on her face as Zack took a seat at her side.

Zane glanced back and forth between Amelia and Zack with genuine curiosity. "I take it you found more than just the blood?"

Zack produced a tablet from his messenger bag. His dark eyes flicked to Amelia, and she offered an approving nod.

As he swiped to the first photo of the ditch, he spun the tablet around to face Zane and Dean. "Agent Storm found footprints in the dirt close to the blood. I made some plaster casts. They appear to have been made by the same person and the same shoe."

Agent Steelman twirled a ballpoint pen in the fingers of one hand, his expression thoughtful. "Willow Nowland's tracks?"

"No." The crime scene tech moved on to the next photo. "Willow Nowland is five-four, so she probably wears about a size six, maybe seven in women's shoes. These prints are approximately a man's size thirteen."

Steelman froze with the pen between his middle and ring fingers. "Thirteen? It seems safe to consider that we have the footprint of the man she stopped to help. What are the odds it could be someone else?"

Zack and Amelia had been over the probability already, and Amelia knew his response before he spoke.

"It's hard to say with one-hundred-percent certainty, but the prints were a couple days old. And they'd have been made after the last rain we had here, so there's a fairly limited period of time where someone could have left the tracks."

Amelia flattened her hands against the table. "Basically, the odds are pretty good, but there's no way to prove it."

"Right. And..." Zack swiped to the next picture, "we found these. Tire impressions not far from the footprints. We can't say for sure if they belong to Ms. Nowland's car because we haven't found it. But we do know from her family that she drives a Honda Civic and had the standard tires on it. And I'm confident the tire tracks belong to a car and not a truck. Once the lab gets a closer look at them, we should know if they are from Ms. Nowland's car or a different vehicle."

Zack went over the remaining photos of the area,

including an empty soda can and a fast-food wrapper that had been found farther down in the ditch. Though neither he nor Amelia had been convinced the items were associated with their case, the litter had been bagged and tagged all the same.

After a few more questions and answers, Amelia and her two FBI companions shook Zack's hand and thanked him for his help. There was a faint shadow of disappointment on his face as he departed, but Amelia had a sinking feeling they'd cross paths again.

As the door latched behind Zack, Amelia returned her focus to Agent Steelman and Zane. "I'm going to take the blood sample back to Chicago for an expedited analysis. The tire impressions and footprints can be handled by the county, but we need a DNA test done faster than they can manage."

Zane's eyebrows knitted together. "You're going to take it to Chicago *now?*"

"Better to get it done sooner rather than later."

"Yeah, true. The sheriff came by while you were gone, though. He was pissed that we were focusing on Willow Nowland instead of the bodies that have been discovered. I suppose I get where he's coming from, but he's just not as convinced that Willow is connected to our other victims."

Amelia stuffed both hands in the pockets of her black hoodie and held back a sigh.

SAC Jasmine Keaton operated the Chicago Field Office with a hands-off management philosophy. She was well-aware of the rigorous training her people had gone through to earn their spots as special agents, and she trusted them to follow viable leads without her guidance.

The Massey County Sheriff must not have shared the same leadership style. Then again, sheriff's deputies weren't special agents. Sure, they had their own physical evaluations and training regimen, but they didn't attend Quantico.

"Doesn't matter." Dean Steelman's voice cut through Amelia's thoughts before she'd even mentally formulated a reply. "By now, we can reasonably assume Willow Nowland is in some kind of danger. If nothing else, we can base that on the fact that she *still* hasn't reached out to any of her friends or family. I'm going to put out an alert for her and for her car."

A tentative sense of relief rolled over Amelia. As confident as she was in the fact that Willow's disappearance was related to their other victims, hearing the same conviction in another agent's voice was vindicating.

Vindicating for her, but what did it mean for Willow?

❄

As I set a plate of spaghetti and red sauce down in front of my youngest daughter, I offered her a cheery smile. The dining room was connected to the kitchen and afforded a view of the living area, including the large-screen television.

When my other daughter and my wife were home, we either turned off or muted the television so we could eat dinner as a family. But for only two of us, a show or film was a welcome distraction.

I sat down beside her and stretched my arm across the dark wooden table to grab the remote. "What do you want to watch tonight, kiddo?"

Twirling some pasta around her fork, she shrugged. "I dunno. Whatever you want to watch is fine."

I turned up the volume and shot her a grin. "What if I want to watch some old people shows, or the *news?*"

"The news!" She threw back her head and let out an exaggerated groan. "I don't want to watch the news."

Snickering, I flicked past the five o'clock broadcast until I reached a cable channel. "What about this? You like *Star Trek: The Next Generation*, don't you?"

She nodded enthusiastically. "Uh-huh. I like the aliens. They're cool."

"*Star Trek* it is." I replaced the remote and picked up my fork.

With my daughter's attention fixed on Jean Luc Picard and the *Enterprise*, my thoughts drifted back to the cabin. Specifically, what was waiting.

The Russian would arrive in two days. Chances were good he'd already arrived in Chicago, or he'd been in the city all along. I wasn't sure where the man called home, and to be honest, I didn't want to know.

In one of my many recordings, I'd caught footage of The Russian after he'd stripped off his shirt. At the time, I hadn't been sure what the nautical star tattooed on each of his shoulders meant, but I'd done my homework since then.

To the Russian mob, the markings indicated a position of authority. Much like the rank insignia worn on the shoulders of a military officer, the stars had to be earned. And from the little I'd learned about the Russian mob, the only way to earn them was through bloodshed.

I didn't want to say that The Russian scared me, but he was the only client whose permission I'd obtained to record his…sessions. And his was the only video I routinely deleted. Fortunately, voyeurism was one of The Russian's many interests.

What had occurred in that man's upbringing to transform him so drastically was a mystery to me—one I never wanted to solve. I suspected the only reason he could function in civilized society was because of the service I provided. Without that release, he'd likely have been locked up for the remainder of his natural life.

"Dad?" My daughter's expectant voice snapped me back to reality.

Blinking away the imagery of The Russian and his many victims, I turned to her. "What's up, kiddo?"

Her cheeks took on a tinge of pink as she paused, looking contemplative. "What happened to that lady from the gas station? The one we saw after my dance on Sunday."

I tightened my grasp on the fork as I forced my expression to remain neutral, but my heart thundered in my chest. My daughter was only seven, but kids were more perceptive than most adults realized. "What do you mean, sweetie?"

She pushed a couple noodles around on the plate. "I saw her when we were pulled over. When the car died...or whatever. She stopped to help us, didn't she?"

Shit.

I'd been certain my daughter was asleep when I'd pulled over on the shoulder of Highway 26. Upon leaving the convenience store, I still hadn't decided whether or not to follow through with my compulsion to take Willow. As I'd contemplated whether or not to act, I'd cruised along the highway in the same direction I knew Willow would soon travel.

My daughter had been the test. I'd told myself that if she fell asleep—as she was often prone to do on even short car rides—then I would lure Willow to the side of the road, incapacitate her, and stuff her in the trunk.

The plan had gone off without a hitch, or so I'd thought.

Panic welled up in the back of my mind, and I took in a long, calming breath.

This was fine. I'd already mulled over the possibility that my daughter could have seen or heard Willow while we'd been pulled over. Though I'd *hoped* that she'd slept through the whole ordeal, I wasn't so shortsighted that I believed there would be no consequences for my knee-jerk decision.

I painted a sheepish expression on my face as I offered my kid a weary smile. "Well, we got the car started without having to jump it, so I assume she just went home like she told us she was going to."

"Oh." My daughter's eyebrows drew together as she appeared to consider my explanation. "Okay. I hope she made it home safe."

"I'm sure she did." Clasping the back of the girl's chair, I leaned closer and dropped my voice to a near whisper. "Hey, let's not tell Mom or Steph about that, okay?"

A flash of worry passed over her face. "Why not?"

I scratched my temple and let out a weary sigh. "Well, you know how your mom worries about the car, right? And about us going on our nighttime drives?"

"Oh," she dipped her chin, "yeah. She's always worried that we're going to hit a deer or something."

I lifted a finger. "Exactly. If she knew the car died and we had to get someone to help us, I think it'd make her worry even more. And, hey, we're okay, right?" I mimed a zipper closing my lips together. "So, let's keep this between us, okay?"

With a grin, she mimicked my movements. "Got it. Secret's safe with me, Dad."

It damn well better be.

16

Sherry Cowen lifted a hand to her forehead to shield her eyes from the glare of waning sunlight. A brilliant splash of orange melded with the golden rays as the sun began to dip beneath the horizon. The exaggerated shadows of a cluster of trees loomed over the grassy clearing like dark paint inching its way down a canvas.

A gentle hill ended in an abrupt fifteen-foot drop-off to the bed of Fox Creek. The area had appeared unremarkable on the topographic map that Sherry and Dean had studied the day before, but in person, it seemed like a pleasant space to enjoy a little nature.

Or it would have if a couple law enforcement personnel and a trained search and rescue dog weren't on the hunt for severed body parts.

She'd already walked through the immediate area to search for any recently disturbed earth, but she'd come away empty-handed. Not that she was surprised. If the man who'd killed Larissa Umber had gone through the trouble of cutting off her limbs, it stood to reason he was capable of concealing a burial site.

Blinking against the sunlight, Sherry pulled her attention away from the view of rolling fields and wooded patches to scan the clearing. Most of the afternoon had been spent wrapping up the search that had been initiated before the FBI was called in for assistance.

They'd had a significant chunk of land to cover, so the three deputies and two canines assigned to the task had split their efforts and performed a methodical grid search. While Sherry had wanted to examine the area she had designated on the map first, they couldn't just traipse through the other areas to get there. Now the waning daylight made her worry they wouldn't be able to fully explore her hunch.

Sherry had accompanied Deputy McCannon and his furry partner, Sir Sniffs, on their search. When McCannon had told Sherry the dog's name, his cheeks had flushed. He'd quickly explained that his daughter, who'd been eight years old when Sir Sniffs arrived at the department, had named the yellow lab.

After spending most of the day in the company of Heath McCannon, Sherry could confidently say she'd come to like the foul-mouthed deputy. The deputy had been professional the day before, and he'd maintained the veneer until he'd tripped on a tree root and nearly face-planted. From there, his sentences had become punctuated by four-letter words.

Shielding her eyes from the sinking sun, Sherry turned to McCannon and his four-legged companion. "Well, this is the spot we identified yesterday. The sun's starting to set, though. When do you suppose we should call it?"

As Sir Sniffs settled back on his haunches, McCannon brushed his fingers through his crop of red hair. "Probably soon. But I think Sir Sniffs can work through this clearing and into the woods a little ways before we have to pack it up."

A smile crept to Sherry's face at the sight of the contented dog, and she could almost forget what they were out here to find.

Almost.

She tucked an errant piece of hair from her short ponytail back behind her ear. "Good plan. We've got a forensic archaeologist and her team on standby in case we find anything. They can be here in less than an hour."

McCannon had assured Sherry that Sir Sniffs had a high success rate, and the number of false positives was significantly lower than average. Though the yellow lab could occasionally be thrown for a loop by the scent of a dead animal or another type of woodland rot, those instances were rare.

The deputy had practically beamed with pride when he'd told her that he and Sir Sniffs often traveled to neighboring counties to lend their assistance. In addition to locating human remains, the dog had been trained to search for survivors in the event of an accident or a natural disaster.

Though Sherry had worked with SAR canines before, the pups never ceased to impress her. All she had at home was a fat, lazy tuxedo cat whose primary talent was the ability to somehow take up the entire couch. More times than Sherry could count, she and her fiancé, Teddy Kielman, had crammed themselves on the recliner because the damn cat was sprawled across the middle cushion of the sofa.

But, on the positive side, the feline's antics had given Sherry an excuse to snuggle up next to the handsome U.S. Marshal she'd met three years earlier. Now, she and that same man were slated to be married in two-and-a-half weeks.

A wedding date in the dead of a Chicago winter might have seemed bizarre at first blush, but the ceremony would be held at a comfortable, albeit not quite luxurious, resort in the Florida Keys. Teddy's family lived in Orlando, and Sherry's family wasn't invited.

Before her mind could spiral, she rubbed her forehead and glanced back to Sir Sniffs. At the lab's side, Deputy McCannon scrutinized his phone. With a sigh, he pocketed the device and knelt down next to Sir Sniffs.

Sherry fought the compulsion to check her cell. She'd switched the sound settings to vibrate only, and she hadn't received an alert in hours. "No good news, I take it?"

McCannon scratched the lab's head, and the dog seemed to smile. "Nothing since Agent Storm found that blood on the side of Highway 26." His focus shifted entirely to the lab. "Let's see if we can change that, huh, bud?"

Sir Sniffs rose to all fours as if to say *"I'm ready when you are, boss."*

The deputy wrapped his fingers around the leash's hand loop, and Sherry looked on, impressed with the synchronicity and cohesion between human and canine. She'd expected the dog to be energetic and excitable, but after almost five years of experience, Sir Sniffs was more patient and well-mannered than most people Sherry knew.

"Ready to work, boy?"

The dog's tongue lolled out of his mouth as he wagged his tail, but his body went on alert.

With an approving smile, Deputy McCannon patted Sir Sniffs's side. The man pushed to his full height and jabbed a finger at the grassy clearing. "Search."

Like the flip of a switch, the simple command turned the yellow lab into a miner hunting for gold. Except in their case, the only gold they sought was decaying human limbs.

Nose to the ground, Sir Sniffs trotted out to the edge of the clearing, just before the drop-off to the creek bed. Deputy McCannon, with Sherry closely behind, was pulled through the search grid like a musher on an Iditarod sled team as the canine feverishly searched for any scent of human remains that would trigger a response.

Aside from the quiet babble of the creek, the area was quiet. Compared to what Sherry had become accustomed to in Chicago, the silence was tomb-like. Only the jingle of Sir Sniffs's collar and the *crunch-crunch-crunch* of his paws and their feet against dry grass cut through the stillness.

Sherry's focus remained glued to the lab as they continued their sweep along the perimeter, with her struggling to keep pace.

Sir Sniffs abruptly halted, and Sherry almost ran into Deputy McCannon. Tail swishing back and forth, the SAR dog plopped down a couple feet from the sharp decline.

Anticipation flooded Sherry's body, and her tired muscles were forgotten. McCannon had explained to her that Sir Sniffs was trained to sit at the site of a scent until his handler rewarded him.

Sherry swallowed and began to ask the deputy. "Did he just…?"

McCannon was focused on Sir Sniffs. He rewarded the yellow lab and patted his side. "Good boy." He held out an expectant hand to Sherry. "You've still got those evidence flags, right?"

Sherry slid the canvas backpack off her shoulders and unzipped the main pouch.

Sir Sniffs might have been thrown off by a dead raccoon or a squirrel or…

Based on McCannon's nervousness, the same thought had occurred to him. Wordlessly, Sherry handed the deputy a small yellow flag.

McCannon gave Sir Sniffs another hearty head rub, planted the evidence marker before giving the command again. "Search."

The dog took a seat at the next spot, less than ten feet from the first, and Sherry could hardly believe her eyes and willed her feet to keep up.

When Sir Sniffs indicated a *third* location, she was unable to put together a coherent sentence.

The fourth flag brought her composure back in a rush. She couldn't stop to be dumbfounded.

They'd just uncovered a graveyard.

❋

RATTLING the ice cubes in his nearly empty drink, Dean lifted the glass to his lips and drained the remainder of the clear soda. He'd barely set the cup down at the edge of the worn wooden table when a young woman swept past to replace the beverage.

Though the few groups of patrons seated throughout the restaurant and bar likely constituted peak business hours on a Tuesday night, the crowd was markedly smaller than what Dean was used to in Chicago. Not that the wood paneling and Mossy Oak inspired décor would have let him think for a second that he was still in The Windy City.

As the petite redhead returned with a new glass of soda, Dean took the opportunity to flash her a quick wink. He didn't make a habit of flirting with servers or women in other customer-facing jobs, but the waitress had offered him a sweet little smile and a wink when she'd led him and Zane Palmer to their seats.

There was no ring on her finger, so he didn't see what harm could come from a few sly looks and friendly banter.

Nothing would come from the back-and-forth. It never did.

Dean told himself he flirted with attractive women so he could stay on his toes. If he ever crossed paths with a woman who captured his interest for more than a single night, he wanted to ensure he could capture *her* interest as well.

An image of Amelia Storm popped into his mind, and he

almost laughed aloud at himself. Even if Agent Storm was emotionally available, or physically for that matter, the last person he wanted to be with was another FBI agent.

As if the thought of the woman from Organized Crime had summoned him, Zane Palmer picked his way past a few tables to reclaim his seat across from Dean. They'd requested an out-of-the-way seat with a relatively unobstructed view of the entire restaurant.

"If you're going to flirt with the waitress, the least you could do is make sure she refills my glass too." For emphasis, Palmer downed the rest of his drink in one gulp.

"Oh my god." Dean rubbed his eyes. He'd forgotten how observant the man could be, but Palmer wasn't the only one with a knack for reading his surroundings. As Dean feigned exasperation, he debated whether or not to trot out the conclusions he'd drawn about the agent's relationship with Amelia Storm.

The two were sleeping together. They *had* to be. And based on the tension that manifested in the air whenever they were in a room together, the encounter had either gone exceedingly well, or it had been disastrous.

Finally, Dean patted the tabletop and returned his gaze to Palmer. "You know what? You're perfectly capable of flirting with people to get your drink refilled faster. I don't see a ring on your finger. Unless flirting is something you stopped doing around Agent Storm?"

A microsecond of worry flitted over Palmer's face before he chortled into his cup. "You're right. I did."

Dean blinked, at a loss for words. "You did?"

Palmer offered him a sarcastic grin. "She laughs at me when I flirt back to waitresses. It got demoralizing, so I stopped."

Well, that was just about the last response Dean had expected. "She *laughs* at you?"

Palmer shook an index finger at him. "Be careful when you're out somewhere with her. She'll do it to you too. I don't know why she thinks it's so damn funny, but she does. She told me one time that she thinks it's cute."

"Wow." Dean spat out an unflattering laugh. "Noted, Palmer. No flirting with waitresses when I'm somewhere with Agent Storm."

"Flirting *back*."

"Yeah, that's what I mean."

"Because if you flirt first, then she'll probably just punch you. In the throat or the shoulder, it all depends on how she's feeling that day." Zane offered a gracious smile as the redhead brought him a fresh glass, but the expression radiated platonic professionalism.

"I guess that's what you get for being a creep. Too bad I don't have her around when some of my buddies from the Army show up in Chicago, and we go to a bar. It'd be nice to see someone knock their heads together. I mean, they're harmless, but I always feel obligated to tip an extra twenty to make up for how cringy they can get." Dean picked at the strip of paper that bound his silverware. "Storm was in the military, wasn't she?"

Dean already knew the answer to his own question, but he was curious to see how deep the bond between Zane Palmer and Amelia Storm ran since he'd apparently misjudged their connection.

"Ten years, or almost ten years. Something like that." Palmer lifted a shoulder in a noncommittal shrug.

He'd seen straight through Dean's intent, and he'd purposefully given a vague answer. Chances were, the man not only knew exactly how much time Amelia Storm had spent in the military but also her exiting rank, where she'd been stationed, whether or not she'd seen combat...

So much for that tactic. Time for a subject change.

Glancing over his shoulder to ensure the booth at their backs was vacant, Dean leaned forward and lowered his voice to a conspiratorial whisper. "Any new thoughts on the killer? Or on the trafficking angle of the whole thing?"

Appearing thoughtful, Palmer scratched the side of his nose. "Not much, honestly. I hate to say it, but the most telling evidence we have is the lack of evidence. We looked for a common thread between Larissa and Heather, and there was nothing. Larissa grew up in the inner city of Chicago, and Heather grew up on a farm in rural Illinois. While Heather was being awarded a full-ride scholarship to UNI, Larissa was facing federal drug charges."

"Which could be consistent with trafficking, right?" Dean paused to wait for a couple to walk past their table. "We found their bodies north of Cedarwood, but neither of them were from here. It could be a trafficker hunting for victims in different areas, couldn't it?"

"Could be." Palmer drummed his fingers against the table. "It's not uncommon for traffickers to target victims in different areas. Storm and I worked a case over the summer where a girl was kidnapped in Janesville, Wisconsin by traffickers based in Chicago. You'll usually see them target kids and younger people in small cities because they're less likely to be on alert."

Dean caught onto the man's reasoning and nodded. "And what we're seeing here is the exact opposite. A killer or trafficker in a rural area who's poaching his victims from larger cities."

"Exactly. It doesn't make sense, at least not according to what we're used to seeing." Realization seemed to dawn on Palmer. "Huh."

Propping his elbows on the edge of the table, Dean leaned in a little closer, eager to hear what had crossed the agent's mind. "Huh?"

"Huh. What about serial killers? Isn't that something they'd do? Search for victims in other cities, so they don't draw attention to themselves. Especially if they live in a rural area like Massey County." Palmer's gaze turned expectant.

There was some logic to Palmer's assertion. Dean could admit that much. But the man was used to career criminals and the mafia, not deranged psychopaths acting alone. "On paper, it makes sense. But..." he flattened both palms on the tarnished wood, "serial killers tend to...*hunt* in their comfort zone. You can almost think of it like a wild animal stalking prey. They won't go too far away from their home because it's unfamiliar territory. Now, over time, that can change. Gradually, they become more familiar with areas that are farther and farther away."

"Well, from everything we've seen so far, it's safe to say this guy has been killing for a while now, isn't it?"

"Yes and no." Dean rubbed his cheek. He needed to shave. "Heather's remains were found four years ago, so we can safely assume that he's been active for at least that long. But...in the grand scheme of serial killers, four years isn't much."

Palmer's eyebrows pressed together, and Dean took the agent's silence as a request to continue.

"Four years isn't long for a serial killer, at least for the most part. Some of them, like Dennis Rader, are active for decades with only a handful of victims. Others rack up a body count in the double-digits before they hit the two-year mark."

"So, you're saying that the four victims we've found could be the only ones, or there could be hundreds."

Before Dean could answer, the pretty redhead returned with their food. She must have caught the somber appearances of Dean and Palmer's faces because she deposited the plates and quickly made herself scarce.

As Dean considered the possibility that they could be dealing with a killer who damn near qualified as a mass murderer, his burger and fries seemed markedly less appetizing. "We've sent everything over to the BAU. It's their job to take jumbled shit like this and make it make sense. We should get a better idea of what we're dealing with when we hear back from them."

Palmer stirred his drink with the plastic straw. "I haven't had a chance to work with them before."

"They're an interesting bunch. A few big egos, but I'm pretty sure you can say the same for any department at the FBI."

Palmer's expression darkened, and Dean figured the remark had reminded him of a particular agent in Organized Crime. "Yeah, that's no shit."

As Dean's phone buzzed in the pocket of his dark jeans, he mentally filed away Palmer's disdain for the mystery ego in Organized Crime. Based on the strength of his reaction, he and the unknown agent must have had more than just a minor disagreement.

Popping a fry into his mouth, Dean retrieved his cell and opened the newest text message. The sender was Sherry Cowen, and he'd only read three words when he froze mid-bite.

"What?" Palmer's voice seemed distant, like he'd moved to the booth clear at the other end of the row.

A wave of equal parts dread and impatience raised the hairs on the back of Dean's neck. "It's from Sherry. They've got more body parts."

Palmer sat up a little straighter. "How many more?"

Dean held up a hand to flag down their waitress. "A lot more. We'd better get boxes for our food."

17

A short hike took Zane and Dean from an infrequently used county road to a veritable hive of activity beside Fox Creek. The drive had been quiet and peaceful, and the sudden transition into the organized chaos of crime scene techs and sheriff's deputies took Zane aback. Between the battery-powered work lamps, tarps, and dozens of men and women milling about the lightly wooded area, he could have sworn the entire damn town was here.

He and Dean had only just flashed their badges to the deputies on the outer-most perimeter when Sherry Cowen trotted over to them.

Even in the low light, the flush on her cheeks was clear. A trained forensic archaeologist was in charge of excavating the newly discovered remains, but Zane could've fooled himself into thinking Sherry had taken on all the manual labor herself.

Smoothing out her ponytail, she nodded a quick greeting. "Hey. You guys aren't going to believe this. Okay, maybe you are, but still, it's…it's a lot to take in. As we worked our way through the grid search from a little way downstream, Deputy McCannon and I arrived here and, well…"

Steelman raked a hand through his hair. "You were right?"

"Yeah. I was. McCannon's SAR dog, Sir Sniffs, found twelve different burial sites. They're all in pretty close proximity to one another, and we just finished digging up the first. I waited to call you out here until after Sir Sniffs had identified multiple sites. The likelihood he found that many false positives was slim."

Normally, Zane would have chuckled at the fact that a trained police dog was named Sir Sniffs, but the good humor had been sucked from his body by the news that they'd discovered the final resting place of up to twelve victims…or at least that many body parts. "You said they just finished excavating the first location, right? I saw the coroner's van parked beside the road. Where are they?"

Sherry's lips twitched in a slight smile. "That's exactly what I was about to tell you. Come on."

They weaved around a series of yellow flags fluttering slightly in the evening breeze. The markers were unassuming, but when Zane considered what might be buried in the earth below them, his stomach sank a little lower. Like the white headstones at Arlington National Cemetery, the sea of yellow flags was sobering.

Past the thin strand of trees, they emerged in a grassy clearing. Beneath the buzz of voices, the quiet babble of the creek was barely audible.

A sturdy work lamp cast a halo of white light on the three-foot-deep hole near the edge of the clearing. The black trash bag and its gruesome contents had already been lifted out of the burial site, and the remains now rested on a blue tarp. Any dirt or other trace evidence would easily be captured by the layer of vinyl. Forensic excavation was a painstaking process, but so far, Zane was impressed with the team's speed and professionalism.

To the side of the grid that had been set up around the dig site, a middle-aged woman gestured to a second flag as she spoke to a group of younger men and women. If Zane had to guess, the archaeologist's team was comprised of graduate students. He didn't envy the work ahead of them.

"Agent Cowen," the coroner waved his hand in their direction, "these must be the other FBI agents from town?"

So much for keeping a low profile...

"Yes." Sherry smiled at Dean and Zane. "This is Agent Steelman, and this is Agent Palmer. They're both from the Chicago Field Office as well."

From where the coroner was crouched beside the tarp, he lifted a gloved hand in greeting. "Evening, Agents. I'm Ray Schaeffer, the Massey County Coroner. I was just about to flag down one of the crime scene techs to cut away this garbage bag."

On cue, a familiar young man hurried up to the little gathering. His brown eyes widened for a beat when he spotted Zane and Dean, but the surprise was soon replaced by a pleasant smile. "Hello, Agents. Nice to see you again. Wish it was under different circumstances, though."

Zane clasped Zack Anders's hand. The tech's grip was strong, and his palm was cool and dry. "Hopefully, this will help us find some new leads to catch this guy."

After Zack had greeted Sherry and Dean, he snapped on a pair of vinyl gloves and retrieved his evidence kit. Aside from the young man explaining the process of photographing and bagging the plastic, they were silent as Zack worked.

Glancing over his shoulder, Zane noticed the forensic archaeologist had already begun to set up another grid around the second flag.

Like a well-oiled machine.

Though Zack's task wasn't quite as daunting, his efficiency was no less impressive. Zane wasn't a trained forensic expert, but he was willing to bet Zack would excel even in an environment as competitive as Chicago.

Zack gingerly removed the trash bag, and the coroner took in a sharp breath. "Is that…?"

"A Y-incision," Zane finished for him. "Yes. Both breasts cut off, just like Jane Doe. Not a lot of decomposition yet, so she couldn't have been here for that long."

The coroner blinked down at the body as he rocked back on his heels. "I'll be damned. I've been on vacation for the last couple weeks. Is this really what we're dealing with? Someone killing girls and performing autopsies on their bodies afterward?"

Zane clenched his jaw, hoping the gesture would hide some of his mounting irritability. In the state of Illinois, only Cook County utilized a medical examiner to inspect bodies at crime scenes. Massey County, along with the rest of the damn state, voted for a coroner each election cycle. The position didn't require any medical experience or even a biology-related degree.

Like plenty of other aspects of government, Zane didn't understand the process of selecting a coroner. The bizarre system wasn't unique to Illinois, either since most states in the country operated in the same nonsensical manner.

Guess it's too much to ask people who dropped a hundred grand on med school to come out and look at partially decomposed bodies.

He wasn't even sure his observation was sarcastic. If *he* had spent one-hundred-fifty-thousand dollars and eight plus years of rigorous training to become a medical doctor, he sure as hell wouldn't be keen on dealing with corpses instead of saving people's lives.

Rather than mentally complain about the poor guy who

was undoubtedly doing his best in an unfamiliar situation, Zane inched closer to the tarp. Retrieving his own pair of disposable gloves, he hunched over and peered at the dismembered torso.

"It's all right, Ray." Steelman's voice was calm and reassuring. "Give us your best rundown, and we'll get everything filled out to have her transferred to Cook County. That's where our other victims have gone too, so it's best to keep them all together."

In Zane's mind, the Y-incision on the newest set of remains was a sure-fire indication they were dealing with the same killer.

The coroner blew out a long breath before returning his focus to the torso. "Well, it's a little difficult to determine the cause of death. At a glance, I'd say she's been dead for less than a month, maybe even only a week or two. The bag she was wrapped in was sealed tightly, so that would've prevented some insect activity. Not that there is much this time of year."

Zane rested an arm on his knee. "We haven't been able to establish a firm cause of death for the other vics, either. Toxicology reports from Larissa Umber showed there was nothing suspicious in her system. If she was drugged, her body metabolized the substance by the time she was killed. We're waiting on a hair follicle analysis to see if that'll give us any more insight."

"Which brings me to the next item on my list." The coroner glanced from one FBI agent to the next. "There's nothing to identify her right off the bat here."

Careful to stay off the tarp and its accumulated trace evidence, Zane waved a gloved finger at a discolored spot on the woman's collarbone. "There was skin removed right here."

The coroner followed Zane's gesture and nodded. "It's

discolored, but that's due to the decomposition. It looks to have been removed post-mortem."

"Larissa Umber had a tattoo in that same location, about the same size. The son of a…" Zane paused to blow out a frustrated breath. "The killer seems to be a fan of removing identifying markers, so he could have cut off her tattoo to make her more difficult to identify."

The realization brought Zane a small measure of relief. They already knew Larissa had been murdered. Better to find another piece of her body than to discover a new, unidentified victim.

He did his best to ignore the sea of evidence flags dotting the area, bobbing like fireflies on a warm June evening.

A camera shutter clicked as Zack snapped one photo and then another.

Only when the tech nodded his approval did the coroner reach down to reposition the woman's torso. "Her arms were severed right at the top of the humerus, but there was no damage to the bone itself. The same technique seems to have been used on the legs, to sever the femur from the pelvis."

"Which is consistent with our other victims. The person who removed the limbs must have pulled on them to slice through the cartilage instead." Dean Steelman crossed his arms, but his focus didn't drift away from the body.

As the coroner turned back to the torso, most of the color seemed to drain from his face. "There are…signs of genital mutilation too. The medical examiner will be able to give you a better idea of the extent, but it looks like a series of cuts."

Zane grimaced as he glanced at Agent Steelman. "Jane Doe Two was sexually assaulted, wasn't she?"

"Yeah. No mutilation, though." His tone was as grim as Zane's mood had become.

Sherry Cowen knelt beside Zane. "If this is Larissa, it could be because she was a prostitute. Could be symbolic."

The coroner's skin blanched another shade lighter.

That's a thing? Zane clenched his jaw and kept the question to himself.

The more he learned about serial killers, the less convinced he became that they'd find Willow Nowland alive.

18

Glass of water in one hand, I leaned back against the couch and propped my stocking feet on the coffee table. The dark wood matched the dining set, though I doubted anyone other than me and my wife ever noticed. Scooping up the television remote, I sipped my drink and selected a local news channel.

I'd kept a vigilant lookout for any news regarding Willow Nowland's whereabouts, but so far, there'd been nothing. Though I was glad for the lack of information, I knew better than to celebrate.

As the segment of commercials came to an end, a familiar anchor appeared.

I snorted to myself. I'd gone to high school with Regina Kimpling. She'd been a stuck-up bitch then, and I doubted much had changed.

During my senior year, Regina had spread rumors to the entire class that my wife—who was a freshman at the time, and whom I'd barely known—had sucked off a teacher for money. That particular instructor had been fired a few weeks before Regina started the tall tale, and the lie spread like wildfire.

I still had no idea what the bitchy news anchor had against my wife back then, but I always let myself imagine that someday I'd pry the answer out of Regina's bruised and bloody lips.

She *was* blonde, and she was also petite.

She wasn't young enough for The Russian, but he could still have some fun with her.

Laughter grew in my throat, and I clamped a hand over my mouth to stifle the sound. Both my daughters were finally in bed, and I didn't want to disturb them.

Regina's colorful rumor had so thoroughly ruined my wife's high school reputation that she was dubbed a pariah for the next two years. When my future wife and I had crossed paths at one of the summer bonfire parties that kids around Cedarwood liked to host, she'd been a complete wreck.

As far as I was concerned, I'd done nothing special to garner her attention, but I hadn't pushed her away, either. She'd just latched onto me, and I'd gone along with her.

We'd been mid-conversation when a muscle-bound jock had strolled up to us. Flashing a wad of singles—likely his entire week's pay from his after-school job—he'd drunkenly asked her for a blowjob.

Without a second thought, I'd stepped in front of her and clocked the guy in the face. He'd made an effort to recover and land a blow, and he hadn't expected me to be as physically capable as I was.

Now, that same jock was a drunk who worked the occasional construction gig and blew all his money at the bar. Every now and then, I wandered into his favorite bar to order a pork tenderloin sandwich and silently laugh at his misfortune. Watching a person drink themselves to death wasn't as riveting as viewing a murder in real time, but his suffering still brought me a measure of joy.

I rubbed my eyes and refocused on the television screen. I could tell by my deteriorating attention span that the time for bed was growing nearer. More than likely, I'd fall asleep on the couch until my wife returned home from her graveyard shift at the hospital to wake me.

As Regina prattled on about a bunch of nonsense she'd cobbled together for a slow news day, my eyelids grew heavy. I shifted my feet from the coffee table to lay along the couch, and my thoughts began to wander.

"Thank you for that update, Regina." The male voice belonged to a fellow with salt-and-pepper hair and a neatly kempt beard, if I remembered right. *"Now, we have some breaking news out of our very own Cedarwood."*

My ears perked up, but I didn't open my eyes.

"Earlier this evening, the Massey County Sheriff's Department put out an alert for a young woman named Willow Nowland. We'll now go to a clip of the short press conference held by Sheriff Mark Thompson."

I was upright and wide-awake before the camera even switched.

The way Mark Thompson wore his uniform had always reminded me of a professional athlete who'd donned a suit for the first time. Though the sheriff had become softer as he aged, plenty of the bulk under the brown and gold shirt was undoubtedly still muscle. I was certain that Sheriff Thompson would be far more comfortable in a football jersey.

Expression somber, Thompson stood behind the podium with its handful of microphones. *"Evening, folks. As you all know, we've been hard at work on the handful of murders that have been uncovered near Fox Creek."*

Even as my pulse picked up, I was amused at the thought of the local law enforcement shitting their pants.

I'd always known that the authorities would find one of the men or women eventually. There was a reason I'd cut them into unrecognizable pieces and stashed their body parts in a handful of different locations. Sure, I enjoyed the process, but it served a practical purpose.

Heather Breysacher had been identified via her dental records, so after her, I'd started to pull out any teeth that remained after my customers had sated their lust for torture. If the cops wanted any shot at locating me, they'd have to figure out the identities of their victims first.

But this wasn't my first rodeo. The same mixture of trepidation and adrenaline had surged through my veins when they'd identified Heather four years earlier.

The sensation was almost impossible to describe. It was a rush, the same high a skydiver got as they plummeted closer to the possibility of their own death. Until the parachute deployed, there was always a sliver of dread that this jump could be the last.

"...any suspicious activity, please don't hesitate to call 911. Now, in a separate announcement, I'd like to ask for the public's help in locating a young woman who went missing late Sunday night or early Monday morning, Willow Nowland. Ms. Nowland's cell signal puts her last-known location at northbound Highway 26, between mile markers 1127 and 1128."

My attention was glued to the screen as the sheriff held up a photo of Willow.

"We have reason to believe that Ms. Nowland may be injured, and she may be in danger. We're still on the lookout for her car, which is a 2010 midnight blue Honda Civic."

I clenched and unclenched the fingers of one hand.

I'd anticipated the development, but I'd hoped for a little

more time before the damn sheriff made an announcement for the ten o'clock news.

Mentally, I walked through my trip to dispose of her car. I'd parked the Civic behind an abandoned barn just off a gravel road, and I'd been beyond diligent in ensuring I hadn't left behind any prints or DNA. The vehicle was difficult to spot but not impossible.

However, even when the car was discovered, I was confident that no trace of my whereabouts would be found. Rainstorms were predicted for the following afternoon as a cold front rolled through the Midwest, followed by a thirty-five-degree drop in temperature between now and Wednesday night. The system would be more than enough to wash away any tracks I might have left behind.

No matter my rationalizations, the leaden pit in my stomach continued to sink.

Between the body parts found in Fox Creek and now Willow's disappearance, the entire town would be on edge. I needed to get rid of Willow sooner rather than later.

I hardly heard another word from Sheriff Thompson as I snatched my cell off the table.

Either The Russian would claim his bounty tomorrow, or I'd kill Willow Nowland myself.

By Thanksgiving, Willow would be nothing more than a bag of body parts.

19

As Amelia set the cruise control of her work-issued sedan to seventy-five, she shifted to a more comfortable position in her seat. She'd crawled out of bed before even a hint of sunlight had brightened the horizon, and she was on the road to Cedarwood a full half-hour before she'd planned.

To her relief, the early morning meant Chicago's abysmal traffic congestion hadn't yet begun, and there were fewer people heading into work the day before Thanksgiving anyway. She'd managed to pick up a latte and hit the interstate in what she mused was record time.

Now, she just had to keep herself sane over the uneventful drive south.

Her night in Chicago hadn't been anywhere near as refreshing as she'd imagined. Though she'd slept in her own bed, Hup had meowed in her face to wake her up at quarter 'til five in the damn morning.

The imminent crisis? No food in the center of the bowl.

But Hup wasn't even the highlight of the night and morning. She'd ignored two separate calls from the same unknown prepaid cell number, and though she couldn't be certain, she suspected the caller was Alex Passarelli.

She didn't know what Alex could possibly want from her. Hell, *he* was the one who owed *her* a favor after she'd exonerated his most-trusted lieutenant from a false murder charge.

Maybe I should just ask him to make himself scarce.

She groaned. If only a relationship with a D'Amato family capo was so simple.

While Amelia had been at the FBI office to submit the DNA from the side of Highway 26 for a rushed analysis, she'd overheard a hushed conversation between Joseph Larson and his current girlfriend...plaything...whatever in the hell women were to a creep like Joseph.

Cassandra Halcott, an Assistant U.S. Attorney, *and* Joseph's newest romantic interest, had been in the midst of encouraging him to brush up on his interviewing skills.

Amelia had been struck with a surge of blind optimism, and she'd feigned nonchalance outside the breakroom so she could listen to the rest of the dialogue. For a beat, she'd allowed herself to imagine that Joseph was applying for a position with a different law enforcement agency—the U.S. Marshals, the DEA, the Secret Service. She didn't give a shit. If he was gone, then he was gone. She didn't care where he went.

Of course, within a matter of seconds, Amelia's hopes had been dashed.

According to the snippets she'd caught while hovering beside the doorway like a creep, Joseph intended to pursue a promotion to Supervisory Special Agent of the Chicago Organized Crime Division.

She still didn't know how she'd kept herself from vomiting on her shoes.

Currently, Spencer Corsaw was the SSA of Organized Crime. Amelia had gotten to know the man better during the

Storey investigation, but most of her knowledge about Spencer had come from Zane. Spencer was the first friend Zane had made when he'd transferred from D.C. to Chicago, and he'd shared a few of Spencer's humorous antics during their downtime.

Amelia wanted to brush off Joseph and Cassandra for jumping the gun. She wanted to roll her eyes at the thought of Joseph trying to snipe the title of SSA from under Spencer's nose.

But as the mile markers flew by, giving her more time to reflect, she drew a new, unsettling conclusion.

Joseph knew something she didn't.

Was Spencer planning to transfer to a different department? Amelia had recently decided she was sick of being shot at by the mob, so perhaps Spencer had the same thought.

Or was he moving to another field office? Like Amelia, Spencer had been born and raised in Chicago. The city was his home as much as it was hers.

I'll ask Zane. Maybe he'd know if something was going on with Spencer.

Amelia tightened her grasp on the steering wheel. *Would he know?*

Joseph Larson had tried to blackmail her. Rape her. She couldn't, *wouldn't* deal with him as a superior.

Amelia knew she needed to report Joseph. She wouldn't be gaslighted into believing what happened was a figment of her imagination. Thankfully, she'd told Zane shortly afterward so her mind couldn't trick her into an alternate reality.

But this was embarrassing. She was an FBI agent, for shit's sake! How could she have put herself into that position? How did it ever get that far? Worse, *why* had she believed that going along with Joseph's coercion was somehow okay? This kind of crap happened to women every damn day. If she couldn't come forward about this…

The skeletons from her past danced in her head, mocking her. Dating a mafia capo all through high school. Concealing that not only from the Bureau but also from Zane. Luca Passarelli's unsettling threats. How was what Luca did any different than what Joseph did? And yet, she hadn't reported either one of the creeps.

The power they held over her—that she was letting them continue to wield—needed to be stripped away. Amelia knew she needed to report Joseph. She'd have to pick the right moment, but it needed to be done. Who knew how many others had been in her shoes and hadn't been able to walk away?

Bile stung the back of her throat, and for a beat, she mentally prepared to pull over so she could vomit, even going so far as to switch lanes to be closer to the right-hand shoulder.

There was no proof of what had happened between her and Joseph, and she knew the ass would deny any and all allegations made against him. To compound the issue even further, the man was dating a *lawyer*. And not just any lawyer. The Assistant U.S. District Attorney.

Amelia's heart knocked against her chest like the thump of a bass drum. She was standing at the edge of a panic attack that threatened to swallow her whole.

The voice of Amelia's therapist mercifully intruded on her thoughts.

Name five things you can see.

Her mind raced. The road. The red truck ahead of her. Clouds. The clock. A fast-food billboard.

Again, her therapist's advice reminded her how to deal with the crippling aspects of PTSD.

Four things you can touch. The steering wheel. Her half-empty latte. The sunglasses she'd moved to the top of her head. The sleeve of her zip-up hoodie.

Three things you can hear. The obnoxious hardware store jingle on the radio. The hum of the car's engine. The rush of air outside the window.

By the time she reached the last item on the list, her heart no longer thudded against her chest like it intended to break free. The taste on her tongue was sour, but the acidic burn of bile had receded.

Feeling much better, she moved into the left-hand lane, ready to move at a quicker pace. She needed to get back to Cedarwood.

Obsessing over the possibility of Joseph being promoted to SSA wouldn't do her a damn bit of good. Reporting Joseph would likewise have to wait. She'd cross both bridges when she came to them, not while she was in the middle of a serial killer-slash-human trafficking investigation.

Taking in a deep breath, Amelia switched the station to her preferred choice of radio, NPR. Though she was a lifelong fan of rap and hip-hop music, the stations on air only ever played edited nonsense. Plenty of the newer tunes were good, but she cringed at every bleep or silenced curse word.

The miles wore on, and gradually, she grew more and more invested in NPR's segment on ocean currents. By the time the discussion wrapped up, she was only ten miles outside of Cedarwood.

She'd taken her and Zane's work car for her trip to Chicago, and though he could easily hitch a ride with Agents Steelman and Cowen, Amelia figured the polite course of action was to at least swing by the hotel. Besides, she was more than a half hour earlier than she'd planned. Maybe she and Zane could grab something to eat before they headed to the sheriff's department. Her now depleted latte wasn't going to be enough to get her through the day.

After parking, she stretched and lazily meandered through the lobby and up a single flight of carpeted stairs. The faint scent of chlorine hung in the air, along with the lemon tinge of cleaning products.

Swiping the keycard through the reader beside the door handle, her mind whiplashed back to a topic she didn't want to think about.

What in the hell am I going to do if Larson is my boss? I need to report him sooner versus later to make sure he doesn't end up with unfettered power.

Yes, she would do exactly that, but no, this wasn't the time or place for that line of thinking.

Blinking to adjust her vision, she eased the heavy door closed. She had drawn the blinds, leaving the space as dark as a starless night.

Her brain wouldn't stay put. She needed a distraction.

Swallowing the unease that threatened to crack her composed exterior, she reached for her phone to do a search of Cedarwood restaurants. Surely, there was some diner around this damn small town that served a decent breakfast.

Some breakfast, another coffee, and work. That's what I need right now. Either that or a stiff drink and a good, long...

She cut the musing short.

I'll get Zane, we'll go eat some food, and then we'll get back to work on this case.

Scrolling through a handful of Google results, she pushed open the door that connected their rooms. She wasn't surprised to find the lever unlocked. They *had* been roommates for more than a week.

"Hey, do you want to go get something to eat?" Stepping over the threshold, she glanced up from her phone.

Right to a freshly showered, mostly undressed Zane Palmer. His back was to her as he shuffled through a pile of clothes on the desk beside the bed.

"Oh, shit!"

Amelia realized too late that she could have avoided the entire embarrassing scenario if she'd simply kept her mouth shut and backed out of the damn doorway.

Toothbrush in one hand, he jumped in place as he spun to face her.

"Oh my god." She squeezed her eyes closed, but she still saw him. All six feet, three inches of his lean muscular frame, save what was hidden by his underwear.

She could barely remember a search result she'd looked up just thirty seconds prior, but every curve, every indentation of his toned body was etched in her mind's eye. A faded scar in the middle of his shoulder blades appeared to have been made with a knife. Another similarly shaped mark on his stomach, and then the nautical stars on his shoulders... and knees.

Wait.

Had she imagined the tattoos?

No. She was tired, but she wasn't in the habit of conjuring images out of the air.

His attention was fixed on where she stood in the doorway between their rooms. She mentally screamed at herself to turn around, but her gaze was drawn back to a blue and black star.

Amelia's throat tightened. Her cheeks were on fire, and even in the relatively low light, she was sure he'd noticed the flush by now.

"I'm sorry. I just...Hup woke me up at the ass crack of dawn, and I didn't want to try to go back to sleep for a whopping thirty minutes. So, I just got all my stuff together and left early. I figured, you know, since you're always at the office before I am, you'd be awake. And, well...*clothed*..."

She trailed off and pinched the bridge of her nose, turning on her heels to move back into her own room.

"It's okay." Even though his voice was muffled, his tone was sincere. The assurance still didn't help curtail Amelia's embarrassment.

Or her curiosity.

One nautical star on each shoulder, just above the armpit, and one on each knee. She'd only come across similar tattoos a couple times during her stay in Boston, but she knew what they symbolized.

A star on each knee means he'll bow to no man, and the other two...

He'd earned those stars. The Russian mob didn't take kindly to impersonators.

An undercover operation? But how long had he been behind enemy lines? He'd been with the FBI for more than a decade, so there was plenty of time for a lengthy stint undercover. Plus, he never mentioned much about his earlier years with the Bureau.

This is the FBI, not the fucking CIA. If he'd done an undercover op, he'd have mentioned it by now.

Why hadn't he?

She rubbed her temples as the questions flashed through her mind.

By the time he appeared in her open doorway, he'd donned a white t-shirt, dark-wash jeans, and a pair of socks. The fresh scent of his hair product wafted over to where Amelia had retreated beside her bed, dumbfounded. Normally, she'd relish any chance she got to inhale that mystery product, but her mind was still spinning.

"Are you okay?" His voice was soft and gentle.

Amelia inhaled a deep breath through her nose before she met his gaze. She was far from okay, but he didn't need to know the sort of turmoil raging in her brain. "It's been a weird twenty-four hours. I, uh…I overheard Joseph talking to Cassandra at the office. They were discussing job interviewing tactics."

Zane's nostrils flared. "What? Why? Is he finally leaving?"

"No." She hadn't intended to bring up the topic so soon, but she was lucky to even be coherent. "They were talking about him going for an SSA position."

"What?" The exclamation was just below an outright shout, and Amelia didn't miss the split-second of embarrassment that followed. Even when they were interacting with suspects or serving warrants, Zane Palmer rarely yelled.

Amelia held up both hands. "I don't know much more than that. SSA of Organized Crime in Chicago. I was tired, but I don't think I hallucinated it, I just…" She bit off the sentence before her voice could crack. God, she sounded like a crazy person, but she knew what she had heard…and seen.

"I'll ask Spencer about it when we get back to Chicago. Larson's not cut out to supervise a bake sale let alone the fucking Organized Crime Division of the FBI."

Though Amelia's mind was still whirling, a wry laugh escaped her lips. "That's putting it lightly."

As the warmth of his touch settled on her upper arm, she dragged her eyes up to his.

The shadows beneath his eyes seemed more pronounced, his expression almost pained. "It'll be all right."

You don't know that.

She forced herself to smile. "It's just been a weird twenty-four hours."

He noticeably relaxed, but she could tell he was still worried. "Yeah, it has been. You got my messages last night, didn't you?"

"About the torso the CSU found north of Cedarwood?" The case was all Amelia had to propel her through the day, and she hoped she didn't sound overeager.

"Yeah. They dug that up last night, and according to the

texts I got while I was sleeping, they found a human femur. The coroner thinks it's a male bone, but we'll know better when all the remains get to Cook County."

"A male?" Amelia pocketed her cell. "Could it be a witness? Or maybe an accomplice?"

"That's what I was thinking too." Zane sighed as he snatched a blue and white flannel shirt from the back of an office chair. "It's older than Larissa and Jane Doe Two's remains but more recent than Heather Breysacher and Jane Doe One."

Renewed purpose propelled Amelia's movements as she and Zane left for the sheriff's department.

Life might go to hell when she returned to Chicago, but for now, she had a killer to catch.

20

With an exasperated sigh, Sherry pulled out a chair and dropped to sit beside her partner. She'd just spent twenty minutes fighting to hook her laptop up to an overhead projector, and she wanted to flip over the damn table.

Hell, she probably could, and Dean wouldn't judge her. He knew how well Sherry and technology agreed with one another. At the ripe old age of thirty-three, Sherry was arch-enemies with almost any sophisticated electronic device. *Especially* printers.

Her head lolled back until she was face-to-face with the drop ceiling. "I'm a boomer. I have to be. Why else would I get shit on by every piece of technology I ever try to use?"

Currently, they were the only two occupants of the conference room or the *war room*, as Dean had taken to calling it. Slats of golden sunlight pierced the opening between blinds, lending the space a warmth that wasn't present later in the day.

With a hapless chuckle, Dean flattened his hands against

the table. "You're four years younger than I am, so I don't buy that for a second. You're just…unlucky."

Sherry shot the projector the middle finger. "That's painfully accurate. I swear, it doesn't matter what brand of smart-whatever I buy. It just *has* to crap out on me five hours after I get it home. Then I spend the next fifty-seven hours googling troubleshooting tips and watching DIY videos, and when I try to fix it, I just make it worse."

Dean pressed his lips together, and she could tell he was suppressing laughter. She went on the same tirade almost once per week, and each time, she added a couple hours to her troubleshooting estimate.

She rolled her head on her neck, stretching out the tight muscles. "You know what, Steelman? I'm just going to go move to one of those monasteries in the Himalayas. Do you think they have to dick around with overhead projectors and Bluetooth connections and routers and modems? I doubt it."

"Teddy and the FBI might have something to say about that decision." He flashed her a charming smile—a grin she'd lovingly dubbed the Steelman Special.

Sherry lightly smacked the tabletop. "I know exactly what they'll say. They'll—"

Before she could finish the thought, the door swung inward. A light flush had crept to Amelia Storm's normally pale cheeks and based on the sneaky smirk on Zane Palmer's face, he was responsible.

"Morning, Steelman. Cowen." Palmer shut the door behind his partner. "Anything come up yet this morning?"

Sherry almost let out a colorful description of her battle with the projector, but she swallowed the words before they could form on her tongue. Though she liked Palmer and Storm well enough so far, she reminded herself that they'd only known each other a couple days.

Just because Sherry was about to marry a Navy veteran

didn't mean her professional colleagues needed to hear her curse like a sailor. "No, nothing new. Just the video call with the BAU in about fifteen. Deputy McCannon said he'd try to make it, but he was out at the dig site until pretty late."

The two agents took their seats, and within a matter of minutes, the laminate table was crowded with crime scene documents, manila folders, and their laptops. As they waited for the call from the Chicago Field Office, the little group went through a recap of what they'd learned so far.

Four different bodies had become five, and one victim was potentially a male. Storm and Palmer suggested that, if the coroner's assessment was accurate, the male victim could have been a witness or an accomplice who'd outlived his usefulness.

To Sherry's relief, Dean took over control of the computer and webcam as an alert notified them of the incoming video conference.

A camera mounted above the whiteboard gave a view of most of the table. Though Sherry had put blood, sweat, and tears into connecting the damn wireless webcam to her computer, all Dean had to do was press a few on-screen buttons.

The projector above their heads hummed to life, and an image of a man in his late fifties flickered onto the whiteboard. "Morning, Agents. I'm Bill Dumke with the BAU here in Chicago. I'm retiring in about six months, and Special Agent Layton Redker here is going to take my spot."

Bill gestured to the younger man who sat beside him at the small, circular table.

"Redker?" Palmer's forehead creased.

Layton Redker offered a cool half-smile in response, but the smile didn't reach his eyes. They looked like they could bore straight into a person. "Agent Palmer. Nice to see you again. Agent Storm, same to you."

Palmer drummed his fingers against a notepad. "What got Cyber Crimes involved in this case? More dark web activity?"

Chuckling, Agent Dumke shook his head. "Not any more or less than we noticed before you all left for Cedarwood. Agent Redker's working with me on the profile of this killer. He's the BAU's newest addition."

Redker's smile radiated so much sarcasm that Sherry almost laughed aloud. "I recently finished my Ph.D. in clinical psychology."

"Huh." Palmer rubbed his cheek. "Okay. Well, Agent… Doctor, Agent Doctor Redker, what've you got for us?"

Though Redker remained largely stoic, his companion laughed. "All right, I'm glad we've gotten that out of the way."

Sherry's focus returned, and she straightened in her uncomfortable chair. "As you can imagine, we've got quite a few questions for you."

A fatherly smile crinkled the corners of Bill Dumke's faded blue eyes. "I hope to be able to answer most of them." He glanced to his laptop, and then back to the webcam. "To start with, let's discuss the location where we've found all the victims so far. The banks along Fox Creek, is that right?"

"Right." Sherry folded her hands to keep from fidgeting. "And last night, we found what we think might be a graveyard. Or a dumping ground, depending on how you want to look at it. SAR dogs identified twelve separate sites, and we think there are likely more in and around the same area."

"Interesting." Dumke unfolded a pair of black-rimmed glasses. "I think it's likely that the killer is based in or around Cedarwood. The fact that he's dumped all these victims here is significant. He keeps going back to the same area because it's familiar to him."

"What about where the victims are from? Do you think they're significant to the profile?" Dean tapped different locations on the map. "Heather Breysacher disappeared from Bloomington, and Larissa Umber from Chicago. Why would a killer based in Cedarwood seek out victims in different areas?"

"That's a good question, Agent. It *is* unusual for a serial killer to 'hunt' outside their comfort zone, but it's certainly not unheard of. There have been plenty of killers who've gone undetected because they targeted victims across the country. Usually, they're men who travel frequently, typically for work. Think of a profession such as a long-haul truck driver or a traveling tradesman."

To Sherry, the assertion made perfect sense. If a person was used to constant travel, then they'd be more confident finding a victim in an unfamiliar environment.

As Agent Dumke slid on his glasses, his countenance sobered. "Based on the state of the victims' bodies, namely the fact that they were surgically dismembered, I think the killer is intelligent and likely well-educated. He can blend in well with others. He might even have an advanced degree, a steady job, and a family. I believe we're dealing with a male, between the ages of twenty-nine and forty-four, who is upper-middle-class."

Just as Sherry had feared.

Not all serial killers were as brilliant as Ted Kaczynski. Contrary to popular belief, the average IQ of known serial murderers was consistent with that of the general population. Sure, there were outliers on both ends of the spectrum, but the same could be said for law-abiding citizens.

"There are two classifications for serial killers," Bill Dumke continued. "Organized and disorganized. Like the names imply, organized serial killers are methodical and meticulous, whereas their disorganized counterparts are driven by urges to kill. That's not to say that an organized killer doesn't have impulses and urges he can't control, and vice versa. After reviewing the case file, I believe I can definitively place this particular suspect in the 'organized' category."

Though helpful, none of Bill's observations so far had come as a shock to Sherry. She'd worked in Violent Crimes since she joined the Bureau at twenty-five, and she'd accumulated a wealth of knowledge about the country's most twisted, vile predators.

Bill glanced at some notes before continuing his presentation. "The pattern of where he selects victims isn't particularly telling. Those locations could be places where he travels for work. But the fact that the two most recent victims were estimated to have been killed within a week of one another makes me think he's escalating."

"There's one other thing."

In tandem, Sherry and the rest of the room turned to Amelia Storm.

She seemed unperturbed. "We think there may be a more recent victim. A young woman disappeared after she'd stopped to help a stranded motorist. She was passing through this area on her way home to visit her family in Mendoza, but she never made it. She's a nineteen-year-old college student from a middle-class family. I wanted to hear your opinion on the likelihood that she's another potential victim."

Leaning back in his chair, Bill appeared thoughtful. "Mendoza is in LaSalle County. It fits the modus operandi, or what little of one we've been able to scrape together. And... its proximity to Cedarwood is consistent with a killer who's become more confident."

"Like you said, a killer who's escalating," Amelia finished.

"Exactly."

The discussion so far had heavily indicated they were dealing with a serial killer, but Sherry still wasn't entirely sold on the idea. Before she put all her eggs in one basket, as the saying went, she wanted to rule out the potential for other options. That was the entire reason Agents Storm and Palmer were here in the first place.

"What about the dark web activity?" Sherry asked.

Bill turned to his companion. "That's not my area of expertise, but fortunately, Agent Redker spent the last nine years in Cyber Crimes. Redker?"

Agent Redker cleared his throat and scooted closer to the table. Clearly, he'd expected the question. "A colleague from Cyber Crimes has been monitoring the dark web activity that we noticed coming out of Massey County. We've been on the lookout for any specific forums or posts that might indicate a trafficking ring but haven't found anything yet."

Sherry lifted an eyebrow. "But there *is* still dark web activity, isn't there?"

"There is." Redker met her gaze through the webcam, and she couldn't help but feel the man's presence in the room.

Now, she was certain she'd never come across the man at the field office. She'd remember a person as intimidating as Agent Layton Redker.

When no one interjected, Redker went on. "We can't pin it down to a specific location other than near Cedarwood. We access the dark web by using something called the Tor network. It's a program that essentially bounces an IP address and any other identifying markers through multiple layers. When the signal comes out the other side, it's unrecognizable, even to us."

Sherry checked her laptop and then looked back to the projected image of Agents Dumke and Redker. "Which is why we can't pin down where it's coming from?"

Redker frowned, and Sherry guessed he was contemplating how technical to get before answering. "Correct. We've been dealing with an uptick in human trafficking across the entire state, even the entire Midwest. We can't rule out the possibility that we're dealing with a trafficker."

"Or both." Dean leaned forward in his chair and pointed at Zane Palmer. "I mentioned this to Palmer yesterday, but we could be dealing with a guy who's something like the Toy Box Killer. Someone who's driven by the need to kill or the need to overpower and own another person completely. But in the digital age, what's to stop them from figuring out some way to monetize it?"

Palmer nodded his acknowledgment before adding his own spin. "Or maybe he's reaching out to other people who share his...interests. Like a social media outlet for murderers."

A shudder worked its way down Sherry's spine.

No matter how they viewed the killer, the dark web activity was troubling.

Even more disconcerting was the enigmatic haze that clouded the suspect. He was nothing more than a wisp of smoke with an indistinct shape. Impossible to grasp hold of.

The one clear certainty was the killer was escalating.

They needed a breakthrough, and soon.

21

Plastic bag of food in each hand, Zane shouldered open the door of the sheriff's department. He nodded a quick greeting to the deputy stationed at the front desk. Only a couple deputies lingered around the front portion of the station, and Zane reminded himself that the skeleton crew was normal for Massey County.

Not to mention that tomorrow is Thanksgiving. I'm lucky there was even any place open for lunch.

He'd drawn the short straw, and as a result, had gone to a barbecue restaurant in the town square to pick up three meals. Sherry had taken off with Deputy McCannon as soon as he'd arrived, which left Zane, Amelia, and Dean to parse through reports of the evidence they'd obtained so far.

They'd spent the day organizing data, but despite the necessity of the task, Zane felt as if all he'd done was run in circles.

With five victims at least—three whose identities they didn't even know—and zero suspects, he wasn't quite sure how they expected to make headway.

They were rudderless.

Cursing under his breath, he elbowed the metal lever to let himself into the conference room that had become their home.

Amelia's eyes flicked up from her laptop, and a rush of apprehension sent little shards of ice through his veins. The crushing dread on her face when she'd told him about Joseph Larson's conversation with Cassandra Halcott had broken his heart.

No one deserved what Larson had put her through and what his existence continued to put her through.

As much as Zane had wanted to offer her some semblance of comfort in what had clearly been a time of need, he'd found himself at a complete loss.

What could he do?

Zane had been through his options to "deal with" Joseph Larson more times than he cared to admit. With all the connections he'd made during his decade in the Central Intelligence Agency, there had to be a way he could deal with the bastard.

But the more he ruminated, the more he realized he'd done a damn fine job of sealing himself off from that life. He'd been forced to call in favors just to return to a semi-normal existence. Now, if he wanted help from those same contacts, he'd be in *their* debt.

From witnessing it happen to colleagues, he knew how quickly those dominoes could topple. One second, he'd be running an errand to repay an old intelligence analyst friend, and the next, he'd be neck-deep in a Russian weapons trafficking operation.

Holding up the bags of food, he tucked the bleak thoughts away in the back of his mind. "I don't know what's what. They told me, but I wasn't paying attention."

Amelia rose to her feet, a glimmer of amusement in her expression. "I appreciate your honesty."

With a grin, he picked the clearest portion of the table between their three seats and deposited the food. The scent of barbecue sauce and roasted meat wafted up to him at the motion, and his stomach grumbled.

"You guys find anything while I was gone?"

Steelman rifled through the first bag, and then the second. "Nothing. They dug up a skull out at the excavation site, but I think you were here when we got that message."

"I was, yeah."

In silence, the three of them doled out lunches and sat down to eat. Without any new developments, save the newest find at Fox Creek, they had no real topic for discussion. They'd done their due diligence, and though Zane hated to admit it, all they could do now was wait.

He hated waiting. Waiting gave him time to think, and when he turned his focus inward, his mind rarely took him anywhere pleasant.

Like his and Amelia's awkward encounter earlier in the day.

The fact that she'd seen him half-naked wasn't much of a point of concern. At least, not for the reasons a normal person might believe.

He liked Amelia, and the more he was around her, the more he realized that those feelings had begun to stray from a platonic friendship. She had her secrets, but so did he.

And this morning, she'd come within a hair's breadth of one. Though he'd love nothing more than to assure himself she hadn't seen the nautical stars on his shoulders and knees, he'd have to be an idiot to lure himself into such a sense of false complacency.

Why hadn't he taken the advice of his old colleagues and paid for laser removal?

Because laser removal doesn't completely get rid of the damn things. And to get them removed, someone would see them. They'd know. He never understood why the agency didn't keep a tattoo artist on retainer who could cover up the telltale marks of the profession while maintaining discretion. With any other tattoo artist, there would be documented proof. So, he was forced to conceal them.

Fighting the urge to rub at the site of one of the stars on his shoulder, he snuck a glimpse at Amelia. Her moss green eyes were glued to the screen of her phone as she scooped up a bite of macaroni and cheese.

In truth, his sentimental side had stopped him from even setting up an appointment with a tattoo removal specialist. No matter how hard he tried to bury the memories of his time with the Russian mob, those experiences were a part of him. A reminder that he could never separate himself from his past.

So, the tattoos stayed. He wore shirts when he'd rather go without, and he wore long pants in the middle of July. He'd only been with one woman since he'd moved to Chicago more than six months ago, and he'd taken special care to ensure she didn't spot the stars.

His gaze shifted to Amelia of its own volition. This time, she looked up from her phone, and her eyes met his.

Before he could either open his mouth to make up a reason he'd been staring at her or jerk his attention away, the door burst inward to reveal a red-faced deputy.

As they all turned toward the door, Zane was tempted to thank the deputy for the interruption.

"Agents." The man's heaving chest and flushed cheeks made Zane wonder if he'd run here. "We've found Willow Nowland's car. I was told to notify you right away."

Amelia was on her feet before the deputy had even finished speaking. "Where? Who's there now?"

The deputy swiped at his forehead with the sleeve of his shirt. "Behind an abandoned barn on County Road 600. A farmer who lives out in the area noticed it a little bit ago when he was on his way into town. He'd caught the description on the news this morning, and he said he called us right away. He didn't touch anything. We've got a deputy out there keeping the area secure."

Zane doubted that anyone would simply happen upon such a rural location to contaminate a potential crime scene, but he was grateful for the competent response. He was also desperate to get out of this damn room.

Shoving away from the table, he wiped his fingers on a brown napkin and fixed Amelia with a look that said, *I'm going with you. Don't argue with me.* "We'll be able to process anything we find faster if I go with you."

Though he half-expected her to protest, she gave a grateful smile instead. "Yeah, you're right. We can have the CSU meet us out there. It's supposed to storm later this afternoon, so we'll need to work fast."

To Zane's side, Dean Steelman dropped his hands to the table and blew out an exaggerated sigh. "I guess I'll hold down the fort, then. Call if you need anything."

❄

THE AZURE SKY and its smattering of puffy, white clouds belied no indication of the heavy storms predicted for the late afternoon hours. In fact, the balmy seventy-degree temperature, the slight breeze that carried the scents of late autumn, and the abundant sunshine struck Zane as the perfect Midwestern day.

Gravel crunched beneath his booted feet as he and Amelia made their way down the unpaved road. Their astute gazes flitted over the surrounding area as they searched for any anomaly in the otherwise serene landscape. Dried grass and reeds rattled in the ditch as the wind whispered past them.

Ahead, a dilapidated barn was positioned behind a couple tall, leafless trees. The outside of the barn had once been a vibrant red, but the elements had stripped the lively shade from the wooden siding over the years, leaving a patchwork of peeling paint as a memory of what once was.

The storage shed that faced the barn was in even worse shape. A massive tree branch, now long dead and mostly rotted, had crashed down on the center of the shingled roof. Though the oak still stood as tall and proud as ever, the shed was less fortunate.

As he and Amelia neared the brown-and-gold-clad deputy who stood at the edge of the abandoned gravel lot, Zane noticed a large, circular patch of ground that was devoid of plant life. "Looks like a UFO landed next to that shed."

The lanky deputy who had been waiting at the end of the gravel road jogged over. The man had surely been told to expect their arrival, but Zane produced his badge for good measure. "Afternoon, Agents. I'm Deputy Jacobsen. I overheard your comment about the dead patch. If I may, I'm fairly certain that a silo used to sit there. It may have been dismantled or been taken out by a storm."

Amelia's attention snapped over to the site of Zane's curiosity and the deputy's explanation.

Zane wiped his brow and glanced at Amelia. "Isn't this the day before Thanksgiving?"

"Unless we drove through a wormhole on our way here, yeah."

He ignored her sarcasm. "It's seventy-two right now. At the end of *November*."

A slight smile crept to her face. "You really don't know much about the Midwest, do you?"

The deputy chuckled before Zane could respond.

"Considering I've only lived here for less than a year, I'd

say I really don't. Tornadoes, seventy-degree days when it's almost December. It's a mess out here."

Her expression morphed into a full-on grin, and for a beat, his heart was lighter. "Just wait until we get some lake effect snow. You're in for a treat."

He snorted. Snow, he could handle. Tornadoes, not so much. Russia had plenty of the former but none of the latter.

To return their focus to the scene, Zane nodded at the deputy. "What do you have for us, Deputy Jacobsen?"

"Willow Nowland's car is behind the barn over there." He waved at the decrepit building. "Parked out of sight of the road, for the most part."

Amelia turned to survey the field that lay beyond a barbed-wire fence marking the perimeter.

Seeming to follow her gaze, the deputy pointed at a cluster of trees and a white house in the distance. The residence was mostly obscured by the skeletal branches, but Zane could pick out a hint of…something. A vehicle, he figured.

"That's the home of the guy who reported Nowland's car," the deputy explained. "His property backs up to this field, but he doesn't own the land."

Zane squinted, but the scene didn't become any clearer. "He see anything a few nights ago? On Sunday?"

Crossing his arms, the deputy shook his head. "No. Said he'd been out of town visiting relatives for an early Thanksgiving. I sent all his info back to the department, and they verified it. He just got back today."

"Shit." Zane scratched the side of his face. "Thanks for checking on that for us, Deputy."

The sound of an approaching engine drew their collective attention back to the road.

A Crown Victoria pulled up behind Jacobsen's cruiser, which was parked at the end of the drive. Zack Anders emerged from the driver's side, evidence collection kit in hand. An unfamiliar woman stepped out of the car, and the pair walked toward them.

After introductions were made, Deputy Jacobsen took up his post in the cruiser at the end of the short road. Zane and Amelia tailed the two crime scene techs to the barn. The chalky-white gravel thinned to reveal splotches of packed earth. Rain and snow had displaced the rocks over the years, and Zane could only imagine what a muddy, soupy mess the place became after a storm.

At the thought, he glanced at his watch. "Quarter 'til two. When are those storms expected again?"

Amelia brushed a piece of dark hair from her eyes. "Five, but it could be sooner. Weather in the Midwest is unpredictable."

He turned his face up to the sky, but there still wasn't a hint of foreboding. "We'll have to work fast."

Zack looked over his shoulder and cocked an eyebrow. "The car is the priority, right?"

Amelia glanced around the old structure. "Maybe we should take a look at the area around it first. Get some photos and see if we can find tracks or anything else that might've been left behind. The interior of the car will be fine once it starts raining, but I can't say the same for the rest of the scene."

"Right. Good idea." Lifting the Nikon draped around his neck, Zack tilted his chin at the ground to their side. "Tire tracks in the dirt, leading around the barn to Nowland's car." The shutter clicked.

Rose Simmons prepared her camera too. "I'll move on up ahead so we can cover more ground."

Amelia retrieved a pair of vinyl gloves from her pocket. "Yeah, good idea. I'll help you." She shot Zane a wicked little wink and started after the tech.

What the hell was that about?

Dropping to a crouch, Anders lowered his camera. "These don't look like the tracks we found on Highway 26." His dark eyes flicked up to Zane. "I'm pretty sure these are from Ms. Nowland's car. If they are, then that means there's a possibility the tracks on Highway 26 could've belonged to whoever she stopped to help on the night she was last seen."

Zane opened his mouth to respond, but Anders continued before he had the chance.

"Not a guarantee, though. Tracking tire imprints in the dirt isn't an exact science. So, even though I'm confident that the marks on Highway 26 would've been left on Saturday or Sunday, there's no way for me to scientifically prove it. Even if I could, we'd need an exact time to prove that the driver was there at the same time as Nowland."

The lengthy observation was followed by the *click, click, click* of the camera's shutter.

Anders rose to his full height. Picking his way along the ground beside the gentle curve of the tire tracks, he fired off another series of remarks about the area.

Now, Zane understood the reason for Amelia's sneaky little wink. She'd spent a chunk of the previous day in Anders's company, and she knew how talkative the young man was.

Anders must have talked off her ear. Not to say Zane disliked Anders so far, nor could he fault the kid for being so chatty. Amelia had endured plenty of lengthy car rides with Zane when he'd been unable to shut his own mouth.

To her credit, Amelia had always indulged him. She'd asked him questions when he'd rambled on about skiing and snowboarding trips with his family, though he was well-aware that Amelia was completely unfamiliar with both activities.

She'd never been to the Swiss Alps, never spent her

Christmas vacation in a luxury ski resort. She'd never so much as thought about the sense of pride and accomplishment someone felt when they moved on to one of the more challenging slopes after learning the fundamentals.

If Zane remembered right, Amelia and her family had only ever taken one vacation to Six Flags before her mother died. Amelia had gone out of the city a couple times with her track team in high school, but they'd never ventured outside of Illinois.

Hell, the only reason she'd been able to sign up for the sport was because a local nonprofit had paid her expenses.

A flicker of sadness had passed over her face when she'd told him about the experience. In her high school social circle, only the rich, privileged kids could afford an extracurricular activity. When she'd been gifted the opportunity by the now-defunct nonprofit, her little group of friends had regarded her as an outsider.

Dammit.

He was at a crime scene. Why in the hell was he thinking about Amelia's life as a teenager?

Pausing beside Anders, Zane rubbed his eyes with the heel of one hand. He blinked to clear his vision and then spotted the shape of Amelia and Rose as they loped along the barbed wire fence. The quiet drone of the women's voices drifted to him, but he couldn't make out a single word.

Anders dropped a small, triangular evidence marker beside the tire tracks. "Just the one set of treads, it looks like. Whoever brought Nowland's car here would have left on foot."

Zane gestured to their parked cars. "Could've had someone waiting for him out on the road."

Tilting his head, Anders appeared to weigh Zane's suggestion as he scanned the tracks again. "True. It's all gravel out there, though. There's no chance we'll find an impression."

The kid was right. "The forensic archaeologist *did* find a bone that the coroner thinks belonged to a male. It could be from a potential witness that our guy killed to keep quiet or an accomplice he decided to get rid of." Zane returned his focus to the not-so-distant road. "Maybe he got rid of one accomplice and picked up another."

Anders fiddled with his camera. "The bone we found could also be a victim. The leg was severed in the same way as all the other victims. Now, I'm not a serial killer expert, but I did my fair share of research when I was in college. Took plenty of classes on the subject, things like that." Shifting his weight from one foot to the other, Anders seemed to hesitate.

"And?" Zane prodded.

CSU or special agent, he didn't care. A theory was a theory, and they'd extrapolated useful information from far less reliable sources in the past. According to Amelia, and based on Zane's observation so far, Anders was sharp. The guy held an advanced degree focused on forensics, which was more than Zane could claim.

"Well, from what I know about serials, they tend to save their ritual for the victims that are part of that hunt, you know? They'll kill witnesses and accomplices, sure, but they typically won't go through the same pattern of activity when they dispose of those people. Their goal is to get rid of them, not necessarily to hunt them."

"You think that our guy targeted males too?"

"I'm not sure. Like I said, that was just a hypothesis. In school, they taught us the ritual of killing is very important to a serial killer. And not every serial targets only one gender. Richard Ramirez, The Nightstalker, he had his ritual of breaking into homes and killing. But he also abducted and sexually assaulted children. That part is usually overlooked by the media."

Zane almost rolled his eyes. "Of course it is. No one wants to read about some creep hurting kids, but they just love a deranged murderer."

Anders's expression sobered. "Exactly. And we both know which happens more often. Something about victims being adults just makes it easier for people to blame them for their own assault or murder, all in the name of reassuring themselves that it'll never happen to them."

"Je-e-sus. That's bleak, Anders." Floating bodies flashed through Zane's mind, and he forced his mind away from other horrors he'd witnessed. "Not wrong, not at all, but holy shit, is it bleak." He hadn't expected such a cynical, albeit accurate, musing from the good-spirited crime scene tech.

A rush of pink tinged Anders's cheeks. "Sorry. I love this job, but it gets to you sometimes. I spent the first half of the day out by Fox Creek, helping the forensics crew process everything. I do my best to stay positive and focus on the good that I'm able to do, but, well…" Lifting a shoulder, he trailed off.

"Yeah, I get it. Cops on TV don't get hit by this stuff. They just always seem to remember that they're fighting the good fight, and apparently, that's enough for them to brush off all the nasty shit they see on the job. And I guess some of us can. Some cops are good at compartmentalizing, but I'm pretty sure they're the minority, if I'm being honest."

Anders moved the camera from one hand to the other as he looked out to where Amelia and Rose were busy scrutinizing the corner of the barn. "Your partner, Agent Storm, she was at that farm in Kankakee County, wasn't she?"

The chill of anxiety trickled into Zane's blood. "We both were."

Anders's gaze shifted back to the tire tracks. "Me too. I

was in Kankakee County to train a few of their department's people on some new tech they'd gotten recently. But when that place went down, they asked for all hands on deck. I was there, so I volunteered to help."

Zane wasn't sure how the conversation had gravitated so far off track, but he was invested. "Six degrees of separation. It's all that separates any of us."

Anders returned his focus to Zane, and the darkness clouding his features began to dissipate. "I guess so. Sorry, didn't mean to get off topic. It's just...no matter how hard I try, I don't think I'll ever forget that place. Those poor girls."

There'll be plenty more just like it, kid.

"Yeah, me neither," he said instead.

A fat, puffy cloud drifted away from the sun, suddenly brightening the landscape. Zane squinted to keep his eyes from watering, and as he turned to face the horizon, he spotted golden light glittering off a shard of glass. A bottle. And it wasn't the only one.

Shading his eyes with one hand, Zane jabbed a finger at the patch of scrub grass. As if the plant life knew it had no hope of conquering the crumbling asphalt that ran the length of the shed, the dried weeds and grass congregated in clumps at the edge of the cement slab.

"There's something over here. Looks like broken bottles."

Camera at the ready, Anders gingerly picked his way to the site. "Beer bottles. Bud Lite, from the looks of it." *Click, click, click.* "And a few cigarette butts. The bottles are dusty, and there are patterns on them that are consistent with rainfall. I'm pretty sure they've been here a while."

"Party spot for underaged kids?"

Anders shot him a grin. "Oh yeah. I grew up in Massey County. Places like this were our preferred hangout spots once the sun went down. Lots of dead branches nearby to make a fire, no one close enough to make a noise complaint. Good times."

After setting another numbered marker beside the site, Zane and Anders circled back to the tire tracks.

They spotted a couple more signs of old parties and notated each accordingly. Though they both expressed their doubts about the items being related to Willow Nowland and her disappearance, they'd bag and tag everything just the same.

By the time they neared the little Civic, dark clouds had amassed on the western horizon like a finger gradually sliding to cover a tiny lightbulb.

Their time was running low, but Zane was confident they'd made good progress so far. Two sets of eyes had helped Anders cover his portion of the scene quickly and thoroughly. On the other side of the Honda, Rose and Amelia's voices were now clear. They were all about to converge on the car.

As Zane produced a flashlight from his pocket and prepared to examine underneath the vehicle, Anders sucked in a sharp breath. Zane spun around to face the younger man. "What?"

Anders hunched down, and the *click* of the shutter followed. "Footprint. It's slight, but it's here."

Zane worked to temper his rush of excitement.

Sure enough, just outside the driver's side door was a faint indentation left by a person's shoe. In the drying dirt, the tread marks were scarcely visible. Zane gave the track a wide berth as he circled around Anders to follow the trail.

"What is it?" Amelia's voice cut through the sudden stillness.

"Footprints." Zane pointed to the second track. "Leading away from the car. There's another one, Anders. Heading toward the..." Studying the scene, Zane barely held back a groan. "Heading toward the gravel. Dammit."

"This is still good." The hitch of intrigue in Anders's tone gave new life to Zane's short-lived optimism. Anders glanced up to Zane and Amelia, and the shutter stilled. "These tracks, they look like the ones that Agent Storm and I found beside Highway 26. It's just a cursory visual observation now, but we'll be able to compare them when we get back."

Zane glanced down to one of his feet and then back to the impression in the dirt. He wouldn't disturb the site by moving any closer, but by his best guess, the person who'd left the print wore almost the same size shoe as he did. "That definitely isn't from one of Nowland's shoes. Unless she's moonlighting as a clown."

So soon after his and Anders's heavy conversation, Zane half-expected the tech to glower at him. To his relief, Anders barked out a sharp laugh.

Thank God. If Zane hadn't found a way to insert humor into this job, he'd have quit as soon as he'd started. As far as he was concerned, any FBI agent who wanted to retain any semblance of their sanity *needed* to find a laugh wherever they could.

"The other side's empty." Sunlight gave an orange hue to Rose's coppery brown hair as she stepped out from the shadow of the old barn. "Agent Storm and I checked the passenger side. It's dirt over here too, but there aren't any tracks."

Zane spared a short glance at the clouds in the distance. "One set of tire impressions leading right up to where the Honda's parked, and then one set of men's roughly size thirteen footprints leading away. No other obvious indications that anyone's been here recently."

Aside from the *click, click, click* of the camera's shutter, the whisper of dried grass swaying in the afternoon breeze, and the occasional cry of a bird, the space lapsed into silence.

Amelia's hands rested on her hips. "That's Nowland's car, but I don't think Nowland was ever here. Whoever had to do with her disappearance is the one who moved this vehicle here, and then they either left on foot, or they caught a ride from an accomplice."

A cold ball formed in Zane's stomach. "Willow Nowland's missing persons investigation is now officially a kidnapping case."

Like the faint grumble of some giant beast, thunder sounded out from the approaching storm. The air itself had become ominous.

They needed to work quickly. Time was their enemy.

※

Ever since Sherry had arrived at the Fox Creek dig site, she'd been asked to remain on the sidelines. But when the first booms of thunder rolled over the hustle and bustle, that all changed.

She'd made her way to the cluster of law enforcement vehicles—deputies' cruisers, CSU vans, and unmarked FBI vehicles. Sherry had been tasked with retrieving tarps to set up a staging area, as well as cover the holes that forensics had painstakingly dug. The open dig sites were priority number one, but the forensic archaeologist, Dr. Daksha Malhotra, had suggested they form a makeshift tent over the entire area.

Sherry appreciated the woman's thorough approach, but she wasn't particularly excited for the tedious process.

As she neared a white-panel van, she offered a smile to the deputy who'd begun unloading tarps to hand off to Dr. Malhotra's team.

"Agent Cowen, looks like you're getting down in the trenches, eh?" The middle-aged man reminded Sherry of a kind uncle, and his tone gave no indication of sarcasm.

She blew a raspberry and held out both arms to receive her bizarre gift. "I guess you could say that, Deputy. Good thing my fiancé loves to go camping. Throwing together a shelter in the middle of nowhere is something I like to think I'm pretty good at."

The deputy grinned as he handed her a rolled-up tarp. "That's old school. My wife and I used to camp in tents like that, then we turned fifty. It's the camper life for us now."

"Ahh, so you like *glamping*." Sherry laughed, a much needed hit of levity after using the term she'd heard applied to upscale camping. Watching forensics personnel unearth dismembered human remains was a bleak task, and she was grateful for the distraction, brief though it might have been. Balancing the rolled-up tarp in her arms, Sherry ambled back through the loose cluster of trees.

Their exact location hadn't yet been revealed to the media, and Sherry took a moment to thank whatever deity might have been listening.

Branches overhead rattled as the wind picked up speed, and the gurgle of the nearby creek was drowned out by the constant drone of voices as Sherry approached the grassy clearing. Well, *dirt* clearing after so much digging.

Crime scene techs, members of Dr. Malhotra's team, as well as the coroner and one of the FBI's own forensic anthropologists had the center stage.

Deputy McCannon and Sir Sniffs were on duty a short distance north of the bustling scene. Word had filtered back to Sherry about an hour earlier that the yellow lab had located more potential burial sites.

The entire ground team functioned like a well-oiled machine, but they had their work cut out for them. Especially if they wanted to preserve their findings in the face of the powerful front moving in from the west.

"Agent Cowen! There you are." A woman's voice cut through the din.

Readjusting her hold on the tarp, Sherry turned to face the speaker. "Oh, hello, Dr. Islas."

A bright blue and green patterned kerchief held the forensic anthropologist's ebony hair out of her face. Her tan cheeks were darkened with a flush, no doubt from the exertion, both mental and physical, of her work.

Though Dr. Malhotra had a group of graduate students and interns to help with excavating each body part, Alicia Islas had only two others from her team back in Chicago. Granted, their task—examining and identifying characteristics of each victim—wasn't quite as laborious as Dr. Malhotra's.

Sherry raised the tarp in her arms. "Is this for you?"

The woman waved a hand. "No, get it over to the techs at site one and site two. They'll want to cover them first since they're the most exposed. But come right back. Mr. Schaeffer and I have some news for you."

Eagerness thrummed through Sherry's body. As quickly as she could manage without tripping and falling, she passed off the vinyl sheet to a crime scene tech who wore a perplexed expression.

Before the man could ask her a question, she slunk off to where the coroner had joined Dr. Islas.

The corners of Dr. Islas's eyes crinkled as she smiled at Sherry. "That was fast."

Sherry was certain her face belied only pinched anticipation. "What news do you have for me, Doctor?"

With a snap, the anthropologist pulled on a pair of gloves and ushered Sherry to a rectangular table that had been set up beneath an awning. The screened sides were rolled up and pinned in place, but Sherry recognized the canvas material.

When she'd last gone camping with her fiancé and a handful of his friends, they'd set up a tent much like this one. The mesh sides could be fastened to the ground to keep out mosquitos, all while leaving campers with a relatively unobstructed view of the world around them.

"Dr. Malhotra is working on the fourth burial site, where she's found a severed arm wrapped in another black garbage bag. I'm waiting for her to finish the excavation before I can take a look. In the meantime, this was found in burial site three." Dr. Islas reached for a stainless-steel container and gingerly scooped up a cracked brown skull.

Sherry had heard of the find, but this was the first time she'd come face-to-face with the remains.

Dr. Islas held up the bones for Sherry to get a closer view. "All the teeth are intact, and the crack at the top is the only real damage I can see. But it's been here a while."

Sherry knew each discovery brought the FBI one step closer to discovering who the killer was. "How old do you think it is?"

"As I'm sure you know, human and animal bones *do* decompose, but at much slower rates than softer tissue. Bones are still porous, though, and that gives fungi, bacteria, and other microscopic organisms an entry point to feed on the nutrients inside the skeleton."

"Like marrow, right?"

The anthropologist tilted her head as her gaze moved to the skull. "Among other things, yes. Bones are formed primarily of collagen, but they're also rich in calcium. That combination is what keeps them sturdy while you're alive, and it's what makes them take longer to decompose. Now, in an arid environment like a desert or some high-altitude climates, a skeleton can survive intact for thousands of years."

As Sherry peered into the darkness of the empty eye sockets, a sense of foreboding coalesced in her gut. "What about somewhere a little more humid? Like Illinois?"

The woman's face had become grave, and as she held the skull in both hands, Sherry could almost picture Dr. Islas as a powerful sorceress prepared to cast a terrible spell. She shook off the image as the anthropologist explained. "It's a bit difficult for me to say out here in the field, but based on the decay, coloring, and taking into consideration *how* she was buried, I'd say she's been underground for at least a decade."

Sherry's heartbeat hammered in her ears. Suddenly, the balmy afternoon was stifling. "This guy could've been active for more than ten years before we even knew he existed." She tucked away the ominous feeling. She'd deal with the implications of their find later. "You said *she*? You think this skull belongs to a woman?"

Dr. Islas's mouth was a hard line as she turned the skull to give Sherry a profile view. "A *young* woman."

Sherry could feel the blood drain from her face. "How young?"

Using a gloved finger, Dr. Islas made a circular motion at the backmost molar. "She has no third molars."

"Wisdom teeth? She could've had them pulled." A memory of a dreadful orthodontic visit floated to the surface of Sherry's mind. "I had to get mine pulled when I was still in high school. Otherwise, they would've crowded my mouth and messed up the perfectly straight teeth I'd gotten from four solid years of braces."

The anthropologist winced sympathetically. "It's possible but look here." She motioned to a squiggly line that ran horizontally along the center of the skull. "These lines are cranial sutures. As humans grow, the sutures close in a relatively predictable order. So, we can get a rough age estimate by visually examining how much the sutures have closed."

"The less visible the lines, the older the person?"

"More or less. Cranial sutures aren't the ideal method to determine the precise age of a skeleton. There's a great deal of variance not only among humans and their physiological development but among the studies themselves. Out in the field, it's still useful, especially when we can combine it with another age measurement."

Sherry saw where the anthropologist's logic was leading. "Like the lack of wisdom teeth."

"Correct. We rarely use just one point of analysis to measure someone's age. Personally, I prefer to review as much information as I can get my hands on. Between the fact that she has no third molars and the fact that the sagittal suture doesn't appear to have closed more than slightly, I'd put her age at somewhere around twelve to sixteen."

Sherry's heart dropped.

Their killer had been active for more than a decade.

And he'd preyed on teenagers.

22

Amelia almost leapt out of her motorcycle boots as a clap of thunder boomed, deep and ominous. Fat raindrops *plunked* against their incident room's only window, and the glass rattled in its pane from the wind that buffeted the side of the Massey County Sheriff's Department. The sky was bruised, the light from between the blinds muddy. Only the sickly glow of the fluorescent fixture overhead illuminated her and Dean Steelman's whiteboard handiwork.

Zack Anders had provided them a flash drive with all of his and Rose's photos from both the abandoned barn and the side of Highway 26. After securing a wireless printer, Amelia and Steelman had set about the task of better visualizing their case while Zane turned to digital research.

The topographic map rested in the center of the veritable collage, now marked with red dots where they'd unearthed victims. Cowen had called not long after Amelia and Zane had returned to the sheriff's department, and she'd advised them that Deputy McCannon's canine partner had found more probable burial sites to the north of the current dig location.

In addition, she'd told them about the more decayed remains that had been unearthed by the forensic archaeologist. The skull of a teenaged girl.

Amelia snuffed out the flicker of rage before the flames could ignite into an inferno. Folding her arms across her chest, she took a step back to observe her and Steelman's organizational efforts.

Beside the topographic map, Steelman had taped a larger depiction of the state of Illinois. The thought was to notate each victim's hometown, but so far, they only had identities for two of the bodies that had been found. If Amelia counted Willow Nowland, they'd identified three out of eight, which left them with four Jane Does and one John Doe.

Each victim had been given their own space on the whiteboard. Below the name, Amelia and Steelman had written as many factual statements about the deceased as they could find. Pictures of the remains were taped beside the meager writeups, and they'd left a chunk of the board blank for the victims who were sure to be discovered over the next couple days.

The *tap, tap, tap* of a pen drew Amelia's attention to where Zane sat at the table behind her and Steelman.

His gray eyes were narrowed in focus as he tapped a ballpoint pen against the laptop. Amelia recognized the gesture. Zane tended to drum his fingers or fiddle with pens when he was in contemplation.

Amelia cleared her throat so she wouldn't startle him when she spoke. "Did you find something? Or a lack of something?"

With a clatter, he dropped the pen and leaned back in his chair to rub his eyes. "Yes."

Amelia didn't bother to hide her confusion. "Which?"

Zane blew out a sigh. "Yes to both. Monday, we visited the gas station Larissa last visited, and yesterday, we sent a request for the security cam footage from the gas station on the night Willow disappeared. The owner of the station said that the camera had been malfunctioning, and since he's in Small Town U.S.A., it wasn't high on his priority list to fix."

Steelman crossed his arms. "Par for the freakin' course."

"That's what I thought." Zane lifted a finger, and his expression was a little less grim. "But our small business owner just sent me an email. He's not all that tech-savvy, so I requested that one of the local tech people go take a look. She's taken over trying to retrieve the footage. Apparently, the camera works just fine, but the hard drive they use to store the video was acting up."

Tentative relief crept into Amelia's thoughts. "Hard drive fixes can be easy, or they can be impossible. Especially if it's a hard disk drive. If the hardware on one of those things is damaged, you might as well kiss the data goodbye."

"My thoughts exactly. We ought to hear back from her in an hour or so to tell us how it went."

Steelman returned his dry-erase marker to the holder and grabbed a paper cup of coffee. "What about the missing persons reports? Any luck there?"

The borderline irritability returned to Zane's demeanor as he paused to study the laptop. "No. Nothing. But we don't exactly have precise timeframes for when the victims would've disappeared, nor do we have any other identifying information. It's like looking for a needle in a stack of needles that's in *another* stack of needles. Needles every damn where."

Steelman swore and sipped his coffee. "Then we focus on the victims we do have, including Nowland."

Amelia's cell buzzed in her back pocket, and she followed Zane and Dean's discussion as she retrieved the device.

"Not that there's much there, either." Zane clicked his

pen. "Heather Breysacher, Larissa Umber, and Willow Nowland couldn't have been more different if they'd tried."

"Ain't that the truth," Steelman muttered. "Only common thread is that they were on the younger side, and they were pretty."

Amelia opened her newest email, and her mouth went dry. "Shit."

The word was barely audible, but both men's attention snapped to her.

Licking her lips, Amelia peeled herself away from the message. "That was the lab. They finished the DNA analysis from the blood we found on Highway 26."

Steelman's vivid blue gaze bored into hers, but his face was carefully guarded. "And?"

"It's a match to the DNA from Willow Nowland's toothbrush."

"Shit," Zane spat. "Anders and Simmons are still working through Nowland's car, but the last update said that it looked like the driver's side had been wiped down. No prints."

Worry licked at the edges of Amelia's nerves. She'd suspected that Willow had been taken by the same killer they were hunting, but to hear forensic confirmation made her heart sink. "Most cars will have at least some fingerprints unless someone doesn't want anyone to find any." She sighed. "And the keys were in the visor?"

"They were." Zane tapped a couple keys on the laptop. "There were a few prints on the glove compartment and the center console, all left by the same person."

"Left by Nowland, more than likely." Steelman scratched the stubble on his cheek. "What about the rest of the car?"

Zane shook his head slightly. "Not much. Long, blonde hairs, consistent with Nowland. A couple even longer dark hairs on the passenger's side. Probably a friend of hers, but

Anders and Simmons bagged them. There's also some glitter on the upholstery of the driver's seat."

Amelia pocketed her cell. "Glitter has cracked some cases wide open."

"It has," Steelman said. "It's usually something a victim leaves behind. Not the other way around, but there's a first time for everything."

The man was right. Amelia doubted they were chasing after a sparkly serial killer. "Well, what now?"

Stretching both arms above his head, Zane jerked around in his seat at another peal of thunder. "Provided we don't get obliterated by a tornado, I think there's only one real thing we *can* do. Breysacher, Umber, and our Jane and John Does aren't going to get us anywhere until we know more about them. We've exhausted all our leads on Umber, and Breysacher's case has been cold for four years now."

Steelman glanced to the whiteboard and then rubbed his eyes. "You're right. We aren't going to get anywhere with either of them."

"Which means we work Nowland's case." Amelia hoped she'd followed Zane and Dean's train of thought.

"It's all we've got. And even there, it's not much." Zane straightened and met her gaze. "Even if we find out down the road that Nowland's not connected, she *is* in danger. There's nothing we can do with the rest of this shit until we get more lab results, so we might as well put our energy into something useful."

The sincerity in his voice squeezed at Amelia's heart. But as the stupid fluttering began in her stomach, she recalled their awkward morning encounter. The nautical stars on his shoulders and knees. A symbol of authority in the Russian mob.

Later.

Zane Palmer was a mystery that would have to wait.

Breaking the eye contact, she looked down and brushed off the front of her plain gray t-shirt.

Dean Steelman's voice broke the silence before the air could turn awkward. "Okay, then. Let's find our girl."

※

Willow twisted the hexagonal bolt and finally managed to move it ever so slightly. Tears burned at the corners of her eyes. For the first time since she'd been knocked unconscious by "Dan," a hopeful rush swelled in her chest.

A dim light had been left on in the room beyond Willow's cell, providing her with a markedly improved visual of the concrete dungeon. She still wasn't sure if Dan had kept the light on intentionally or if he'd simply forgotten. Though she had no way to track the passage of time in this pit, by her best estimate, the kidnapping prick had been gone for six or seven hours.

Probably working his desk job or taking care of his kids.

Nausea churned in Willow's gut.

How long before the sweet little girl she'd come across at the gas station became a suitable target for her vile father? Would he chain *her* in a lightless room with nothing but a water basin, a rusty metal toilet, and a paper-thin mattress?

Willow had tried to pull apart the sink for an item she could turn into a makeshift weapon, but the fixtures were reminiscent of what she'd expect in a maximum-security prison.

She shook herself away from the musing and returned her focus to the pair of heavy-duty bolts that bound her shackles to the cement wall. The contraption was old-school like it had been pulled straight off the set of *Game of Thrones*.

But it was effective.

Two loops were welded to a metal plate, and the chains

were similarly fastened in place. A bolt on each side kept the entire device secured. She could have pulled and pulled and pulled, but she wouldn't have gained an inch.

Licking her dry lips, Willow spun one of the bolts. A reminder of what she'd accomplished. The significance hadn't fully dawned on her, and she doubted she'd experience any true sense of relief until she was above ground again.

She was on the cusp of freedom. She'd finally be reunited with her mother, her brothers, her father. Odds were good that her mom would never let her leave the house again. And Willow doubted she'd object. Staying indoors with a warm bed, home-cooked meals, and loving parents didn't seem like a bad way to spend the rest of her life.

Stop. Jaw clenched, she scolded herself.

You're not out of here yet. Get your shit together. Undoing those bolts is just the first step.

With a long, steadying breath, she lowered herself to sit on the floor. Though she wanted nothing more than to rip the shackles off the wall and make a run for it, she had to be smart. Dan had been gone for a while now, and if his routine held, he'd be back at any moment with food. Dinner or lunch, hell if she knew.

She'd stay in front of the loosened bolts as much as she could, and she'd pretend to be wary and anxious like she always was. There would be no change in her demeanor. Dan was a sick bastard, but there was an unnerving intelligence in his indigo eyes.

He was smart. He'd be well aware that she was searching for a way out.

Willow slid a hand into the pocket of her hoodie. A sense of grim consummation greeted her as she closed her fingers around the makeshift lockpick she'd forged from the underwires of her bra. She was far from a professional, but she'd had a few successes in her younger years. As long as the handle of the door wasn't too heavy-duty or complex, she'd have a fighting chance.

A distant, metallic *clang* ripped her out of the mental planning. She knew that sound.

Blood pounded in Willow's ears.

He was here.

23

Stephanie Gifford closed and locked the front door as her younger sister, Kaitlyn, pulled off her orange and green patterned rain boots. Orange was Katie's favorite color, though Stephanie was almost certain her sister had merely copied *her* favorite color. Kids were like that, she'd come to realize.

Not that Stephanie viewed herself as a kid. She was thirteen, and she'd be fourteen in a few months. Fifteen was the legal age to obtain a learner's permit, and her dad had already assured her he'd teach her to drive. How could she think of herself as a kid when she was only a year away from being able to *drive*?

Once she and Katie had hung up their coats and backpacks in the mudroom beside the garage, Stephanie procured snacks for the two of them. For Katie, she made a peanut butter and jelly sandwich, and for herself, she cut up an apple.

Though Stephanie had always been on the slender side, she figured it never hurt to cut out a few carbs where she could. At least, that's what she'd heard some of her fifteen-year-old friends say.

Her sister chattered for most of the time, but Stephanie paid little attention. Something about a boy who'd been caught copying her friend's homework.

As Stephanie deposited their dishes in the sink, Katie hurried to the living room to claim the television remote for herself.

Again, Stephanie didn't particularly care. Katie's shows were for little kids, but Stephanie hardly paid attention to them. She either messed around on her phone or played games on the computer. Unfortunately, as she wandered down the hall to peek into the shadowy den, the widescreen monitor was dark.

Stephanie sighed.

One of these days, she'd convince her parents to give her the password. For now, she was stuck with her sister and the television.

"Hey, Steph, what do you want to watch?"

Glancing to where her sister had commandeered the recliner that was comically large compared to her tiny frame, Stephanie shrugged and flopped on the couch. "I don't care. You can pick."

Truly, Stephanie didn't care. They'd arrived home before two, and they were free from school until the following Monday. And most importantly, Stephanie's teachers had shown mercy on her eighth-grade class. Not a single one of them had doled out an assignment. Finally, for what felt like the first time since the beginning of the school year, Stephanie didn't have to spend the first chunk of her night with her nose buried in some boring old textbook.

Plenty of her friends skipped out on homework or cheated on tests, but Stephanie had always cared about her grades. Her parents had come to expect high marks, and they gave Stephanie money for each A and B she earned.

As the flicker of the television lit up the room, high-pitched cartoon voices echoed from the speakers.

Stephanie cringed at the volume. "Turn it down a little, will you?"

Katie's cheeks turned pink. "Sorry." The younger girl jabbed the remote a few times before settling back into the plush recliner.

All in all, Stephanie could definitely do worse for a little sister. One of her best friends had a younger brother who liked to steal items from her room while she was gone. Katie wouldn't even dream of such a thing.

Tuning out the colorful show, Stephanie started to scroll through a supernatural webcomic that her friend had recommended. She'd only made it to the third page when her sister's voice cut into her brain.

"That girl isn't missing."

Stephanie propped herself up with both elbows to look at her sister. "What?"

She expected Katie to apologize and wave away the comment, but Katie was dead serious. She jabbed a finger at the television. "There. Her. That girl isn't missing. I saw her Sunday night after my dance."

As Stephanie tried in vain to put together the puzzle pieces, she turned to the screen.

A news anchor straightened a stack of papers on her shiny desk. *"We have a news update for our viewers. Law enforcement officials located the vehicle of a missing nineteen-year-old girl who'd disappeared late on Sunday night. Jessica Trundle is live on the scene at the old Gibby property. Stay tuned for more on the discovery, as well as new information we've learned about the remains that were found near Fox Creek."*

The image switched to a photo of a pretty blonde with a flawless, white smile.

"Her!" Katie scooted to the edge of her seat, her eyes like a pair of saucers. "After my dance, me and Dad stopped at a gas station, and he bought some candy bars. I saw that nice girl there. Then Daddy and me went for a drive. We were pulled over on the highway, and I saw—" Katie slammed a hand over her mouth.

"Wait." Stephanie pushed herself to sit and stared at her little sister. "You saw that girl on Sunday?"

Katie worried at her bottom lip as her gaze dropped to her lap. "I'm not supposed to talk about it."

Alarm bells clanged in Stephanie's mind with the force of a sledgehammer.

This entire scenario was *off*. Something was wrong here, and though Stephanie was partially inclined to drop the subject altogether, to put as much distance between herself and the discomfort as she could manage, her desire to understand the situation was overwhelming.

"Katie, look at me." Leaning over the arm of the couch, Stephanie placed a hand on her sister's shoulder. "What's going on? What aren't you supposed to talk about? Did something happen?"

Fidgeting with the hem of her t-shirt, Katie cast a paranoid glance around the living room.

Now, Stephanie was *really* worried. Had her sister been hurt? Had she seen another person hurt the missing girl from the news? *Who* had she seen?

She said it was after her dance. Dad picked her up from the recital because Mom was working a late shift, and they let me stay home to study for my big test the next day.

Stephanie had been neck-deep in studying when her sister had arrived home on Sunday, but their father hadn't been with her. At the time, Stephanie had paid little attention to his absence. He liked to keep the same hours as their mother, and his departures at night weren't unusual.

Pushing aside the slew of what-ifs, Stephanie gave her sister's shoulder a gentle shake. "Katie, come on. You can't just say that you recognize a girl who's missing and then not say anything about her."

Katie wrung her small hands. "I'm not 'sposed to say."

Stephanie tucked both knees beneath herself and turned to fully face her sister. "Why not?"

"Dad asked me to keep it a secret."

Anxiety smashed into Stephanie like a bolt of lightning. She clutched the arm of the couch to conceal the sudden tremble in her hands. "To keep *what* a secret? Something about that girl?"

"Uh-huh." Katie's voice was small.

"Katie." Stephanie now spoke from between clenched teeth.

At the firmness of Stephanie's tone, Katie's head snapped up, worry flickering across her pale face.

"Tell me, Katie." Stephanie took a deep breath and forced herself to speak evenly. "The news says that this girl is missing, okay? That means that she could be hurt, or she could be in danger. If you know something, *any*thing, you need to tell me so we can tell the police. They're looking for her right now."

Katie worried her bottom lip before finally nodding. "Okay. But…just so you know, Dad wanted me to keep it a secret. He didn't want me to say anything to Mom because he didn't want her to worry. Promise you won't tell Mom?"

Stephanie rested a hand over her heart. "Scout's honor."

The answer seemed to set Katie at ease. "After my dance on Sunday, me and Dad stopped at the gas station to get some candy bars. Dad said that since I'd done so well at the dance, we could go for a drive."

"One of your country drives?"

"Uh-huh. That girl from TV was there, at the gas station. She liked my glitter and said she wanted to be a ballerina just like me. I think she said she was from...um...Men...? Mend..."

"Mendoza?" Stephanie finished for her.

Katie's face lit up like a Christmas decoration. "Yeah! She said she was on her way to Mendoza for Thanksgiving. Then, me and Dad left, and we drove around for a little bit. I fell asleep, but I'm not sure when."

Stephanie was finding it hard to breathe. "And when you woke up?"

She scrunched her feathery eyebrows together. "We were pulled over. It was really dark. I wasn't sure where we were, but then I heard that girl talking. She was...saying something to Dad. Something about cables? I saw her when she walked past my window to talk to Dad. Then when she went back to her car, I closed my eyes and pretended to be asleep."

Unease burned low in Stephanie's stomach. "What happened then?"

She hoped her sister would simply say that everyone had gone their separate ways, but she could tell by the focus on Katie's face—the effort to remember—that there was more to the story.

"Dad walk by my window, and he was holding one of those metal wrench things. You know, the kind they use for fixing tires."

Stephanie wasn't knowledgeable about cars, so she guessed. "A crowbar? A tire iron?"

Katie pressed her lips together. "One of those. I'm...I'm sorry, I don't know what it's called."

"It's okay." Stephanie forced a reassuring smile to her face, but her mind burned to look in the direction of the front door. The garage made plenty of noise when it opened, but their father didn't always use the parking space. Stephanie still wasn't sure what had happened between Katie, her dad, and the missing girl, but she knew for certain she did *not* want him to walk in on her and Katie's conversation.

Stephanie dug deep to find her voice. "What happened after that?"

Hanging her head, Katie shrugged. "I'm not sure. I fell back asleep, and when I woke up, we were home."

"It's okay."

A single tear slid down her sister's cheek. "Should we call the police?"

Should they?

"I…I'm not sure."

Could their father have had a hand in the girl's disappearance? Katie had witnessed him interacting with her, and then walking after her with a tool in his hand.

He was probably just helping her. Katie didn't say who stopped first, just that she woke up and they were on the side of the road. Dad could've just stopped to help her, and then left. It's nothing. Nothing happened.

No matter the logic Stephanie used in her head, her gut told her that Katie's recollection was significant.

It wouldn't hurt to call the police, would it?

What if he finds out that we told the cops about that girl?

Goose bumps dotted Stephanie's forearms.

She loved her dad, but there were times when his temper flared. Never when their mother was home, and the rage was never directed at her or Katie. Usually, he'd claim to be frustrated with his work or with one of his friends. There was a modest home gym set up in the basement, and Stephanie had caught her father punching vigorously at a heavy bag while he swore under his breath.

Then, there was the fire pit.

Her body grew cold at the memory.

Three years ago, when Stephanie was ten and Katie was four, both girls had caught a flu-like bug that had been circulating through town. The subsequent fever and chills were among the worst Stephanie had ever experienced. Sleep had come at odd hours, and she'd awoken in the dead of night covered in sweat.

In an effort to cool and calm herself, she'd gone downstairs for a glass of water. She'd noticed a glimmer of orange from between the blinds that covered their kitchen's French doors, so she'd snuck a peek.

Alone in the center of the patio, a fire skipped in the iron bowl like a dancer on a stage. The sight had confused Stephanie, and as she'd turned around to go back to bed, she'd come face-to-face with her father. His eyes had been as wild as the flames, but the expression wasn't what stuck out in her memory.

He'd clutched a shirt and pants in his arms, both of which had been covered in a dark substance that resembled blood.

After he'd shooed her back upstairs, Stephanie had promptly fallen asleep due to her illness. The next morning, her father had asked that she keep the night's events to herself.

She'd had no reason to doubt him, so she'd done as he requested.

The mechanical whine of the garage door pulled Stephanie back to reality. Mom wasn't due home from her shift until six in the morning, which meant...

"Dad's home. Should we—"

"Shhh..." Stephanie firmly shook her head. "No. You were right. It's nothing. Don't tell Dad you told me, okay?"

Katie agreed with a sigh of relief.

They were better off pretending that their conversation had never occurred.

24

Raindrops still pattered against the window of the conference room, but to Zane's relief, the storm's unseasonal bluster was gone. Amelia had repeatedly reassured him and Steelman that they wouldn't experience a tornado at the end of November, but neither Zane nor the West Virginia native had been convinced.

For the past hour, the three of them had combed through Nowland's social media accounts, call records, and text messages, searching for any new contact that might have been their killer. Zane had called Nowland's friend and roommate, but the young woman hadn't spotted any recent oddities.

Neither had Nowland's academic advisor, nor anyone else in Nowland's life. She'd exhibited no propensity for self-destructive behavior like bar-hopping or drug use. Her older brother had a couple arrests in his past, but both were for nothing more than teenage mischief. All charges had eventually been dropped.

By all accounts, Willow Nowland had been a kind, mild-mannered young woman who was focused on obtaining her degree in engineering. She'd not dated since a breakup with her high school sweetheart, a young man who'd moved to Los Angeles to attend UCLA.

Simply put, there was nothing.

The majority of crimes, including kidnapping and homicide, were perpetrated by someone who was close to the victim. When strangers were thrown into the equation, the problem became exponentially more difficult to solve.

A tense silence had descended over the incident room. Zane, along with Amelia and Steelman, had all busied themselves with retracing Nowland's life leading up to her apparent abduction. No one had made the observation aloud, but Zane had the sinking feeling hope was waning.

As Zane's thoughts started their inexorable shift toward Amelia, a popup in the bottom right-hand corner of his laptop screen told him he had a new email. He clicked the icon, and as he scanned the message, he damn near leapt out of his chair. "Oh, shit."

"What?" Amelia and Steelman chorused.

"I just got a response from the tech that was working on the hard drive at the Cedarwood Gas 'N Go." He opened the attachment and swiveled the screen to face the two agents at his side. "It's the security camera footage from the night Nowland was there."

Amelia and Steelman exchanged fervent glances and moved closer.

Once Zane was satisfied all three of them had a view, he pressed play. Though he'd been concerned about the quality of the feed, they were greeted with a fairly clear view of the Gas 'N Go's front counter. Double-checking the time of Willow Nowland's transaction, Zane moved the video to a half-hour before her arrival.

"This is a small town." Dean Steelman gestured to the young cashier who'd busied himself with organizing packs of gum. "If we get stills of the people who were in there around the same time as Nowland, one of the deputies here might recognize them."

Amelia tilted her head, appearing thoughtful. "Huh. That makes things easier. We've already got the printer set up."

Steelman quietly snorted. "According to Cowen, that's more than half the battle."

One of Amelia's eyebrows arched. "She really hates printers, doesn't she?"

"Oh, you have *no* idea." Steelman chuckled, and the room drifted back into silence.

For a solid five minutes, not a single soul entered the convenience store. Two counter clerks were listed on the employee schedule that night, and Zane made a mental note to reach out to them next.

The first visitor who appeared on screen was a petite, elderly woman with neatly curled white hair. After fueling her SUV, she picked out a bottle of iced tea and chatted with the cashier for a couple minutes before she left.

Zane paused the video. "I don't think she matches the profile, nor would she have been able to abduct Nowland without help. I think we should take a screenshot, though. She may have seen something."

Dean Steelman shrugged. "Can't hurt."

Within moments, the printer buzzed to life as it spat out a photo of the woman.

Less than a minute after her departure, a young couple arrived. The woman was at least seven months pregnant, and her partner was lanky and rail thin. Regardless, both stills went to the printer.

Next came a burly fellow with tattooed arms and a hard hat in one hand—likely a construction worker from the repairs underway on Highway 18. He was much closer to Bill Dumke's profile than the previous three customers.

The air buzzed with unspoken excitement. They were getting somewhere.

Approximately fifteen minutes before Nowland's transaction, a middle-aged couple swung through to gas up their car and purchase a six-pack of beer.

The killer either walked back to his car, or he had someone drive him.

Was the woman an accomplice? She wouldn't have been the first spouse to aid a serial killer in hunting victims.

In the remaining time, a teenager and her two female friends passed through, along with a late thirties man wearing a plaid shirt. Another idle period followed, during which one of the two employees stepped out back for a smoke.

When they returned to their duties in the store, a sleek, black sedan stopped at a fuel pump—a man and his daughter. The pair waited patiently as a second car pulled up to the stall catty-corner to the sedan.

"That's Nowland's car." Zane peered down at the screen, watching Willow gas up her little Honda Civic.

She strolled inside, and Zane switched to the interior camera.

"Guy and his kid." Steelman rubbed his chin. "Guy's probably mid-forties. Clean-cut looking. Matches the demographic from the BAU's profile."

Once more, the printer hummed to life. Nowland exchanged a few words with the man's daughter, and then the pair were on their way.

An agonizing period of downtime followed, forcing Zane to speed up the footage. Almost twenty minutes later, a couple more teenagers wandered through the doors. Then more nothing, and more teenagers. Twelve minutes after the last patrons drove away, the employees locked the front door and went about closing up shop for the night.

Anticipation thrummed through Zane's veins as he rose to his feet and collected the printouts. One of the people in these photos may well have had a hand in Willow Nowland's kidnapping.

Setting aside the laptops, Amelia and Steelman cleared a space for Zane to position the images side by side, starting with the elderly woman and ending with two teenaged girls.

"All right. We'll start with a narrow focus and work our way out. Like a pyramid." He tapped the table beneath the still of the older woman. "We're going to exclude her for now, but we'll circle back if none of the others pan out." He pushed the photo up and out of the orderly line.

Steelman waved at the pregnant woman and her partner. "This one's iffy. The male could've done the physical labor, and the woman could've helped."

Zane agreed. "They stay, then. We'll see if we can get names for them."

"Construction worker is next." Amelia crossed her arms as she examined the burly man. "I'd put him around mid-thirties. He's got a hard hat. Could be a tradesman, which is one of the occupations that Dumke mentioned in the profile. I'd say he's on the short-list."

"I second that," Steelman said. "After him was another couple. They're about…early fifties, maybe? Could be older or younger. It's hard to tell at that age. They're dressed pretty average, and they look polished enough."

"They stay." Zane waved at the next three faces. "Teenaged girls. About as far out of our demographic as the first customer."

Wordlessly, Steelman pushed the photos up to the same level as the older woman's. "Then we've got this guy. Normal looking dude, plaid shirt, driving that puke-green Jeep. Didn't Anders say he thought the tire treads were from a car?"

Amelia tilted her head. "He did, but I don't think that's enough to rule out our pal and his weirdly colored vehicle."

"Which brings us to this guy and his kid." To Zane, the presence of a small child meant little in terms of suspect elimination. He'd worked in Organized Crime long enough to understand that traffickers didn't shy away from using kids to lower their victims' guard.

However, he was curious to see Steelman's take on the father-daughter combination.

"He fits the demo." Steelman frowned. "Weird for a serial to have a kid with him, but not unheard of. Otherwise, he's clean-cut. Drives a nice car, probably has means. I'd put him on the short-list too."

"All we've got after him is more teenagers." Zane twisted the expensive watch around his wrist. "We can go back earlier in the video to see if anyone else matches the demographic. They could've waited for Nowland on the side of the road somewhere, but let's save that for the next step. It's getting later now, so we should knock out what we can before we start throwing a wider net."

Steelman nodded. "Right. Pyramid."

Rubbing his hands together, Zane hoped they were finally making progress. "All right. Let's figure out who these people are."

The process of obtaining identities for the seven individuals was straightforward. Though Zane worried that the lack of deputies present in the building might yield fewer names, he quickly realized he was mistaken.

Having lived his entire life in one major city or another—save a couple isolated Russian villages—Zane was unfamiliar with the intimacy that came with life in Small Town, U.S.A. When citizens mused that everyone in Cedarwood knew everyone else, they weren't lying. They weren't even exaggerating.

Everyone. Knew. Everyone.

He'd never been quite so glad to call himself a city-dweller. The sense of community was comforting, but the prospect of his neighbors knowing the ins and outs of his personal life set his teeth on edge.

The older fellow who manned the desk nearest the front doors gave identities for all but two of the Gas 'N Go patrons. Thanking the deputy for his expertise, Zane set off in search of another pair of eyes while Amelia delivered the list of names to Dean Steelman.

By the time Zane had flagged down a deputy, showed the photo to the woman, and jotted down the couple's name, Amelia was still nowhere to be found.

Must have gotten sucked into some research with Steelman.

Zane walked down the hall to their incident room, and the drone of a male voice filtered out to him. The speaker wasn't Steelman, nor was he Deputy McCannon.

The second he pulled open the door, the commanding tone of the Massey County Sheriff reached up like a slap to the face. Sheriff Thompson wasn't shouting, but the irascibility was plain in his tone.

His flushed face snapped around to Zane. "Agent Palmer. There you are. Could you give me an update on what you and your colleagues have been working on?"

There was no doubt in Zane's mind that the man already had the answer he sought. What was less clear was why Thompson had suddenly deigned Zane the leader of the town's FBI presence. The day before, Dean Steelman had stepped in to address the sheriff before Zane could bite off the guy's head.

With measured, purposefully slow movements, Zane eased the door closed. Being obnoxious and taking one's time when the counterparty was expressing obvious agitation was a tried-and-true interrogation tactic. He firmly believed people displayed their true colors when they were pissed.

The door latched, and Zane cleared his throat. "We're doing what we're here to do, Sheriff. We're following leads."

"You know how many bodies we've found out by Fox Creek?" Color continued to seep into the larger man's cheeks. If he sprouted a white beard, he'd bear a striking resemblance to Santa.

Body parts without names, without ages, without any details beyond the fact that they belong to someone who's dead. Pray tell me, Sheriff, what in the fuck *are we supposed to do with that? We're the FBI, not a coven of witches.*

Striding over to set the printed photo on the table, Zane allowed the angry sentiments to run their course. When he finally met the sheriff's glare, he was confident his poise had returned.

He didn't have time for this shit. Willow Nowland had been kidnapped and was undoubtedly in danger. "I'll do us all a favor and cut to the chase. This is about the Nowland case, isn't it?"

"We've been over this, Agents." Thompson's voice cracked like a whip. "There is a *massive* investigation piling up as we speak, and it sure as hell isn't the one that you all are chasing after. And now, you're all about to go waste time talking to these...these people from the gas station? Why? Because you think they had something to do with a missing girl?"

Amelia crossed her arms. "I told him we were all going to go do these interviews."

For a beat, Zane's brain struggled to piece together the reason the words had sounded so strange.

They sound weird because she said them in Russian.

He flashed her a warning glance before replying in the same language. "No. You're adding fuel to the fire by saying shit he doesn't understand." As he returned his focus to the sheriff, Zane held up both palms. "Agent Storm is going to follow up on this by herself."

Thompson narrowed his eyes but didn't speak. He bobbed his head between the two agents who were speaking to each other in a foreign language. Russian nonetheless. His growing agitation indicated he wasn't pleased he felt like an outsider in his own precinct.

"Look." Zane swallowed a sigh. "This is frustrating for us too. We don't know who these remains even belong to, and without IDs, there's not a lot we can do. We've got to wait for the forensics lab to give us *something*. Something we can run with. Until then, yeah, we're going to follow up on the Nowland case. She's missing, and we've plenty of reason to believe there was foul play. Her case has been changed from missing persons to probable kidnapping."

In the silence that followed, Zane could almost hear the gears grinding in the man's head.

"All right," he finally said, his voice calmer. "Let me know if there are any new developments."

As the sheriff turned around to leave, suspicion thudded in the back of Zane's mind.

Was there a reason the sheriff was so dead set on dissuading them from investigating Willow Nowland's disappearance?

Or had Zane's time working undercover left him paranoid?

25

Amelia brought her car to a stop by the curb in front of a two-story house complete with an attached, three-car garage. With its wide, sloping driveway, covered front porch, and large, picture windows, the place was cloaked in an elegance Amelia hadn't expected to find in Cedarwood.

She pushed open her door and sighed. Her breath misted in the newly arrived cold. A faint humidity clung to her cheeks, and a haze created halos around the harsh streetlamps. The white lights glinted off the narrow stream of water that still rushed toward a storm drain, and damp concrete glistened. In the stillness of the small-town evening, her footsteps echoed off the sidewalk as she approached the looming house.

After crossing out the first two names on her list—the construction worker and the pregnant couple—she felt a familiar hole open in the pit of her stomach.

Lifting her chin, she refused to let the hopelessness take hold. She had three addresses left, and if she didn't find what she was after, she'd go back to the drawing board. The sheriff might not be fully convinced that Willow Nowland had been kidnapped by a serial killer or human trafficker, but Amelia was certain. Every investigative instinct in her body screamed the girl's disappearance was connected.

If they found the person who'd snatched Nowland off the side of the road, they'd find their killer. She had no doubt.

Amelia climbed the final step up to the porch and pushed back the hood of her jacket. Clearing her throat, she pulled open the outer glass door and rapped her knuckles against hardwood.

A muffled voice responded almost immediately. "Who is it?"

The speaker was a kid. Before Amelia could leap to judgment, she reminded herself that culture in quiet places like Cedarwood was much different than Chicago. In towns like this, parents allowed their children to answer the door for strangers.

"I'm a special agent with the Federal Bureau of Investigation. I'd like to ask you a few questions." Provided the kid was old enough to know what the FBI was.

Amelia's pulse echoed in her ears as the seconds dragged on in silence. She didn't even have the drone of the city to keep her company out here. There was no wail of distant sirens, no rush of traffic. There was just...nothing. An occasional vehicle on the main street a few blocks east, but little else. She missed the white noise.

Just as Amelia raised her hand to knock a second time, the heavy door creaked inward. A sliver of light escaped onto the pristine concrete, as if the glow had been eager to escape all along. In the slight opening, a pair of wide, blue eyes emerged.

She was right. The girl was no older than thirteen, fourteen at the most.

"Hi." Amelia reached into her coat for her badge. "I'm

Special Agent Amelia Storm with the FBI. Are your parents home?"

Hinges creaked quietly as the opening widened. "Um... no. My mom is at work, and my dad is...um...he's not home."

"Your dad is Daniel Gifford, correct?"

"Um...yeah." Even in the low light, the flush on the girl's cheeks was plainly visible.

Amelia relaxed her tone. "What's your name?"

"I'm Stephanie." The first hints of sweat beaded along the girl's brow.

The kid was terrified. Was her fear the result of coming face-to-face with an FBI agent for the first time? Or was there more at play?

Amelia tucked away her badge. "Okay, Stephanie. Would you mind if I came inside for a moment?"

Obvious worry pinched her face as she appeared to war with herself. "My parents don't like for us to have people inside when they aren't home."

"Us?"

"Me and m-my sister, Katie."

Though Amelia considered pressing the issue—reassuring the girl that she was a federal agent and it was safe to let her inside—she decided to respect the boundary. "That's fine, then. We can talk right here. Do you know when your mother or father will be home?"

Stephanie gnawed at her bottom lip and shook her head. "Mom is working a night shift at the hospital. She won't be home until the morning. My dad went out for a little bit, but I don't know when he'll be home."

"Does he leave you and your sister home alone often? Does your mom know you're here by yourselves?"

The girl swallowed hard. "Y-yeah, she knows. She allows us to be home alone since I'm almost fourteen. My dad...he works at night sometimes too. I think that might be where he is right now."

Another red flag unfurled in Amelia's mind, but she kept her outward appearance calm. "Well, like I said before, I'm with the FBI. Right now, I'm investigating a missing girl. I'm looking around to see if people have run into her lately. She's been missing since Sunday night." Holding the girl's gaze, Amelia took her sweet time fishing a photo of Willow from her jacket.

Stephanie Gifford's eyes shot open wide, though only for a split-second. She swallowed once, twice, and then three times in rapid succession. With the back of one trembling hand, she swiped at her forehead.

Terrified *and* nervous.

What the hell was going on with this kid?

Amelia offered her a warm smile and held up the printout of Willow Nowland's senior picture. "Have you seen this girl? Around town, maybe?"

The flush vanished from the girl's cheeks as her face turned ghost white. For a beat, her eyes seemed to glaze over, and Amelia was convinced the teen was about to faint.

"Stephanie? Are you okay?"

Stephanie's knuckles turned white where she grasped the doorframe. "Y-yeah. I'm okay. I've, uh, I've never seen her before."

Amelia was struck with a twinge of guilt as she pinned the girl with a scrutinizing stare. "Are you sure? You don't know anything about her? How about your sister?"

"N-no. She's asleep right now. S-s-she can't talk. I'm sorry. I should go to bed too."

It's barely even seven.

Amelia bit off the remark before it could slide out into the open.

Asking questions to children in the capacity of interviewing a witness was legally permitted, but with their case poised to shoot straight to the top of every mainstream media outlet in the country, Amelia would do well to mind her *P*s and *Q*s.

"All right, Stephanie. Do me a favor, okay?"

The teen's eyes popped open so wide, Amelia expected them to roll from their sockets.

"Call me if you remember anything." She held out her card. "Anything at all, any time of day. Okay?"

Stephanie swallowed. "Yeah, yeah, okay."

"You and your sister stay safe. And again, call me if either of you think of *any*thing."

"I will."

Holding Stephanie's gaze for a moment longer, Amelia finally turned to make her way down the stairs. She still had two names left on the list from the Cedarwood Gas 'N Go, but she suspected neither visit would be fruitful.

Stephanie Gifford was hiding something, and her secret could be deadly.

26

A decisive chill had taken over the air around Willow. She wasn't sure if the change in temperature was a figment of her imagination—some externalized manifestation of the task that loomed before her—or if the weather had undergone a drastic shift. Seated as close to the door as her chains would allow, she tucked both knees beneath her chin and hugged herself to ward off the creeping cold.

Her stomach was in knots, and ever since she'd eaten, she'd had to fight to keep herself from puking.

This was insane. Everything about her predicament was absolutely, unilaterally crazy.

Was she *really* about to rip a pair of metal shackles from the wall, pick a lock, and escape from an underground bunker?

No, not a bunker...a dungeon.

Though she'd sat with her ear turned to the door, straining to make out even the slightest noise, she still had no earthly idea what awaited her on the other side. For all she knew, she'd stumble out into a den of camouflaged mercenaries who'd been hired to do Dan's bidding. Or perhaps a supernatural predator like a wendigo—the monstrous remnants of a lost traveler who'd been forced to cannibalize his companions.

Maybe she was in the bottom of a missile silo, and Dan was a scientist with the U.S. military who'd captured her to perform gruesome experiments in the name of advancing civilization.

Squeezing her eyes closed, she pressed on her ears and shook her head.

No, no, no. None of that is true. Dan is a sick freak who kidnapped me and chained me up in a basement somewhere so he could give me to his...friend, or whoever in the hell he keeps talking about when he's down here. That's all this is. There are no wendigos, no secret military prisons, none of that.

She'd been down here alone for too damn long. Years ago, she remembered watching a documentary about the effects of solitary confinement on incarcerated persons. The film had featured a handful of experts who asserted that extended periods of isolated lockup were tantamount to torture. Some lawyers had even argued that solitary was a violation of the Eighth Amendment of the U.S. Constitution.

That's it, then. I'm losing it.

All the more reason for her to get the hell out of here. Wherever *here* was.

Pushing away all the morbid scenarios that played through the theater of her mind, Willow straightened her spine. Dan had left on the dim light—this time—allowing her to make out the shape of her hands, as well as the shackles that bound them to the wall.

She preferred the dim light to Dan's more recent games. There was the time he entered the room without turning on the light. Had it not been for the sudden creak of the hinges, she'd have been caught loosening the bolts.

Then when he'd left, he had kept the light on. She worried

he had witnessed her efforts to free herself and wanted to be able to monitor her somehow, though he'd not indicated he'd seen anything. She wouldn't put it past him to have a peephole somewhere. Was she like an artifact in a museum, displayed under bright lights she couldn't shrink from?

With the blinding light filling her dungeon, it somehow felt more dangerous than the darkness. How much time had passed? How would she know when he returned, unable to notice the tell-tale light under the door in the fluorescence of her cell?

Yes, Willow's warped psyche had decided the dim light was her preferred setting. *How messed up was that?*

She needed to refocus her drifting thoughts. The metal cuffs were locked closed around her wrists, and each was soundly welded to a length of chain. She wouldn't be able to rid herself of the binds, but she didn't care. She only needed the bolts to come loose from the wall.

Swallowing in an effort to return some moisture to her mouth, Willow held her breath and listened.

She'd waited well past Dan's departure, and then she'd waited some more. The man typically didn't return for an extended period of time after bringing her food. If his routine held, she was in the clear.

If his routine holds.

She silenced her inner skeptic and climbed to her feet. There was no other option. The escape was risky, but so was sitting idly by and awaiting her fate.

Gritting her teeth, Willow shuffled to the wall, took a deep breath, and brushed her bruised fingertips along the first bolt.

In case Dan was lying in wait or in case he'd decided to spend more time in the bunker, she moved diligently to avoid excessive noise. With each metallic *clink* of her shackles, she winced.

But she didn't stop. She spun the loosened bolt until she was able to pull it free from the concrete. After another pause to ensure nothing outside the cell had changed, she went to work. Renewed fervor and determination guided her, her heart pumping the first traces of adrenaline through her tired body.

Holding the metal plate in place with one hand, she jerked the second bolt free.

The moment of truth.

Willow's breath caught in her throat as she slid her fingers beneath the rough metal. Part of her expected, *dreaded*, that there was an epoxy or an unseen screw that affixed the plate to the wall.

Heart thundering in her ears, she hooked a finger through one of the loops that held the chains. She planted her feet firmly on the ground, said a quick prayer, and pulled.

A yelp of surprise escaped her lips as she stumbled back, nearly tumbling ass-first onto the cement floor. Though she'd put as much force behind the motion as possible, she hadn't actually needed to use *any* force. Odds were, the metal plate would have fallen to the ground if she'd not held on to the damn thing.

Swearing under her breath, she made her way to the door. Her heart was in her throat as she listened for movement.

Nothing but an eerie silence greeted her.

Willow retrieved the improvised lockpick from her hoodie. Back when she'd been a freshman in high school, her older brother, a junior at the time, had gone through a rebellious phase. He'd befriended a few of the shadier kids at their school, and he'd periodically sneak out of his room in the middle of the night to go smoke or drink in an abandoned parking lot.

As the little sister, Willow had admired her brother. And

as a teenager, she'd wanted to earn herself a spot with his "edgy" clique.

Though her brother hadn't gone as far as bringing her to hang out with his sketchy friends, he had made an attempt to pass on some of the skills he'd learned. Among those abilities was lockpicking.

Now, more than five years later, many of the specifics eluded Willow. All she could recall was the need for a sturdy, slender object. Plenty of retailers sold kits, but Willow had never bothered with one. From what she could tell, the underwires from her bra were similar in size and shape to the picks she'd seen online.

Sliding the first wire into the bottom of the tumbler lock, she clenched her jaw and forced herself to take deep, even breaths. With the second wire, she began to poke at the pins along the top of the lock. She'd paid special attention to the door handle the time Dan had tormented her by leaving on the light until his next visit. She was confident that the teeth of a key, the jagged edge that pushed the tumbler pins into the proper location, was located at the top of the lock.

But when seconds stretched into minutes with no headway, she started to second-guess the observation.

No. I know I'm right. I know the pins are at the top.

Tears of frustration sprang to her eyes. She *had* to unlock this door. There was no alternative.

Willow rested her forehead against the cool metal surface and focused on her breathing. She'd used the same technique before stressful exams, as well as nights when she had trouble paying attention to a tedious assignment.

Breathe in, breathe out. In, out.

Gradually, the wave of despondency subsided, and the clouds of melancholy rolled away.

"Press the pins until they all reach the shear line," she heard her brother say. *"Start by taking them one at a time. It's a*

guessing game when you're learning, but you'll get a feel for it. If you listen closely, sometimes you can hear the pins move."

Willow pulled out the top wire to start fresh. Slowly, millimeter by agonizing millimeter, she wiggled the makeshift pick until she thought the pins had reached their shear line. She was forced to start over once and then twice, but her concentration didn't waver.

After minutes or hours, she couldn't tell, she clutched both wires and twisted.

The tumbler moved.

Adrenaline poured into her bloodstream like a party drug. Before the tremors could threaten her steady hands, she turned the lock and then the brass knob.

Rusty hinges creaked, and the dingy light fell along the sleeve of her sweatshirt. Her throat was tight, and a thousand little needles jabbed at her rapidly beating heart.

She'd done it. She'd picked the damn lock.

Now what?

Blinking repeatedly, she peered through the crack in the door to allow her vision time to adjust. Her cell was set back in a short hall, and in the sliver of the room visible beyond, she spotted the dark screen of a computer monitor.

Not a wendigo. Not a mercenary. Not a missile silo.

An office.

Was holding her captive really just another normal part of Dan's life? Did he return home to his wife and kids to tell them all about the college girl he'd chained up in the basement? Did the family throw back their heads and laugh at his sarcastic observations about Willow's refusal to eat?

Willow had seen horror films—plenty of them. In more than one, the protagonists were chased after not just by a single madman but by an entire family of lunatics.

She would trust no one. Not until she was in a real town full of cameras and computers and smartphones and cops.

She wouldn't let down her guard, and she'd operate like Dan was lying in wait around every corner.

It was time to leave.

As quietly as humanly possible, Willow gathered up the lengths of chain still attached to her wrists. The binds were cumbersome, but the sturdy metal could work as an improvised weapon.

Clutching the chain with one arm, she used her free hand to pull open the door. Thanks to her slow, measured movements, the hinges emitted little more than a mouse-like squeak.

The soles of her Chuck Taylors were silent against the cement floor. At the end of the hall, she stopped to take in the room before her.

She couldn't be certain that the exit lay beyond the corridor at the far end of the office. However, she couldn't recall the sound of a door opening outside her cell when Dan came to bring her food. She'd also grown accustomed to the quiet drum of his footsteps as he neared the closed door. If he'd used either of the doors across from her cell to reach her, she wouldn't have heard him walking.

Satisfied with her logic, she swept her gaze over the room one more time.

A corner desk held two widescreen monitors, a mechanical keyboard, and a computer tower. The mesh-backed chair was pushed in, and all surfaces were polished and pristine. Even the file cabinet beside the doorway looked as if it was brand new. Apparently, Dan was a neat freak.

The curiosity burning in the back of Willow's head whispered for her to snoop through the man's belongings, but her sense of self-preservation screamed at her to get far away from this godforsaken place.

She ignored the desk and focused instead on the open doorway at the other end of the room. Balancing on her tiptoes, she crept forward. To Willow's ears, each minute clatter of the chains in her arms was as loud as one of the dinner bells that rural households had once used.

As far as she was concerned, she might as well have been yelling, *"come and get it while it's hot."*

Blood pounded in her ears and sweat beaded along the small of her back. More of the hallway came into view with each inch she traveled, and she fully expected to spot Dan looming in the shadows at any point. Swallowing the nausea that threatened to crawl up her throat and bring her to her knees, she rested her back against the cold cement wall beside the doorway. At least for a moment, she'd be partly obscured from view.

Though her imagination still roamed wild, Willow realized she had no idea where in the hell she was headed. She glanced back to the short hall that led to her now-open cell, as well as the pair of doors on the opposite side.

She didn't *think* either entrance led to a way out of this pit, but she might be wrong.

Clamping her teeth together, she shook her head resolutely.

You're second-guessing yourself. Knock it off. You've spent the last god knows how many days listening to that asshole walk through a room to get to your door. This is where Dan came from. It has to be. You don't have time for this. You need to keep moving.

Willow inhaled a long, silent breath to provide her body with much-needed air.

Before she could renege on her mental assurance, she took the first step into the open doorway, then the second.

To her right, a dim emergency bulb cast a muted halo over a metal door at the end of the hall. For all she knew, that door led to a furnace or a water heater. Or another office.

Her jaw ached from how tightly she'd clenched her teeth, but she couldn't, *wouldn't*, let her body relax. Not now.

When she swiveled her head to face the right side of the hall, she almost cried out in victory.

Stairs.

The other door could have led anywhere, but the stairs led one direction. Up.

Since she'd decided near the beginning of her captivity that she was underground, she knew she *had* to go up.

Shifting the weight of the chains to rest in the crook of her left arm, Willow forced the onslaught of doubts, the warning bells, and the incessant voice that suggested she simply go back to her cell, to the back of her head.

She cast one more paranoid look over her shoulder, then picked her way down the concrete hall. The glow from another dim bulb shone on the cement floor of a landing. After ascending the first few steps, Willow paused before she snuck a peek around the corner.

More stairs led to a second landing, and from her awkward viewing angle, she *thought* she caught the shape of a doorknob in the gloom above. Holding her breath, she squinted into the darkness but spotted no movement.

Balancing one hand against the wall, she hurried up the final length of the stairwell. No light shone up here, but she *was* face-to-face with another windowless metal door.

A faint rush from beyond the door froze her in place. Mouth dry, throat aching, she held her position and strained her hearing to its limits.

She didn't have to wait long before the same noise greeted her again—a *whoosh*, like a distant machine, or...

The wind.

A fresh surge of adrenaline pounded through Willow's veins, and she could hardly hold her hand still as she reached for the first of a series of three locks. She didn't stop long to ponder why this door had locks on the inside. *Maybe to keep his wife or daughter out?* Her chains clinked together softly as she reached for the first lock, but she ignored the disturbance.

Once she'd thrown the final deadbolt, she hovered her hand over the lever handle. She considered taking a few seconds to compose herself. To prepare to face whatever might await her on the other side.

The moment of consideration lasted only a split second.

Muscles tensed, she wrenched open the door.

Cold air rose to greet her like a slap to the face. The mournful sigh of the wind was muffled from the wooden structure into which she stepped.

Willow blinked to adjust her vision to the darkness. Slowly, the shape of shelves and the slight shadows of hanging tools came into focus.

Along with crisp, freshly cut wood, she caught the scent of wet leaves and woodland detritus. A smell she'd once associated with hide-and-seek adventures with her friends, she now took as a tentative sign of freedom.

Carefully placing each footstep, she walked to a workbench, scouring the floor for any shape that could be a trap.

A handful of tools hung on pegs spaced out above the table—a wrench, pruning shears, bolt cutters, a handsaw, a hammer, and a couple other items she couldn't identify in the low light.

Are those surgical tools? A scalpel? What is *this place?*

She could have used the bolt cutters to sever the burdensome chains from her wrists, but she didn't want to waste the time. Dan's routine wasn't set in stone, and he could return at any second. Besides, something about this room sent a chill through her.

After swiping the hammer from the wall, she crept to the outline of a set of double doors. She disengaged a pair of locks, breathed deeply, and shoved her way into the blustery night.

Branches rattled overhead, and a short stretch of dried grass led to a patch of woodland. The shadows of tree trunks rose to either side of the shed like the oversized bars of a prison cell.

Though the chilly wind nipped at her flushed cheeks and exposed skin, Willow was grateful for the constant gusts. She had no idea how to traverse the area, but the creaking tree branches would drown out the scuffles of her movements.

Tightening her grasp on the hammer, she started for the woods, eyes darting back and forth. Twice, the moving limbs of an oak or a maple almost caused her to whip around and bring the hammer to bear.

Her entire body trembled from the combination of cold and the surge of adrenaline, but she kept her strides even and purposeful.

When the third shadow flickered in her periphery, she jerked her head toward the site of the movement. A towering tree, its branches swaying against the inky black sky like skeletal fingers, was all that greeted her.

Or so she thought.

"I've been waiting for you."

Willow's feet, like the trees that loomed ahead of her, suddenly grew roots. Her skin crawled like she'd been covered in carpenter ants, and her heart thundered so hard against her chest she thought her ribs might crack.

The speaker wasn't Dan. She knew that right away. His words were tinged with an accent, but her scrambled brain couldn't place the source.

Cold, sharp tendrils of dread threaded around her stomach.

He was the man who Dan had reverently mentioned ever since she'd woken up in this hellish nightmare.

No matter how many times she urged herself to move forward in those crucial seconds, her body wouldn't obey.

Her fight or flight reflex was malfunctioning when she most needed it to work.

Muffled footsteps grew nearer. She could *feel* him at her back.

Numbness began to buzz into the tips of her fingers, a testament to how hard she still gripped the hammer.

Do something!

He was too close. She couldn't run.

Swing the damn hammer!

Like the antidote to a fast-acting poison, the thought shattered her crippling indecisiveness. She gave the idea no further consideration.

She just acted.

Planting one foot solidly on the damp ground, she spun on her heel, the claw end of the hammer leading the way. She'd been certain that the man was close, but as she watched him hop out of reach, she realized just *how* near he'd gotten.

Her stomach turned as she made note of his towering height.

Dan was also tall, but this man was a giant. Where Dan's lean frame hinted at muscle, the man in front of her was a hulking *mass* of muscle.

And he moved with the agility of a cat.

For the second time, the all-encompassing fright nibbled at the edges of her consciousness. With or without the hammer, she was no match for this monstrous creature.

A grating sound emitted from low in his throat. Willow thought at first that the noise was an expression of anger, but renewed terror sawed through her gut when she realized what the sound actually was.

Laughter.

You can still run. Lose him in the woods. Make it to a town and call the police.

The thought hadn't even finished forming when she

turned and launched herself toward the trees. Their skeletal shapes were ominous, but tonight, they'd be her saving grace.

A big hand clamped down around her right bicep, jerking her slight momentum to a halt. Willow hated the pitiable cry that slipped from her lips as the man's fingers dug painfully into her skin.

She tried to pull away from him with all her strength, but he didn't budge. Before she could even attempt to shift the hammer into her left hand, he yanked her arm behind her back, bent it at the elbow, and pushed.

The sound that ripped its way out of her throat was nothing like what she'd heard in horror movies. Willow's scream was primal, the same type of cry that had erupted from cavemen as they'd been mauled by saber-tooth cats.

Burning pain lanced up and down her arm, and she could do little to maintain her hold on the hammer. Over the thundering of her pulse, she barely registered the thump of the tool falling to the ground.

The brute of a man slammed her body into his. As the bulge of his erection pressed up against her back, she almost forgot about the agony in her arm.

Reflexively, she tried to pull away, but his grasp only tightened. She might as well have been trying to wrest herself out of an iron maiden.

This couldn't be real. This couldn't be happening. How had she gone from pulling over to help a stranded motorist to being at the mercy of this monster?

She couldn't get away. Her makeshift weapon was gone. There was only one option remaining.

Pulling as much air into her lungs as possible, Willow let loose a high-pitched shriek for help.

In response, the man relinquished his hold on her arm, tightened his grasp around her waist, and clamped a large, calloused hand over her mouth.

"Remember what I told you the first night you were here?" Dan's quiet, unnerving tone pierced the chilled night air, and Willow swore her heart skipped a few beats. Ice water rushed through her veins as Dan's familiar figure stepped out from behind a tree.

Even if Willow had been able to speak, words escaped her.

Rubbing his hands together, Dan paused about ten feet in front of her. "You were far more clever than I'd expected. Using the underwires of your bra to pick that lock?" A sinister smile crept to his shadowed face. "I can't say I've seen that before."

In the few seconds it took Willow to process his statement, all the remaining bluster drained from her body.

He'd been watching her the whole time.

Her "escape" had been part of their game.

She'd never stood a chance.

27

Zane didn't realize he'd been sitting in absolute silence until the metallic *click* of Amelia's door pulled his focus away from the screen of his laptop. Rubbing his tired eyes with the back of one hand, he pushed the computer aside and stretched. The queen-sized bed of his hotel room had become his makeshift office after he'd returned from the sheriff's department.

While Amelia had gone to talk to the handful of people who'd been ID'd from the video surveillance at the Cedarwood Gas 'N Go, Zane had combed through all the security footage they'd collected in relation to Larissa Umber's case.

As he'd anticipated, there were no new leads waiting in the grainy videos. No revelations lurking in the shadows between buildings, no epiphanies hidden on the streets of downtown Chicago. All he'd accomplished by staring at the computer screen for more than an hour straight was drying out his eyes.

The clatter of Amelia's knuckles against the doorframe pulled him the rest of the way out of the haze. "Are you, uh...*clothed?*"

His snort of laughter was muffled by the hand he still held over his face. "Yes, Amelia. I am. You can come in."

Despite the obvious sarcasm, a twinge of unease still plagued him when he thought back to the awkward encounter.

It's only a matter of time before she asks about the stars.

He shoved the thought into the far recesses of his mind. That was a bridge he'd cross when the time came.

Amelia poked her head through the doorway, and the comedic sight pushed away the rest of his trepidation.

Stretching both arms above his head, Zane yawned. Maybe the bed was a comfortable office, but the spot was also a prime site for the allure of sleep. "Did you find anything?"

With a sigh, Amelia stepped over the threshold and shucked off her coat. "Well, I made it through all the names. The pregnant couple let me inside and fed me chocolate chip scones that the husband was baking. Turns out the wife is a true-crime writer, and she was actually excited to talk to someone from the FBI."

A pang of jealousy zinged through Zane. He hadn't been privy to a homemade baked good since the last time one of the Chicago Field Office's lead tactical agents, Tom Harris, had brought a platter of muffins up to the Organized Crime floor.

He moved the laptop to a nightstand to make room for Amelia. "Do you think they were trying to pay you off with treats?"

Lifting a shoulder, she took the silent offer and dropped down at the edge of the mattress. The faint scent of strawberries and coconut wafted over to him with the movement.

"I mean, if there's anything I can be bribed with, it probably *is* food. Especially right now. Those scones were a couple hours ago, and I'm starving." She waved a dismissive hand. "Anyway, the construction worker was at home with his wife and their teenaged son. We couldn't see it in the video, but his son was in the vehicle when he went inside the gas station. They both came home right afterward, which the wife verified."

Zane scooped up a water bottle and twisted off the top. "She could be covering for them."

Amelia wrinkled her nose. "No, I don't think so. They seemed genuine, you know? Like they really wanted to be helpful. That guy and his son also left the gas station about ten minutes before Willow even got there."

He was familiar with the type of person she'd described, and he trusted Amelia's judgment. "What about the next guy?"

As Amelia turned to face him, a glimmer of suspicion flared to life in her expression. "That one was weird."

Curiosity piqued, Zane straightened.

Amelia took the nonverbal cue to continue. "A thirteen-year-old girl answered the door, and she said her parents weren't there."

"We *are* in Small Town, U.S.A. That doesn't seem off to me."

"Not by itself, no. But when I showed her a picture of Willow, she was scared shitless. Said she had to go because she needed to go to bed, but it was barely seven. I don't know many teenagers who willingly go to bed that early."

Zane replaced his water and grabbed the laptop. "I hear ya. What was her dad's name?"

"Dan Gifford. We saw him and his daughter in the video, and they were there at the same time as Willow. I didn't get to talk to him since he wasn't home, but he's definitely worth a follow-up visit. The girl didn't know when he'd be home, but we can try again in the morning."

His fingers flew over the keyboard as he typed Dan's name into a handful of different applications.

"Do you want some help with that?" Amelia gestured to the computer.

He motioned to the room's miniature fridge. "I'm fine. You go ahead and eat. Leftovers are in there. I need something productive to do before I lose my damn mind."

Amelia pushed to her feet. "I don't understand how the sheriff expects us to dig up new leads without including Nowland's disappearance in our investigation. We've been digging up body parts left and right, but it doesn't help us much when we don't know who any of them are."

"You're preaching to the choir, my friend." He left out how he'd mentally gone over the evidence collected so far from the remains at Fox Creek five-hundred times, hoping against hope that they'd all simply missed a glaring clue that would point them in the right direction.

But in truth, there was a fat lot of nothing. The killer who'd dismembered and dumped his victims' bodies along the banks of Fox Creek had gone to great lengths to destroy any identifying markers. They'd only found Larissa Umber because her DNA was in the system, and they'd been able to ID Heather Breysacher through dental records because the killer hadn't pulled her teeth.

Even then, the killer had learned from his mistake. No additional bodies would be identified by their teeth.

The aroma of cooked bacon filled the air as the microwave in the corner beeped three times. Amelia had eaten less than half of her hearty breakfast earlier that morning, which Zane had found peculiar. Normally, the woman was a bottomless pit. Though he had at least sixty pounds on her lithe frame, he was confident she could out-eat him if they entered a contest.

A reminder of the nautical stars niggled in the back of his

mind, but he pushed aside the reflection before it could take hold.

Zane cleared his throat as Amelia resumed her seat to his side. "Here's what I've got so far. Daniel Terrance Gifford, age forty-one, has lived in Cedarwood his entire life. Both his parents were from the area, and he only left for a few years when he went to college. Which..." As he spotted the man's occupation, excitement bloomed in his chest.

"What?" Amelia paused, plastic fork midway to her mouth. "What did you find?"

"He's a salesman...guess what he sells?"

Her eyebrows scrunched together. "I don't know. Vacuum cleaners?"

Zane flashed her a quick smile. "Not quite. He represents a corporation that sells *surgical supplies*. And I don't mean scalpels and stethoscopes. I'm talking top-end, technologically advanced robotics."

Amelia's eyes shone as she locked her gaze on his. "Salespeople in those types of fields travel all the time. It's a huge part of their job. Does he have a degree?"

"Yeah. A master's degree in biomedical engineering. Hold on, let me find his college records." A leaden silence hung between him and Amelia as he clicked through a handful of windows and typed in a new search query.

Neither of them had uttered the observation aloud, but so far, Dan Gifford was a dead ringer for Agent Dumke's psychological profile.

"Okay. Here." Zane scooted closer to Amelia and angled the laptop so she could see the screen. "He started out in med school at The University of Illinois College of Medicine. But about a year into it, he left the program and changed his major. Graduated three years later and moved back to Cedarwood."

Amelia appeared thoughtful as she chewed. "What about his wife?"

"She's a nurse at Cedarwood Hospital." Zane clicked over to the window that displayed Natalie Gifford's DMV photo. The woman's pale eyes held a youthful sparkle, and her smile seemed genuine. "She's worked there since she graduated with her nursing degree."

"And they've got two kids. Stephanie, who is the one who answered the door, and the younger daughter. Kaitlyn." Amelia let out a long breath. "Jesus, if Dan Gifford is our guy, he's been living one hell of a double life. He'd put Dennis Rader to shame."

Trafficker or serial killer, Amelia's reference to BTK was spot-on. "Dan and Natalie are both listed as owners on the house that you visited, but Gifford owns another property. And this one is…"

As Zane trailed off, Amelia leaned in closer to peer at the map. "Shit. It's pretty far from Fox Creek."

"But…" Zane shifted the cursor to a neat line that connected Gifford's rural lakeside cabin with a far more familiar location, "this road is gravel, but it's almost a straight shot to Fox Creek. Doesn't look like there are many other houses along the way, either. It'd be easy to drive back and forth without anyone noticing."

Amelia's shoulder brushed against his upper arm as she cradled her container of food and stared at the laptop. "Let's see if we can find out where he was on the night Larissa went missing. Since he travels for work, you know? Cedarwood's only about a three-hour drive from Chicago, but maybe if he had a work event in the city…"

Though she left the sentence unfinished, Zane caught onto her thought process right away. "We can't get into his phone history without a warrant or a subpoena, but…" He opened a new browser and pulled up a popular social media platform. "We know where he works. If there're any company events in Chicago, they'd likely list them somewhere online."

Amelia scooped up a bite of egg and potato. "If he is our bad guy, I seriously doubt he'd post about it on his own accounts. But he can't stop his company from posting information about an event."

Zane was silent for a beat as he scrolled. As Amelia had suggested, the company for which Dan worked updated its event schedule regularly. "Let's see, they're part of an upcoming event in Milwaukee. That's in about a week. Otherwise, the most recent was in Chicago. And it was…" The hairs on the back of his neck stood on end. "Shit. It was held at the Sheraton in downtown Chicago."

Amelia spat out a handful of colorful obscenities as she spotted the date. "That's the same night that Larissa went missing. Do they have any pictures from the event?"

"Yeah." An image of a balding man in an expensive suit posing beside a more youthful fellow populated the screen. "According to the caption, the suit is the company's chief financial officer, and the guy who looks like he's being forced to pose for a holiday Christmas card is a surgical resident at Chicago Methodist Hospital."

He clicked to the next photo, which displayed the same balding executive, this time shaking hands with a taller, middle-aged woman. An oncologist who worked for the same hospital as the surgeon.

The fourth and fifth photos both included the CFO with various medical personnel. But when Zane moved on to the sixth picture, Amelia sucked in a sharp breath.

"That's him. That's Dan Gifford. Since the image from the gas station wasn't a great image of his face, I looked him up before I went to his house." She pointed the handle of her fork at a tall man with bright indigo eyes and a neatly styled head of caramel-brown hair. His high-boned cheeks were clean-shaven, his suit pressed, his smile as photogenic as most models. In an odd way, he reminded Zane of Agent Dean Steelman.

Sure enough, as Zane focused on the man's likeness, recognition crept into his brain. The father in the gas station security footage had been clad in a blue button-down shirt and casual slacks, but there was no mistaking his identity. Dan Gifford held a commanding presence, no matter if he was in a tux or casual dad attire.

Without interacting with Gifford, Zane could already tell he would be more than capable of tricking or persuading even a street-smart woman like Larissa Umber. Someone like Heather Breysacher would have never stood a chance.

Zane scratched his cheek. "Heather Breysacher went missing from Bloomington, Illinois, right?"

Amelia nodded while she continued chewing.

"Four years ago, in late September." He returned to the photo album and scrolled back in time. "November, October…here, September. Do you remember the date Breysacher went missing?"

Balancing her food in one hand, Amelia swiped at her phone with the other. "Yeah, I took notes of the dates before I went out to interview those people. Let's see, Breysacher was in class teaching on Thursday, the twenty-second, and then she didn't show up for work the next day. So the working theory is that she must've disappeared on that Thursday night."

Zane's mouth went dry as he reached a cluster of images dated the twenty-second of September. "Here they are. There was a small fundraising event for the St. Joseph Medical Center in Bloomington, held at a conference center not far from the hospital."

"Wait." Amelia shoved her phone in Zane's face so

abruptly that he almost leapt out of his seat. "Look. Breysacher's grandmother was, *is*, an administrator at St. Joseph's."

Blood pounded in Zane's ears. They were finally getting somewhere, but a single inconsistency could derail all their fragile progress. If Gifford had been out of the country, if he'd been skiing in Colorado or fly-fishing in Montana, if he'd accompanied his family to Six Flags that week. Anything to place the man elsewhere at the time of Breysacher's disappearance would send them back to square one.

Zane worked to put a cork on the rush of anxiety. "Why would Heather attend an event for her grandmother's hospital?"

"There's a photo of Heather's grandma, and the caption identifies everyone at that table as members of her family. Apparently, she was being honored by the hospital for her fundraising efforts, and her family came to support her. But I don't see Heather."

He was struck by the sense that he was an observer outside his body as he clicked on another picture from the medical center's fundraiser. "Gifford's employer gave St. Joseph's a pretty sizable donation, it looks like. St. Joseph's is a regular client of theirs, and they were raising money to open a new wing. Here's the CFO again, in the middle of a speech. And the CEO."

Zane moved to the next image, and Amelia swore.

Raking a hand through his hair, Zane was overcome with a sense of grim relief. "The company's top salesman for that year. Dan Gifford. The caption says St. Joseph's is his client."

As quickly as he could manage without losing any attention to detail, Zane sifted through the remaining images from the fundraiser. The administrator of St. Joseph's was indeed Heather Breysacher's grandmother, Faye, though her granddaughter didn't appear in any of the photos.

"Go to Heather's page," Amelia said. "If she was going to an event like that, she might've posted a picture of herself."

Though Zane hated elaborate galas and fundraisers, Amelia's suggestion served as a reminder that there were plenty who viewed such events in a more positive light.

But when he navigated to Heather Breysacher's social media accounts, all he received was a notification that the account had been deleted.

"Try Faye Breysacher's account." Clearly, Amelia was unperturbed by the setback.

Zane complied, and they remained silent as he scrolled through years of unrelated posts. When he reached the twenty-second of September four years earlier, the anticipation flowed back into his veins. "There's Faye, and there's Heather. The post says they're at a St. Joseph's fundraiser, and she's thrilled that her granddaughter and the rest of her family will be present when she's honored for her fundraising efforts at the evening's gala."

The spell of quiet returned in force, and Zane assumed Amelia was processing the new information, just as he was.

In his gut, Zane knew they'd just come across a major breakthrough. But on paper, all their evidence was circumstantial. Sure, Gifford met Bill Dumke's profile to a T. And sure, there was photographic evidence of Dan in the same geographic location as each victim on the same nights they'd disappeared. However, that was *all* they had.

"This can't be a coincidence." Amelia's tone was firm and resolute, echoing the musings that skittered through Zane's mind like drifting leaves. "He was in the same building with Umber and Breysacher on the nights they vanished. There's no way in hell that was just something that happened. What are the odds?"

"I agree, but I'm not the one we have to convince. We have to convince a judge so we can get a warrant, and right now, we don't have enough to get them to look past the Fourth Amendment."

Amelia set her emptied container of food on the wooden nightstand. "Then we need to find something. We probably won't be able to find much security footage from when Breysacher went missing four years ago, but we *can* get the surveillance video from The Sheraton on the night Umber disappeared."

"We can, but what will that give us that we don't already have? We know Gifford was at the hotel that night. There're already pictures to prove he was there."

Eyes widening, Amelia snapped her fingers. "The parking garage. We didn't pull the footage from there because we knew Larissa Umber didn't drive. If we can find video of him leaving at the same time she did, then maybe we can trace a path where he followed her."

As much as Zane wanted to praise Amelia's suggestion, they didn't have the time. "Okay. I'm going to keep looking here. Do you want to go bang on Cowen and Steelman's doors and let them know what we found?"

She was on her feet right away. "Yeah, I can do that. Let's get this bastard."

28

Pausing to adjust my vision to the dim foyer, I eased the door closed and gingerly flicked the deadbolt into place. At quarter past eleven, both my daughters would already be in bed. And though none of Willow Nowland's blood was on my hands—in the literal sense, at least—I didn't have the energy to deal with my daughters tonight.

As I stepped out of my shoes and hung up my jacket, my mind was still back at the bunker.

The Russian never ceased to deliver a spectacular performance, and tonight was no exception. Not all my clients were driven by their baser, sexual instincts. Some merely wanted to exact pain and suffering on their subject, whether as a cathartic release or as a source of pleasure.

Either way, I didn't judge. I merely observed. The power of life and death, of a *god*, was what compelled me to continue this line of work.

Viewing not one but two people at their most vulnerable was enthralling. The captive was quite obviously laid bare, but the sense of vulnerability for my clients was more nuanced. They fancied themselves entirely in control of the situation, with the power to snuff out another human's life with a single movement.

They were anything but. The weakness manifested differently, but to me, it was clear. When my clients stepped into that subterranean room with their specified subject, they revealed who they truly were.

The cool façade was stripped away, and only their primal selves remained. A side they'd never show the world, but they were more than happy to display to me.

Hell, they *paid* me for this vulnerability.

I knew the weakness for what it was, and I suspected The Russian did too. I'd never anticipated that a client would establish trust with me, but The Russian had gone far above and beyond any expectations I'd had when I started this business.

In some respects, I was conducting a twisted social experiment. Watching The Russian and others like him repeatedly brutalize women half their size didn't get my rocks off. Viewing a corporate executive pull the teeth of a man young enough to be his son didn't excite me. Not in a paraphilic way.

As far as I was concerned, I was no worse than the psychologist who'd conducted the Stanford Prison Experiment or Stanley Milgram and his infamous studies on obedience and conformity.

Maybe if I'd collected data all these years, I could use the analyses if I ever went on trial.

I snorted aloud at the prospect.

No, I lived in a world inhabited and dominated by the small-minded. Men like me and Ted Kaczynski had to blend in, lest we be chased down by a mob of nitwits armed with torches and pitchforks.

Rubbing my forehead, I cast aside the observations and started for the shadowy living room. Guided only by the meager light of the cable box's clock, I padded over to an end table and flicked on a small lamp.

All I wanted to do was shower and crawl into bed, but the sight of Kaitlyn's sweatshirt draped over the arm of the recliner reminded me that I'd assured my wife I would take care of the kids' laundry. Couldn't have the little lady being cross with me or wondering why I wasn't here to do the chores I'd promised.

I hadn't dealt with Willow Nowland's body. Truth be told, I was certain she was alive, at least when I'd left her. I'd caught a faint pulse when I'd bound her wrists to the sides of the exam table in my small morgue, and even through the ringing in my ears, I'd noticed her shallow, ragged breaths.

Would she survive the night? The Russian had beat the hell out of her, but he didn't do much to her head or face. Brain damage was unlikely. If she didn't bleed out, there was a real possibility she'd make it through the next twelve or so hours before I returned to put her out of her misery.

Blowing out an exhausted breath, I wiped a hand over my face. I *should* have killed her before I left, but I'd just wanted to get home. Kaitlyn and Stephanie had been left alone long enough, and if I was absent for too much time, they'd become curious.

After almost twenty-four hours awake, I was running on less than fumes. I needed rest so I could craft a believable cover story.

Laundry first. Then a shower before I'd allow myself to sleep.

My stocking feet were silent against the wooden stairs as I ascended to the second floor. Hanging on the wall at the top landing was an autumn-themed family photo my wife had coaxed us into a couple months earlier. The memory was still vivid. We'd taken the pictures, and then we'd driven thirty minutes to one of Illinois's many pumpkin patches.

All on the four-year anniversary of pretty little Heather Breysacher's death. The third of The Russian's selections and the one that had solidified our bond.

Like Willow, Heather had tried to escape. But unlike Willow, I'd been blindsided by the effort. I'd been bringing captives to the bunker for more than six years at that point, and until then, none of the attempts to escape had ever come remotely close to fruition.

But Heather had been a clever one.

I'd met her and her grandmother at the Eastland Conference and Event Center in Bloomington, Illinois. Though my interactions with both women were brief at the St. Joseph fundraiser, I'd followed Heather out to an upscale bar later in the night.

She'd been in the company of a few friends, and I'd almost left when I'd spotted them. But The Russian was becoming antsy for his next purchase, and Heather—with her brilliant white smile, golden curls, and sparkling blue eyes—had been an exact match to his specifications.

Knowing she was perfect, I'd waited for her friends to leave. Keeping my face turned away from any security cameras in the building's vicinity, I'd made my move.

Despite my disdain for the general population, I was well aware of the fact that I was conventionally attractive. I went for a run every morning, practiced good dental hygiene, and ate real food. None of that dollar-menu garbage that others were so delighted to cram down their gullets. I'd been thirty-seven at the time, but I could've easily passed for a man in his late twenties.

I'd taken a seat next to Heather before she could pay her tab, bought her a drink, and laid on the charm. She was a wholesome woman who'd exuded "sweet country girl" vibes, but I'd noted quickly that she had an itch to scratch. And with my wedding ring securely in the locked glove compartment of my car, I'd offered to scratch that itch for her.

An hour later, I'd paid cash for three hours at a seedy motel on the edge of Bloomington.

Was the move risky? Very.

My cognitive resources had been stretched thin as I'd searched for security cameras any time Heather and I were within a couple feet of one another.

But was the experience worth the effort? Absolutely. Heather had been an unassuming grade school teacher, but she'd let me use her limber body in any way I wanted.

That night wasn't the first time I'd brought one of my subjects to bed, and it wasn't the last, either. I wasn't beholden to the same fetishes as some of my clients, but I did have needs that my wife couldn't fulfill. Acts I viewed as slightly too depraved to request from the mother of my two children.

Plenty of my clients, The Russian especially, were fine with utilizing force to satiate that desire, but I didn't count myself among them. Only lesser men permitted their baser instincts to drive them to such lengths.

Besides, I'd known what awaited Heather at the hands of The Russian. The least I could do was give her a few hours of pleasure before the beginning of the end of her life.

As memories of her sculpted ass and those perky tits floated to the surface, my weariness was all but forgotten. My growing erection strained against my pants, and I almost turned around to go downstairs to the master suite.

Laundry first.

I shook myself out of the lustful thoughts, rubbing my eyes for good measure. Starting the laundry before I showered was the more efficient method and would ensure the clothes were in the dryer before I fell asleep.

Happy wife, happy life.

I smiled. Happy alibi too.

Steps measured, I picked my way down the hall, careful to avoid the sections of the floor I knew were creaky. Kaitlyn and Stephanie slept like a couple rocks, but I had a personal need to attend, and I'd rather not risk waking either of them.

Fortunately, from my vantage point in the hall, I could tell that neither Kaitlyn nor Stephanie had allowed their doors to latch.

Breathing a silent sigh of relief, I pushed in Kaitlyn's door and tiptoed through her room to the mesh hamper. The golden glow of a scented wax warmer fell over the lump in the center of her bed. When I paused on my way out, I caught a light snore.

I left the door to Kaitlyn's room unlatched, set her clothes next to the landing, and went a little farther down the hall to collect Stephanie's laundry.

Stephanie's space glowed with the same soft light provided by another wax warmer, and the air was scented with the pleasant aroma of apples and cinnamon. I hadn't understood my wife's obsession with the warmers when she'd first situated them throughout the house, but over the years, I'd come around. I'd even bought a couple of my own for the cabin near Billsbach Lake.

I crept to a hamper identical to Kaitlyn's and spotted a hooded sweatshirt, jeans, and a pair of socks that had been tossed on the floor in front of the bed. Biting off a growl of frustration, I scooped up the clothes, tossed them in the hamper, and headed back downstairs.

When I flicked the light switch of the downstairs laundry room on, tears stung the corners of my eyes. The harsh white fluorescence was a stark contrast to the relatively unlit second floor, but they shouldn't have affected my eyes so harshly. I really needed to get some sleep.

I was tempted to dump both girls' clothes into the

washing machine, but I recalled the eight-hundred dollars I'd forked over to buy a new phone for Stephanie when I'd made the same mistake four months earlier.

Absentmindedly, I scooped up Stephanie's purple and pink hoodie and fished through the kangaroo pocket.

The corners of a piece of cardstock poked my fingertips, and I was glad I'd taken the few extra minutes needed to do this search. Finding tiny pieces of paper strewn throughout the load would have seriously pissed me off.

Dropping the sweatshirt into the washer, I turned over what turned out to be a business card.

All moisture left my mouth, and straw replaced it. For a moment, the only sound was the cacophonous thudding of my pulse as my heart threatened to crack through my sternum.

Special Agent Amelia Storm
Federal Bureau of Investigation
Organized Crime Division, Chicago, Illinois

"What the fuck?"

In a rush, I remembered the diner that morning. The tall man had worn a plaid button-down, but his hair—parted slightly to one side and then neatly brushed forward—was styled like I'd expect from a resident of Los Angeles, not Cedarwood.

At the same time, I'd noted a cunning in his gray eyes that I didn't see in most people. I didn't know his story, but I strongly suspected he was dangerous.

And the woman who'd been with him...she *definitely* wasn't from this town. I'd have remembered a bombshell like her. The Russian typically preferred blondes, but I guaranteed he'd have made an exception for her. With her full lips, porcelain skin, forest green eyes, and those tits she'd hidden beneath a damn hoodie...

I was certain most of my clients would have made an

exception for her. An exception for which they'd happily drain their bank accounts.

But there was a reason I hadn't recognized either of them. They weren't just out-of-towners passing through.

They were Feds. Or at least I was fairly certain. I needed to know for sure. I grabbed my cell phone and launched a web browser. Her name was unique enough, and several news articles quickly populated my screen. I clicked on the most current one—an article about the events at a farm in Kankakee County—and found her picture. *Damn, she was stunning.* Definitely the woman from the diner.

Feds then.

Considering the recent discovery of body parts along Fox Creek, I knew there was only one reason the FBI would be in Cedarwood. The Massey County Sheriff's Department had handed jurisdiction over to the federal government. Either that or the Feds had followed The Russian.

Or both.

Organized Crime flashed in my mind's eye.

I had the utmost confidence in my ability to outsmart and outplay the Massey County authorities and their shoestring budget, but the vast resources of the federal government were a different story. Once upon a time, I'd looked into becoming an FBI agent. I knew from personal experience that the Bureau was far more selective in their hiring than a rural sheriff's office.

The laundry could wait. I needed to get rid of Willow Nowland, and I needed to do it yesterday.

❄

As the muffled hum of a car engine drifted up to Stephanie Gifford's room, she sat bolt upright, clutching the teal and gray comforter to her chest as she struggled to breathe. Her stomach was in knots, and she held perfectly still as she willed away a bout of nausea.

When her father had arrived home, she'd been on the verge of sleep, but the quiet footsteps in the hall had ripped her fully away from the land of dreams. To witness her father collecting her and Kaitlyn's laundry in the middle of the night wasn't unusual, especially when their mom was working a late shift, which she often did.

But when her dad had shut the door behind himself, the first tendrils of sheer panic had sprung to life in Stephanie's chest.

The card. She'd left the FBI agent's card in her sweatshirt pocket.

What would her dad do if he found out she'd spoken to a federal agent while he was gone? Not that Stephanie had even *said* much to the woman, but her dad didn't know that.

She'd hoped and even prayed that he'd toss the hoodie in the washer without checking the pocket, but she knew better.

Maybe I should call that agent.

Her father might have taken the business card down to the laundry room, but Stephanie had stared at the stupid thing for so long she'd memorized every single word and number.

I don't have to tell her anything about Dad. I can just tell her what Kaitlyn told me. Then if Mom or Dad find out, I'll tell them the truth. I was just trying to help. Mom always says that as long as your heart's in the right place, everything will work out in the end, right?

Stephanie was confident her mother would understand, but she was less sure about her father.

With a trembling hand, she pulled her phone from the charger and entered her PIN.

Call if you remember anything. Anything at all, any time of day. The FBI agent's words echoed in Stephanie's mind like a shout through a tunnel.

What would the FBI say when they found out that Stephanie had lied, though? Would she get in trouble?

Thumb hovering above the phone call icon, Stephanie swallowed hard against the bile that threatened to burn its way up the back of her throat.

According to the episodes of *Law & Order: SVU*, Stephanie had only recently been allowed to watch with her mom, lying to the police was referred to as obstruction of justice. Though the detectives in *SVU* wouldn't be eager to go after a teenager who'd withheld information, she couldn't say the same for cops in the real world.

She *had* lied to the FBI. She'd told the agent she didn't know anything about Willow Nowland's disappearance, and that wasn't true.

Stephanie wiped a sweaty palm on her t-shirt, brushed the tears from the corners of her eyes, and stared at the phone in her hand. She tapped the edge of her phone screen to keep the phone from going dark. Indecision stabbed at her heart like a hundred little needles.

All she had to do was set down her phone, snuggle down into her covers, and pretend none of this had ever happened. Tomorrow, the sun would rise, and she'd help her dad with preparations for Thanksgiving dinner while her mom napped. They'd put football on television, and Kaitlyn would ask their dad a billion and one questions about the rules of the sport.

Life would go on. Everything would stay the same. That FBI agent would go back to Chicago, and Willow would just be another picture on the missing persons bulletin board at the grocery store. Days would turn to weeks, weeks to months, and months to years.

The photo of Willow's smiling face would fade, and eventually, the image of another missing person would obscure part of the flyer. Then a new piece of paper would block out another section, and another, until no one saw Willow's face at all. She'd be a footnote. Another young person who'd vanished into thin air.

Stephanie and Kaitlyn would enjoy Thanksgiving and Christmas with their parents and a handful of other relatives, but what about Willow's family? How would her mom and dad handle Thanksgiving without their daughter?

How would Stephanie's mom feel if she or Kaitlyn went missing? If someone else's daughter knew about the incident but didn't come forward?

A new round of tears burned in Stephanie's eyes. Her mom would cry. Her heart would crack. She'd be sad, but she'd never stop searching for her daughter.

Stephanie didn't want to believe that her father could be capable of harming anyone. And maybe he wasn't. But the possibility remained that he knew *something* about Willow.

Dabbing at her cheeks with the sleeve of her t-shirt, Stephanie typed in the FBI agent's number. She swallowed to return the moisture to her mouth. And before she could talk herself out of the decision, she pressed the call button.

While the dial tone filled her ear, part of her hoped the agent wouldn't pick up. Then, at least, Stephanie could say she tried.

Shortly after the second ring, the line clicked to life.

"This is Agent Storm." The woman's voice was crisp, cool, and collected. The exact opposite of the white-hot panic that had invaded every vein in Stephanie's body.

Nevertheless, she cleared her throat. "Hi. This is, um… this is Stephanie Gifford. I don't know if you remember me, but you were at my house earlier, and we talked for a little bit. I'm sorry it's so late, but you said to call any time of day if I remembered anything."

"It's okay, Stephanie." The voice was softer now, more comforting. "I remember you, and I was still awake. Did you remember something? About Willow?"

Stephanie clamped her hand down around the edge of the comforter. "I...kind of."

"Okay. I'm glad you called. Now, I need you to tell me everything."

After taking a very deep breath, Stephanie did.

29

Less than an hour later, Amelia and Zane—along with elite members of the SWAT team—arrived on the perimeter of Dan Gifford's Lake Billsbach cabin. They'd pulled over to the side of the gravel road that led to the property, and they'd shared a pair of binoculars to stare into the gloom while they waited for the rest of the team to surround the cabin.

Though trees loomed thick just beyond the ditch, obstructing the view, two recon teams had already gone in to survey the situation. Their chatter filled Amelia's head as they all moved into placed like the well-oiled machine they were.

Dean Steelman and Sherry Cowen approached, each sporting the same bullet suppression vest as Zane and Amelia. Tension and anticipation radiated off both of them in waves.

Despite the chill night air, sweat had begun to bead against Amelia's skin where her t-shirt was concealed by the lightweight Kevlar. She'd shrugged on a dark-blue jacket with "FBI" emblazoned on the back, though she wished she could forgo the outerwear.

But in the middle of the night, if all hell broke loose, she wanted to make damn sure that everyone knew she was a friendly party. Considering the block letters could be seen from the International Space Station, she figured the coat would serve that purpose.

Clouds blotted out the stars that might have otherwise dotted the night sky, leaving them with only the illumination from flashlights and vehicles. In Chicago, the only comparable darkness came from enclosed spaces. To Amelia, the ruddy glow of the city's lights reflected on a cloudy sky was comforting. The glow served as a reminder she wasn't alone, that she was *home*.

Out here, there was no such reassurance. Chicago was only a few hours north, but she was overcome by the same sense of isolation she'd faced during much of her time overseas in the military.

She shook off the eerie remembrance and turned to face Steelman and Cowen. "Where's McCannon with the warrant?"

Sherry Cowen jerked a thumb over her shoulder. "Just pulled up. The warrant encompasses the entire property and isn't just limited to the cabin, so any garage or shed or other type of storage area is fair game. We aren't permitted to start any excavations just yet, but we've got the all-clear to conduct a thorough search."

Zane checked his service revolver, reassuring himself the sidearm was ready for action. "We haven't heard anything else from Natalie Gifford since the sheriff's department notified her. She and her two daughters are at the house in Cedarwood, but they're being guarded by a couple deputies who're also collecting their statements. Last we heard, she was being cooperative. Powerfully confused but cooperative."

Rubbing her hands together, Sherry nodded. "Good. If Dan Gifford tries to contact them, we ought to know about it right away. We've got a warrant for his arrest too."

Uncertainty nibbled at the edge of Amelia's thoughts. Probable cause for arrest didn't equate to proof beyond a reasonable doubt in a courtroom. Just because they were able to slap a pair of cuffs on Dan Gifford didn't mean any of the charges would stick.

Testimony from a seven-year-old witness, a pile of circumstantial evidence, and a BAU profile did not translate to a guaranteed conviction.

Before the doubts could sink their teeth too deeply into Amelia's mind, Deputy McCannon jogged up to the little gathering. As he came to a stop, he produced the warrant and shot them all a grin. The bobbing flashlight beams and figures of a half-dozen additional deputies closed in at his back.

"Here it is, Agents." McCannon tucked the papers back into the top of his own Kevlar. Unshouldering a matte-black shotgun, he glanced to the other deputies and offered them a crisp nod. "We're ready whenever you are."

Amelia wanted to ask where the hell *her* shotgun was, but she bit her tongue to suppress the smartass remark. Though procurement of the search warrant had taken less than a half hour, they were still closing in on midnight, and she'd been awake since before five that morning.

Caffeine, adrenaline, and spite were her only sources of energy currently. Spite for Dan Gifford and all the sons of bitches like him.

Wolves in sheep's clothing, as the saying went. If he was their killer—and Amelia strongly suspected he was—then he'd not only destroyed the lives of all the young women and men he'd chopped to pieces, but his own family would never be the same after tonight.

Maybe his wife would receive a book deal and a sizable chunk of cash. Perhaps, years down the line, his daughters would be recruited for a documentary about their experiences being raised by a serial killer-slash-human trafficker.

But Daniel Gifford's mark would never go away. His children's children would feel the shame of their grandfather's heinous actions.

Rubbing her forehead, Amelia mentally shook herself. First, the proof. Then, the aftermath.

"We're ready." Zane's decisive tone re-anchored her to reality.

She met his gaze and unsnapped the holster of her Glock nine-mil. "Yeah. We knew from his oldest daughter that Gifford wasn't at the address in Cedarwood and the deputies on the scene there confirmed that. The cabin here has a windowless barn-like structure serving as a garage, according to city blueprints, so we're not going to know if he's home until we knock on the door."

"All right." McCannon turned to the leader of the SWAT team. "What do you need us to do?"

Tristan Reyes frowned. "Stand back until we've secured the building. I'll call you in once we have the situation contained."

McCannon looked disappointed, and Amelia wanted to comfort the young man. Though barging into a building sounded exciting, it was better to leave it to those who were highly trained.

Zane indicated the four agents. "We'll have your six." He zipped up his jacket a little higher, and Amelia couldn't help but wonder how in the hell he was even remotely cold.

Reyes doled out orders to the remaining team while two

CSU vans and a couple ambulances lurked a few miles away, the techs waiting patiently until they were needed.

"Going dark," Reyes said through Amelia's earpiece, and all trace of light disappeared as they started the trek down the gravel road to Dan Gifford's cabin. Aside from the crunch of boots against gravel and the rattling of tree branches overhead, the air was quiet. The crunching echoed a memory from a distant land when she and her squad were moving through what intelligence reports said was an abandoned village. The reports had been wrong...

The silence weighed on Amelia like a lead blanket. No distant wail of sirens, no hum of traffic. Nothing but them, the weather, and the wildlife.

Focus.

She tightened her grasp on the Glock, resting her index finger along the frame of the weapon just above the trigger. Goose bumps prickled her forearms, and the sensation had little to do with the late-night chill.

Though the journey past the slight curve in the road took only a minute or two, Amelia felt as if she'd been walking the same trail for a half hour. Her nerves were wound as tightly as the strings of a poorly tuned guitar. At any second, she fully expected an ambush to swarm down around them before they reached the cabin.

Clenching her jaw, she willed the memories out of her head. She was always struck with the same sense of impending doom when she and her fellow agents approached a potentially dangerous situation. Rather than let the bizarre anxiety control her, she had started to teach herself to harness the paranoia. To make the hyper-awareness work in her favor.

As they approached the covered porch of Dan Gifford's cabin, Amelia noticed a single window glowed faintly, the interior light blotted out by a set of drawn curtains.

Adrenaline coursed at the base of Amelia's scalp.

Gifford was home, after all.

Pausing at the beginning of a short set of stairs, she and Zane exchanged knowing looks. Wooden beams creaked beneath the team's footsteps, and the cry of a night bird drifted over to them.

Deputy McCannon passed the search warrant to Amelia, and they waited as Reyes and his men were in position. And for a beat, the world was completely, utterly still.

Amelia's stomach twisted into knots, her hearing on hyperalert.

The eerie, pseudo-serenity was all wrong. This quaint, single-story cabin, the accompanying chunk of woodland. It was just...*wrong*.

She assured herself that the change of scenery—that going from one of the largest, most populous cities in the United States to the rural Illinois countryside—had thrown her for a mental loop. Like she so often did during raids or high-risk warrants, she was overreacting.

This was the United States of America. This was Small Town, U.S.A., not Baghdad. Not the Afghani desert. They were about to enter a home owned by a single man, not a group of armed insurgents. There weren't landmines in the backyard, or traps attached to doors and light switches.

Dan Gifford was one man. He wasn't a Mexican drug cartel, nor was he a group of radical militants trying to overthrow the government. He wasn't even part of a well-connected Chicago mafia family.

That's all true, but something about this isn't right.

She gritted her teeth. Strong as she was, she was only human, not some comic book superhero. She couldn't shoot webs from her wrists nor climb walls like a spider. She was a paranoid combat vet who went through a predictable onslaught of PTSD whenever she approached a dangerous location.

Reyes nodded to Zane, who moved into position beside the door. The crack of Zane's fist against the wooden door brought her focus back to the present before she could employ her therapist's PTSD trick, the ominous warning clanging in her head.

"Daniel Gifford, open up. This is the Federal Bureau of Investigation." Zane hadn't shouted, but his voice carried. The silence that followed his words was even more complete than the initial spell of stillness.

Amelia's heart knocked against her ribs as she listened for a response. When none came, Reyes moved closer and twisted the knob. The damn thing didn't budge, but it was worth the attempt.

"Why would a man in the middle of nowhere lock his door?" someone muttered from behind her.

"Because he's paranoid, or he's hiding something," Amelia said as Zane knocked again. "This is the FBI, Mr. Gifford. We have a warrant. Open up."

Amelia held her breath as if the gesture would summon a response from Gifford.

Nothing.

Just more branches, and another bird.

When Zane stepped back, a middle-aged SWAT member moved in, a lightweight battering ram in hand.

Reyes held his hand up for a moment in time…then two… before giving the signal.

There wasn't so much as a beat of hesitation before the man swung the battering ram. Metal crashed into the heavy door with a raucous retort, and the crackle of splintering wood followed. A slat of light pierced through the slight opening, and then the door flew open wide upon the second hit.

The team had been briefed to watch for tripwires, and they did just that before rushing into the room. Around the other side of the cabin, another door was breached, and Amelia prayed that team remembered the safety rules as well.

After the team had entered, Amelia swung her weapon to bear and stepped over the threshold. The glow of a floor lamp forced her eyes to quickly adjust, but she was grateful for the illumination.

As she entered the foyer, Amelia noted for the first time the level of luxury housed within the cabin. A vaulted ceiling, a galley kitchen fitted with glittering marble counters, and top-of-the-line stainless-steel appliances. Benches were built into the wall to form a cozy breakfast nook beside a pair of elegant French doors that would have looked out over the woods if the blinds hadn't been drawn.

The spacious living area held an overstuffed sectional, along with a wingback chair to either side of a brick fireplace. The hearth was dark, and based on the unlit logs piled neatly in its center, flames hadn't been stoked recently. The décor was rustic but modern, and Amelia was certain the owner had paid a pretty penny for the furnishings.

Do we have the wrong guy?

At the far end of the room, a loft shadowed the entrance to a hallway. She knew from a cursory glance at the cabin's blueprints that the corridor led to two bedrooms and a second bath.

Zane's eyes met hers, and he gestured toward the living room, advising her he would go left. With a silent nod, she crept toward a doorway on the right. The remaining deputies entered the cabin and set off toward the bedrooms.

After flicking on her mag light, Amelia carefully entered the laundry room, checking each corner for movement. Once she was satisfied that space was empty, she similarly checked a half-bath and then stepped into the breakfast nook.

Taking in the sight of the still kitchen, Amelia brought her Glock up to position when she caught a hint of movement in her periphery. As she jerked her head around to the pair of French doors, she spotted the source...a familiar pair of riding boots visible in the slight opening between the blinds and the floor.

Sherry Cowen's boots. She and Dean Steelman, along with the deputies who'd accompanied them, must have already cleared the backyard.

"Shit." Amelia's surge of anger subsided, though her own voice sounded muffled by her pulse rushing in her ears. She hurried to open the doors, and as the brisk November air rushed past Amelia, she waved Agents Cowen and Steelman inside.

"Clear!" came a voice from the other side of the cabin.

Another man's call came shortly after the first, followed by others up in the open-air loft.

Tentative relief unfurled in Amelia's mind, driven by the realization that her paranoia might have been unfounded. "We're clear here too."

Zane descended a set of steps as the two deputies emerged from the hall.

Lowering his Glock, Zane's eyebrow arched. "Nothing out back?"

Sherry Cowen shook her head. "Nothing so far. McCannon and one of his guys are out around the tree line right now. Trying to see if Gifford was hiding in the woods."

Amelia was as hesitant as Zane to holster her handgun. "No sign that anyone else has been here recently, though."

"McCannon checked the garage." Sherry pulled a pair of vinyl gloves from her pocket. "The side door was unlocked. It fits two cars, and there was only one inside. Could be that Gifford just keeps one vehicle here and drives another."

Steelman frowned. "Might be why the light in here was still on. If he's driving a different car, he might've stopped here before he left. You think his kid tipped him off?"

"Maybe."

Steelman's theory made logical sense, but then where in the hell was Nowland? Where was Gifford? Had he taken Nowland and fled the area? Or was she already dead, her surgically removed body parts strewn around some new location?

The first traces of resignation trickled through Amelia's veins, weighing down her extremities until standing felt like a chore. "What's next?"

As Steelman started to respond, the French doors at their backs burst open to reveal a red-faced Heath McCannon. Anticipation and excitement glittered in his eyes. "You guys aren't going to believe this. We let ourselves into the shed out back, and it's…well, it's not *just* a shed. There's a concrete wall at the back and a door. Not like the front door there, either. This thing's reinforced steel."

McCannon's determined tone sent a much-needed flare of energy into Amelia's tired body. "What the hell is it? A storage room?"

The deputy held both arms out to his sides. "I don't think so. I've seen a setup like this before. My granddad was one of those prepper types, and he stored everything he thought he'd need in a bunker he had built during the height of the Cold War. He hid the door to that thing in a rickety ass shed."

Zane looked as hopeful as Amelia felt. "If that *is* the door to a bunker, then there could be another entrance. It's not listed on the blueprints the county has, so we've got no idea how big it is. Could be like a cellar, or it could be massive."

Reyes had joined them, listening closely. "You're right. My

granddad used to say that if you build a place with only one way in or out, you might as well be locking yourself in a tomb." He beckoned two SWAT members toward them. "I'm going to have you guys comb through the yard for anything that could be a trapdoor, got it?"

The men nodded in unison.

Sherry handed her vinyl gloves to her partner. "This place is big for a cabin, but I don't think it quite warrants all four of us. I'll go help these guys with the search outside."

"All right. Stay sharp out there. We still don't know if Gifford's on the property somewhere." Steelman's sapphire eyes flicked from Amelia to Zane. "Guess it's the three of us in here, then." He focused in on Reyes. "Let us know when you're ready to breach. We'll take another look around here until then."

Though the indoor task seemed cushy at first-blush, Amelia would have rather wandered around in the cold breeze. In here, she was liable to roast beneath her Kevlar. She considered taking off the bullet suppression vest to let her skin breathe, but the paranoid voice in the back of her mind shut down the idea.

Her intuition was something Amelia tried never to ignore.

She caught Reyes as he was about to head outside.

"Be careful," she told him. "You're about to break down a door that might lead to a serial killer human trafficking lair."

She didn't add, *my PTSD thinks that there might be something wrong here, so, you know. Watch your back and stuff.* She thought the SWAT leader probably had some PTSD issues of his own.

He nodded. "Will do."

"And be sure to let us know when you're ready to go inside."

Another nod before he hurried off, Sherry on his heels.

Amelia flexed the fingers of both hands and breathed in to the count of four. "Is it just me, or does something feel off about this right now?"

Steelman's expression turned grim. "I don't know. *If* Gifford's on the property somewhere, then he has to know we're here by now. And if he's here, and he knows we're here, and he *still* hasn't come out with his hands up? Then, yeah. Something doesn't feel right." He checked the cabinets for wires. "Might just be that too many years of this's got me paranoid. It's just as likely he's hiding out in that bunker somewhere, hoping we won't find him."

Amelia doubted that a person as smart as Dan Gifford would utilize such a ridiculous tactic to avoid arrest, but criminals acted in unpredictable ways when they were cornered.

Which was exactly why Amelia was on high alert.

"Like you said, Steelman." Zane pulled on his own set of vinyl gloves. "Stay sharp."

"Always." Steelman gestured to the hallway on the far end of the living area. "I'll take those two bedrooms. See if he doesn't have a hidden door in the back of a closet or something."

Knowing that she wasn't the only one with her hackles raised gave Amelia a renewed sense of purpose. "I'll do the same with the foyer and…" she waved a hand at the breakfast nook. "This side of the house. There could be a trapdoor hidden in the floor."

"Guess that leaves me with the kitchen and the living room." Zane tapped his mini-mag light in an open palm. "Just yell if you find anything."

After Amelia and Dean muttered their affirmations, the three of them split up to attend to their chosen sections of the spacious cabin.

Cautious of not disturbing the scene, Amelia didn't

bother to flick on the overhead fixture as she scoured the half-bath and then the laundry room with her flashlight. Other than the washer and dryer, a few built-in shelves above the appliances and more storage mounted to the far wall, the space was unremarkable. Floors made of smooth ceramic tile, pale blue drywall, and various laundry supplies arranged on shelves. She even went as far as peeking inside the front-loading machines, but as expected, nothing was out of the ordinary.

Mag light trained on the floor, she walked slowly back toward the foyer. A heavy-duty mat rested just inside the door, followed by a longer rug that ended in front of the doorway to the laundry room.

A hatch hidden in plain sight?

She dropped down to a crouch and peered at the hardwood. Shuffling alongside the rug, Amelia examined the floor carefully until she reached the start of the tiled foyer. Aside from the seam that separated hardwood from ceramic, the surface was undisturbed.

Rising to stand, Amelia passed the flashlight around the foyer. A bench ran along one wall, and the other held a handful of coat hooks, most of which were empty. The only garment present, a black parka, was covered in a thin layer of dust. More than likely, it had been in the same location since last winter.

The same was true for a pair of snow boots beneath the bench. Aside from the faint tracks left by her and the others, there were no obvious signs of recent use.

Had Dan Gifford even *been* here in the last month? Did his lamp automatically turn on and off at the same time each night?

"What the fuck?" came Zane's exclamation from the kitchen. The genuine pang of anxiety that underscored his words brought her heartbeat to a rapid crescendo.

Spinning on her heel, she took a swift step toward what she could see of the open-air kitchen before she froze in her tracks.

With both hands raised, Zane stood at the end of the kitchen farthest from the breakfast nook. Recessed lighting illuminated a rich, wooden liquor cabinet behind him, but Amelia hardly registered the sight.

Instead, her attention snapped to a tall man who stood with his back facing her, clutching a handgun.

No, not just clutching a handgun but jamming the barrel into the temple of his captive. Amelia couldn't see the other man's face, but she recognized the chestnut brown of Dean Steelman's hair.

Which meant the man with the pistol and the black canvas jacket was...

Dan Gifford.

Damn.

Adrenaline rushed through Amelia's veins, and she mentally swore as she hurried to the bare drywall beside the coat hooks. Service weapon in hand, she pressed her back flush with the wall, inching forward until she could peek around the side.

"Relax, Dan." Zane's voice was soft and controlled. "Let's talk."

"He was in the damn closet," Dean Steelman said from what sounded like between gritted teeth. "There's a door in there that must lead down to—"

Gifford jammed the handgun harder into the side of Dean's head. "Yeah, thanks. Now that you two are all caught up." Obvious irritability simmered in Gifford's voice, but the man exuded a level of calm unmatched by almost any suspect Amelia had encountered to date.

Christ, this guy really is a psychopath.

If Gifford was this calculated as he held a gun to a federal agent, then what? Was he level-headed because he had a plan, or was this just his usual mode of operation?

Amelia's thoughts whipped through her brain in a hazy whirlwind, processing all the options. Gifford stood to lose everything—his freedom, his wealth, his family, potentially even his *life*...

And he was as calm as if he were waiting in line at the grocery store.

As Amelia turkey-peeked around the wall, Zane's eyes flicked to her for a split-second. Controlling her breathing and heart rate, she offered him a slow nod in return.

Then she watched...waited...for Dan Gifford to slip up.

Her quick assessment confirmed that Gifford was standing behind Dean Steelman, pointing a gun at his temple, the other arm circling the agent's throat.

"Take it easy, Gifford." Zane's hands moved a little higher. "What are you trying to do right now? You know this place is surrounded, right? How do you think you're going to make it out of here?"

Gifford scoffed and backed up another step, dragging Dean backward with him. "I was hoping you'd be able to help me figure that out, Agents." Keys jingled, and Amelia intuited what Gifford would try to do next. "These are Agent Steelman's keys. I'm not stupid enough to think anyone would let me back out of the garage, but me and Steelman look a little bit alike, don't we?"

Zane's mouth was a hard line, but he didn't move. "What's that supposed to mean?"

With a light *click*, Gifford pulled back the hammer of the weapon in his hand and yanked the agent back another couple steps closer to Amelia. "Here's the deal, Agents. I'm going to take this one's jacket, his keys, and his wallet. After that, I'm going to go outside, and I'm going to take his car, and I'm going to drive away. Don't worry about where. Your work is done as soon as I walk out that door."

"You can't honestly think that's going to work?" Steelman's muffled voice was gravelly, and Amelia wondered if he'd taken a blow to the throat.

"I don't know if it will or not, but I guess that's half the fun, isn't it?" Another step. Fifteen feet or less now separated Amelia from Gifford and his hostage.

Think. You've got the element of surprise.

Gifford was calm, but he hadn't hesitated to pull back the hammer of his handgun. If Amelia didn't time her move just right, she had no doubt that Gifford's itchy trigger finger would get to Dean Steelman before she could act.

Her own weapon was in her hands, and she had a clear shot at the back of Gifford's head. But there was no guarantee that the shot would stop at Gifford. If the bullet pierced through their suspect's skull, it would hit Steelman in the head too.

As for a body shot, Amelia couldn't tell if Gifford was clad in a bullet suppression vest. Even if he wasn't, shooting him in the chest carried the same risks as aiming for his head. A through-and-through shot might hit Dean, though she doubted he had removed his Kevlar. But Gifford could pull the trigger before he succumbed to a shot from Amelia.

She patted the pockets of her jeans. Aside from a pocketknife, she had no alternate weapon. If she'd had a longer blade, she could attempt a high-risk maneuver to kill Gifford by piercing the base of his skull. Unless he spotted her before she reached him, in which case, she and Dean would both be as good as dead.

Grating her teeth, she dared another glimpse of Gifford and Dean. By her best estimate, there was less than thirteen feet between them now.

Come on, you son of a bitch. Get a little closer.

Amelia couldn't risk shooting Gifford in the *head*, but she could aim for his hand. A higher caliber weapon would have been preferable to completely disable or even sever the wrist, but a nine-mil was still capable of rendering the hand useless. Especially at close range.

The shot itself would need to be precise, but Amelia had hit smaller targets at longer distances with a Glock. Her service weapon wasn't made for sharp shooting, but it was reliable.

As Gifford heaved a sigh, she ducked back behind the wall. "We're running out of time, Agents. You let me go, and you can just say I overpowered Steelman here and took all his shit. You were busy looking for something, and you didn't even see me leave. Easy. No one gets hurt, and we all live to fight another day."

"Even if that works, how far do you even think you'll make it out there?" Zane's voice had taken on the *let me help you* tone he used in interrogations. "You're wanted by the FBI now, Gifford. You clock an agent and steal his ride, and you'll be in the top ten most wanted before the morning news tomorrow."

Keep him talking. Keep him focused on you.

Amelia rolled her shoulders and breathed in a deep, silent breath. If she missed, or if her shot didn't sever the right nerves in Gifford's wrist, Steelman was dead.

They had an obligation to catch the sick bastard and put him away, but was stopping him now really worth the gamble?

Amelia's stomach twisted. She pictured Willow Nowland's smiling face. Pictured the way Larissa Umber's mother had sobbed when Amelia and Zane had broken the news about her daughter's death. She recalled how Larissa had pulled herself out of a downward spiral. How the young woman was attending college classes, and how she'd scored well on all her assignments and exams so far that semester.

She silently blew out a calming breath and ran through her options. What about Dean Steelman? What if Gifford maintained enough use of his hand to pull the trigger and snuff out Steelman's life?

The agent's death would be on Amelia's hands. Her poor decision-making could potentially doom Dean Steelman to a gruesome fate.

No. I'm a sharpshooter. Don't doubt the shot. Question whether it's the best course of action.

If Gifford fled, they could find him. With the resources of the U.S. Marshals' fugitive recovery team as well as the expertise of the FBI, Gifford's days of freedom would undoubtedly be numbered.

Right?

Or would he slip through their fingers, assume a new identity in a new location, and hunt down another innocent girl? Whether or not Gifford could elude them was debatable, but in the event he went free, the grisly murder of another young woman was inevitable.

There was no guarantee of success, no matter the path Amelia chose.

The only certainty was that she *had* to choose. And she had to choose now.

Releasing another steadying breath, she flexed her fingers against the textured grip of the Glock. Spinning on her foot, she side-stepped from behind the wall and started to bring the handgun to bear.

But the sights never made it to Gifford's arm.

A concussive blast exploded from the backyard, yellow-orange light flaring along the bottom of the French doors. Glass panes rattled in their sills so violently, Amelia was sure they would shatter. Even the floor beneath her feet trembled.

For a beat, her mind slipped back in time.

As the shockwaves from the newest explosion rippled through the cement building, light fixtures swung wildly from side to side. Plumes of dust erupted from newly formed cracks along the ceiling, and Amelia wondered if this was it. If she was about to meet her end not from the bullet of an enemy's rifle, but from the crumbling ceiling of a building that hadn't been meant to withstand direct mortar fire.

The mental imagery was so stark, she swore she could smell the dry desert air and the stench of sulfur.

Her flashback—if that's even what she could call it—lasted only a split second. When her focus returned to the real world, she knew the raucous boom was an explosion.

Zane's wide-eyed stare shifted to the French doors, though in Amelia's mind, the entire world was moving in slow-motion.

Ten feet in front of her, before the rumbling had even receded, Gifford forcefully shoved Dean Steelman to the side. As he cracked the agent across the side of the head with the grip of his handgun, Amelia reflexively backed behind the wall.

He was about to make a break for the door.

No!

Amelia Storm's wrath needed to be sated. This time, at least.

Blood racing through her veins, her attention sharpened to a pinprick as she tracked Gifford's shadow as he hustled toward the foyer. He was moving at just below an outright sprint. Amelia's window of opportunity would be mere seconds, if that.

Despite Gifford's rapid pace, she could have sworn she waited for an eternity, her lungs burning, perspiration beading on her forehead.

The instant his body came into her field of vision, Amelia burst into action.

Sweeping one leg low, she caught Gifford just above the ankles. As he began to totter forward, she tightened her grip on the Glock, arced her arm backward, and swung like she was pitching underhanded in one of the two varsity softball games she'd bothered to attend in high school.

Gifford had started to bring his weapon to bear, but when Amelia's Glock collided with the underside of his chin, the weapon went wide. A single shot ripped through the enclosed foyer, and white chunks of drywall exploded where the slug slammed into the ceiling.

The force of the blow to Gifford's chin reverberated up Amelia's arm as the man plummeted face-first toward the ceramic tile.

At the last possible second, Gifford snapped his elbow out to break the fall. His fingers tightened around the grip of the wood and steel finished handgun, as if he thought to try to turn around and take a shot at Amelia.

She jammed her Glock into the back of his neck before he had the chance.

"Don't move, Gifford. Don't even twitch."

As the ringing in her ears began to subside, she caught Gifford's labored breathing, as well as a few droplets of blood that splashed onto the tile beneath his face.

"Let go of your weapon. Slowly." Her voice was icy and commanding, even to her own ears.

Gifford hesitated, and a lump of dread coalesced in the pit of Amelia's stomach. With memories of Alton Dalessio's refusal to obey her orders so recently engraved in her mind, the last thing she wanted was for Gifford to make one final stand.

Besides, she wanted this bastard to stay alive and let them

know the identities of his victims so that their families could have some semblance of closure.

Millimeter by agonizing millimeter, Gifford relaxed his fingers from where he'd held so tightly to the handgun. As Gifford pulled his hand away, Zane's tall frame threw a shadow over the foyer. Wordlessly, Zane kicked the gun out of his reach.

Cautious relief threaded its way through Amelia's body.

"Daniel Gifford, you're under arrest…"

30

As Dean pushed open one of the two French doors to step out onto the wooden deck, his temple throbbed painfully with each beat of his heart. Gifford's blow hadn't drawn blood, but Dean suspected he'd be stricken with a headache for several days. Cradling the side of his head, he turned his attention to the shed.

His breath caught in his throat.

The acrid stench of burning debris wafted past him on the chilled night breeze. Beams of flashlights bounced as men and women scurried around the perimeter of the smoldering ruin that had once been a shed. A faint, reddish glow pierced through the rubble of crumbled cement and wooden beams —a subterranean fire.

Dread increasing, Dean unsteadily weaved his way down the short set of stairs. He waved urgently to the nearest deputy, a young man who couldn't have been older than thirty. "Hey…" he squinted at the man's name tag, "Jenkins. What happened out here?"

Even in the gloom, Dean didn't miss the haunted shadow in the deputy's eyes. Some called that look the thousand-yard stare. Some referred to it as shellshock. More modern circles had officially labeled it as posttraumatic stress.

The man's Adam's apple bobbed. "There was an explosion. I...I was just outside the shed. I don't know what caused it. I wasn't really close. But...I saw..." Squeezing his eyes closed, the deputy rubbed his forehead. "They're dead. They're all dead. One minute, they were getting ready to breach the door, and the next..."

Clasping the deputy's shoulder, Dean willed some semblance of moisture back to his mouth.

"Did you call in the medics?"

The deputy swallowed again. "Yeah."

Dean nodded, then grimaced as a wave of dizziness assailed him with the movement. "All right. I'll go see what's going on. Just stay back here and have a seat."

With a weak nod, the deputy made his way to the edge of the wooden deck.

The irony of Dean's request wasn't lost on him. Here he was, telling Deputy Jenkins to sit down because he was in shock, all while fighting to keep a series of tremors from completely overtaking his basic motor functions.

Sherry. He needed to find Sherry. She'd volunteered to assist the deputies in their search of the bunker, and according to Jenkins...

They're all dead.

Dean's stomach churned. Ignoring the shouts all around him, he lurched toward the charred remains of the shed. The front of the structure was largely intact, both doors open wide as figures rushed in and out.

They were in the middle of nowhere, and an explosion had caved in the entrance to Dan Gifford's bunker. Based on the slight depression in the ground behind the shed, the blast had done far more damage than met the eye.

Since they'd set out to serve a search warrant, not to raid

a gang stronghold, paramedics, EMS, and the fire department had remained a few miles away on standby with the crime scene techs.

As the beam of Dean's flashlight fell on a familiar brown-and-gold-clad deputy lying on the dusty floor, he couldn't draw breath.

Fresh blood was spattered along Heath McCannon's pale face, glinting in the halo of light. Sherry Cowen knelt at his side, her expression pinched as she pressed a towel to a garish wound on the deputy's neck. Both her hands were covered in crimson as McCannon's heart pushed out blood, and she desperately tried to hold it all back with a makeshift bandage.

Dean didn't think the sight of the poor man could get any worse, but as he took stock of the remainder of McCannon's injuries, he realized how wrong he'd been.

Blood pooled beneath one shredded leg, and a tourniquet tied around the other did little to stem the flow from the stump of ruined flesh just beneath his knee. The tang of iron mixed with the stench of gunpowder. For the first time, Dean realized how much blood stained the cement floor of this little slice of hell. Not just from McCannon, either.

The last time Dean had witnessed this much blood in one place was outside the city of Fallujah in Iraq. He'd been a Marine back then, and the title had made him confident that he was one of the baddest sons of bitches east of the Mississippi.

Until they'd been ambushed. Until he'd watched his best friend from grade school bleed out in his arms.

"Dean?" Sherry's voice was a hoarse croak.

He was grateful to hear his friend speak, but gratitude didn't last long as he returned his focus to the present. "What...happened?"

With tears in her eyes, Sherry pulled her hands away

from the bloodied towel draped over McCannon's neck. "I'm not sure. I didn't see what triggered it. Could've been a tripwire, or it could've been remote or timed. But as soon as they started down those stairs, it detonated."

"Is McCannon...is he?" Dean couldn't bring himself to finish the question. Of the four FBI agents investigating the trail of body parts, Sherry had spent the most time with Heath McCannon.

Sniffling, Sherry pushed to her feet. "Dead. Yeah. Shrapnel hit his carotid. I knew as soon as I saw him, but I had to...to try." She waved a hand at the open doorway to indicate they should leave the shed.

Dean was more than happy to comply. As they stepped back into the breeze, smoke and gunpowder were still present, but the scent of iron was gone. "What about the others?"

Sherry's gaze drifted back to the ruined shed, and she gave a slight shake of her head. "The first and second in line died as soon as the blast went off. The third, well...you just saw him."

He was afraid to ask the next question, but he forced it out into the open anyway. "Any sign of Willow Nowland?"

"No. They didn't get very far down the stairwell, though. She might be down there somewhere, but if she is..." Sherry blew out a very long breath. "I don't know if she's still alive. I think it'll take a while to get down there. That blast seems to have collapsed the whole entrance. What about Gifford? Was he even here?"

"Sure was. The bastard was hiding behind a false wall in a closet, and he jumped out and put a gun to my head. Took my weapon, then marched me out into the living room and used me as a human shield while he tried to talk Palmer into letting him go. Then the explosion happened, and the son of a bitch pistol-whipped me. Just another day in the life of me."

"He *was* here, then? Did he...did he detonate this?"

"No. At least I don't think so. He was too preoccupied turning me into human Kevlar to have a free hand to press a detonator. Whatever was down there had to have been something he'd rigged up ahead of time. My guess is he set a timer before he left. I think he thought he'd be long gone before the explosion went off. We're going to have to wait for the bomb squad to clear the second exit of the bunker to make sure he didn't booby trap that too. Storm read him his Miranda rights, and he hasn't said a word since. He's cooling his heels in the back of a squad car. I think he'll be going to County today, then up to MCC Chicago tomorrow, since it's..." Dean glanced at his fitness tracker and confirmed the date. "Thanksgiving."

"I guess we should be thankful he can't continue his killing spree." She stole a quick glance back at the remnants of the shed where Deputy McCannon lay dead. "Who'll take care of Sir Sniffs?" When no one answered, she growled low in her throat. "I hope Gifford fries."

The distant wail of a siren cut through the smattering of voices. Fire and EMS had arrived more quickly than Dean had expected, but for Heath McCannon, they were too late.

31

Plunking his black duffel bag on the foot of the queen-sized bed, Zane set about the task of double-checking the hotel room to ensure he hadn't forgotten any important items. After the events of the previous night—Dean Steelman's near-fatality, a tripwire that had triggered an explosion right beneath the feet of the first few men who'd breached the door to Gifford's bunker, and the stony silence of Dan Gifford after he'd been tossed in an interrogation room—Zane couldn't wait to return to Chicago.

For the entirety of Natalie Gifford's time in an interview room separate from her husband, the poor woman hadn't stopped crying. She'd come close at one point, but then the Massey County Fire Department and the Peabody bomb squad had cleared the remaining booby traps in the emergency exit to Dan's underground lair.

Though the front-most area was collapsed, the farthest cluster of rooms was mostly unscathed. In one of those rooms, a novice's morgue, the firefighters had found Willow Nowland. By that point, both of her arms had been severed, and much of her blood flushed down a drain.

Zane hadn't had the displeasure of viewing her body, but his imagination had no trouble painting a detailed image that had stuck in his head. A scene too reminiscent of one that still clung to his psyche from his undercover past. Their arrival that night had caught Gifford in the midst of cutting the poor girl apart.

What if they'd arrived earlier? What if they'd found Gifford *before* he'd set the explosives to collapse the front half of his bunker?

Stop it. It's done, and there's nothing we can do now except move forward.

He heaved a sigh and massaged his temples. Two SWAT members and one deputy were dead, and a fourth was in critical condition. Before the incident at the cabin, the forensics team had uncovered the remains of at least two more victims, and they anticipated many more.

The lead forensic archaeologist expected she and her team would be at the location for another couple of weeks, at the least. Her goal was to retrieve the bodies before the cold temperatures made the task of digging nearly impossible.

Once Zane was satisfied he hadn't left behind any personal items, he strode over to the door that separated his and Amelia's rooms. He figured she was as eager to go back home as he was.

Home.

Was that how he viewed Chicago now? He'd only been in the city for about eight months. For nearly three years, he'd lived in Washington, D.C., and he'd *still* never thought of the capital as any sort of real home. All he'd done during his time there was work and lose himself in video games or veg out watching movies.

Suppressing another sigh, he knocked on the doorframe.

"Come in." Amelia's response came right away, but her voice was thick with sleep.

"Hey, are you about ready to..." he stepped over the threshold at the same time Amelia propped herself to sit upright in the bed, "go. I guess I just answered my own question. We've got to leave in the next half hour if we want to make the check-out time."

She rubbed her eyes and yawned. "I'm not going. I'm staying here for another day or two with Steelman to help wrap things up. Gifford's going to be here at least until tomorrow, so we'll get a chance to talk to him again before too much time passes."

A pang of something akin to jealousy stabbed at Zane's stomach. Stuffing both hands into the pockets of his zip-up hoodie, he gingerly took a seat on the edge of the mattress to Amelia's side. "That's kind of...last minute. Why didn't you say anything about it?"

She fidgeted with the edge of the blanket. "Because you and Cowen had already left the sheriff's department when Steelman and I told the sheriff we'd stay to help and to deal with Gifford. I figured you'd be asleep when I got back to the room, so..." She trailed off and lifted a shoulder.

Though he was confident that Amelia's words weren't disingenuous, he was also sure that her choice to prolong her stay in Cedarwood had been driven by more than a random desire to help.

He knew this, but he also knew he could drop the subject. He could wish her the best, grab his duffel bag, and head back to Chicago with Sherry Cowen.

The easy route.

If he never bothered to delve deeper into Amelia's thoughts, then whatever *thing* had developed between them would gradually wither and die. Eventually, one of them—more than likely him—would transfer to a different department or a different field office.

Maybe, years down the line, they'd find one another on

social media. Maybe he'd add her as a friend and then stare at her profile picture and lament what could have been. He'd watch her life from afar as she married, as she posted pictures of herself holding her first kid.

Or he could stop being a baby and talk to her like a fucking adult.

He cleared his throat and shifted to face her. "Something's been bothering you." He didn't need to ask that question. He'd already discerned that there was a weight in the air between them.

Combing the fingers of one hand through her disheveled hair, Amelia dropped her gaze to the comforter.

Slowly, he reached out to brush some of the strands from her face. Her skin was soft and warm as he traced his thumb along her cheekbone. "Tell me, please. I want to help."

With a quiet sniffle, she touched the back of his hand and lifted her chin. "Yeah, I guess something has been bothering me. I just…ever since that night I was staying with you, and I went to show you that revised article that Real Chicago News had written. I opened my laptop, and all this research I'd been doing on Luca Passarelli was still on the screen."

How could he forget that night? The only time he was aware of when Amelia had kept something from him, she'd brushed off a deep dive she'd conducted into a D'Amato capo's background. Before then, he'd noticed how she paid a little extra attention when anyone at the Bureau mentioned the D'Amato family, but he hadn't attributed much meaning to the piqued curiosity.

As one of the two major Italian crime families that called Chicago home, the D'Amatos weren't uninteresting. Their businesses had shifted over into the twenty-first century. No longer did they rely entirely on funds from trafficking copious amounts of heroin or cocaine. Where the rival Leóne family had its hand in various crimes that carried a mandatory minimum sentence in the double-digits, the D'Amatos bought and sold counterfeit designer handbags.

The profit margin was enormous, and the industry of knockoff sales was far less treacherous. A person caught hocking fake Louis Vuitton handbags might be fined or popped with a misdemeanor. That same person selling heroin, however, faced hard time in a federal prison.

He'd assured himself that the D'Amatos' unorthodox business practices were what had drawn Amelia's interest, but on that night, his outlook had been permanently altered.

Whatever the reason for her attachment to the well-entrenched crime family, his instincts told him the connection ran far deeper than professional interest.

"Yeah." Zane's voice was barely above a whisper. "I remember."

He half-expected her to double-down on the evasion she'd offered that night or berate him for prying.

She did neither.

As she squeezed his hand, her eyes met his. "You know I'm hiding something. I tried to tell you that it's not something that defines who I am, and I asked you to trust me, but..." She licked her lips and swallowed. "I can tell that you don't. Not completely. And I can tell that you're...you're *watching* me somehow. Like you're judging me."

He started to respond, but she held up a hand, and the words died on his tongue.

"That sounds harsh, I know. But it's how I feel. Normally I wouldn't give a shit if someone was judging me. I'd roll my eyes and move on with my life. But when it's you...it's different. I care what you think because I care about you."

Taken in any other context, the statement would have washed him in warm fuzzies. But as he peered into the depths of those sad, forest green eyes, his heart broke.

"And then yesterday, when I walked in on you..."

Oh, shit. Here it comes. He fought the compulsion to rub the star tattooed on his shoulder.

"I know what those stars mean, and I know how someone gets them." She tightened her grip on his hand and swiped at the corners of her eyes. "Look, I get that you might not be able to tell me everything. I get that there are things you probably *can't* tell me. But I…I trust you, you know? That if there's anything big, like if you've secretly got a wife and six kids…you'd tell me."

His snort of laughter sounded more akin to a cough. The little snippets of humor Amelia tended to insert into otherwise serious conversations were one of the reasons he'd grown so fond of her.

"No wife. No ex-wife, and no kids, unless someone's keeping a really big secret from me." He winced at his semi-sarcastic remark. "Sorry. That made me sound like a creeper, didn't it?"

To his relief, Amelia's lips curved into the slightest smile. "No, not really. I didn't exactly think you'd been committed to a life of chastity. You're not a monk or a priest."

"No. No, I'm not." In truth, after high school, he'd only come remotely close to a real long-term relationship once. He'd spent so much of his adult life pretending to be someone else that he'd forgotten such a thing was even possible.

As the room lapsed into silence, Amelia worried at her bottom lip. Being vulnerable wasn't a trait that came naturally to Zane, and he'd learned over the course of his and Amelia's friendship that she shared that characteristic.

Rather than prod her to reveal what had plagued her mind as of late, he rested his hand on her shoulder and waited.

She pulled the comforter up over her lap and traced the shape of a dark green leaf printed on the fabric. He came close to mentioning that she might not want to touch the comforter without gloves or a black light.

Best not to know what happened in this room before their arrival. And even better not to think of how he wished he and Amelia could leave their own evidence of lovemaking on this bed.

He shook away the thoughts. They were having an important conversation. He couldn't risk deflecting with humor or desire.

"I guess," Amelia's voice held so much vulnerability that it tugged at Zane's heart, "it feels to me like I'm trusting you, but you aren't reciprocating. Almost like you've been judging me for keeping a secret when you have so many of your own. I mean, I don't know anything about you after all the middle and high school stories you've told me. You've worked for the Bureau for more than ten years, but you've never told me anything about what you did. About the cases you've had in the past, or the people you worked with."

A pang of anxiety wedged itself into Zane's thoughts. He was under orders from the CIA to reveal none of the details of his tenure as a covert operative, and the Agency had even covered for him—in conjunction with the FBI—to make it seem as if he'd worked for the Bureau for the past thirteen years.

But they didn't provide him fake stories to tell. They didn't give him a list of acceptable activities to regale to his close friends or a rundown of how to fill in all those years he'd spent in Russia.

Sure, he could claim he'd worked undercover for the FBI, but he couldn't expect a fellow special agent to believe he'd spent a decade behind enemy lines. There was no SAC in their right mind who'd ever authorize such a high-risk, lengthy endeavor.

What did he tell her, then?

The truth. Or at least as much of it as he was able.

"I'm sorry, Amelia. You're right. I've been a hypocrite, and that's part of what's been making me so...*distant*, if that's the right word." He squeezed her shoulder where his hand was resting and rubbed his eyes with his other hand. "There's a lot about my past, about my *life*, that I can't tell you. And when that whole thing with your search into Luca Passarelli happened, my knee-jerk reaction was to be suspicious. Mistrustful. And I unconsciously put distance between me and you. But I knew, deep down, that I was being a jackass."

Her gaze met his in a silent bid for him to continue. The sincerity in her expression, coupled with her diligent attentiveness, lessened the stranglehold of trepidation that had threatened to consume him.

"I can't expect you to trust me without returning the favor. Navigating interpersonal relationships isn't something I've ever been very good at. Not that it's an excuse, but more of an explanation." He dropped his hands into his lap and stared at them, unable to meet her gaze.

"Trust is hard," she said quietly. "But it's worth it if you find the right person."

His heart seemed to stutter. Did she mean him? He couldn't say for sure, but he *wanted* her to be referring to him.

If you want her to trust you, then you have to stop acting like a petulant child and return the damn favor.

He peered into her eyes and managed a wistful smile. "Thank you, Amelia."

She wrinkled her nose. "Thank me? For what?"

"I know that wasn't easy for you to bring up, so thank you for being the adult in this relationship and bringing it up anyway. I'll do better, for you and for myself. I promise."

Leaning forward, she slid both arms around him and rested her cheek on his shoulder. "I'll see you in a couple days."

He returned the embrace and pulled the warmth of her body closer to his. If he'd been given the opportunity, he'd have held her like that for hours. After what had happened at Dan Gifford's cabin, he was sure both of them could use the hit of oxytocin.

The moments passed by in silence, but the quiet wasn't awkward or uncomfortable. It was peaceful.

But Zane was running on about three hours of sleep, and his eyelids soon felt as if they were weighted.

Rubbing Amelia's upper arm, he buried his nose in her hair and kissed her head. "All right. I need to leave before I fall asleep."

I'd rather lay down at your side and drift off holding you in my arms. But there was still a massive workload ahead of them.

Amelia tightened her grasp around him and yawned. "And I need to sleep. There's an ATF agent heading down here in a few hours. Figured I'd try to get a few hours of sleep before they get here."

He pushed to his feet and smoothed out the front of his sweatshirt. "Get some sleep. Let me know when you and Steelman get back out to the cabin, okay?"

"Okay." She looked like she was going to say something else, then settled on, "Drive safe."

"I will. Talk to you soon."

As Zane turned to go pick up his bag, his body was weary, but his heart was lighter.

Maybe he had hope for a real life after all.

32

Amelia set her phone on the edge of her apartment's granite breakfast bar and made her way to the living room window. Like her old place, her new residence was located on the second story and gave her a view of the building's entrance. She loved the open floorplan. Between her previous apartment and her new one, she knew she could never go back to living somewhere she couldn't see the television from the kitchen.

In fact, the ability to watch a show or movie while cooking had reduced her takeout ordering by at least half since she'd moved back to Chicago.

Parting the semi-sheer curtains and the blinds, Amelia peered down to the surface parking lot. She missed the view of a grassy courtyard instead of a patch of worn concrete and the front of another apartment building, but alas. She *didn't* miss the knowledge that a stalker had broken into her place and planted hidden cameras throughout each room.

A shudder worked its way down her spine at the thought. The working assumption was that Glenn Kantowski—the woman who'd assassinated Ben Storey and then tried to frame Amelia for the crime—had situated the tiny cameras with the intent to spy on Amelia's daily routine.

Amelia wasn't convinced.

Why in the hell would Glenn have *needed* to know what Amelia did when she was inside? Especially inside her shower. She shivered at what the crime team had found inside the showerhead after a secondary search.

Sure, more robust knowledge of her prey's regular activities wasn't *un*helpful, but what exactly had Glenn gained with such a high-risk maneuver?

But if the culprit wasn't Glenn, then it begged the question…who?

Only one name came to Amelia's mind.

Joseph Larson.

A supposed fellow agent, a manipulative son of a bitch, and a former friend who'd come within a hair's breadth of raping her. The thought of the near miss made her stomach clench even now, almost three months later.

I need to report that bastard before he gets promoted. But who will believe my word versus his?

Shaking off the unpleasant thoughts, Amelia shifted her attention to a familiar silver Acura. Zane emerged a moment later, balancing a white box in one hand as he elbowed the driver's side door closed.

Amelia rubbed her chin in thought as she walked over to the buzzer in the foyer. As far as she recalled, her and Zane's plan for the night was to celebrate Daniel Gifford's swift plea arrangement and subsequent sentence to life without parole by ordering pizza.

That morning, Amelia and Zane, along with Dean Steelman and Sherry Cowen, had sat in a courtroom as a federal judge formally handed down Dan Gifford's sentence. The process had been fast—far quicker than any of them had anticipated.

Amelia and Dean had stayed behind to help the Massey County Sheriff's Department with the aftermath of the explosion that had killed three deputies and critically injured one other. However, they'd not been permitted to access the bunker until the Peabody bomb squad and the fire marshal had declared the area safe to traverse.

By the time they tailed the CSU down to the veritable house of horrors, the crime scene was already contaminated. Gifford's electronics were scorched and soaked, his office area partially covered with rubble, and the so-called "murder room" littered with debris from a shattered wall. The only room that had survived was Gifford's amateur morgue, but virtually every surface—save the silver table on which Willow Nowland's dismembered body had lain—was spotless.

Their hopes had been low in those first few hours. Though there was no doubt Gifford would serve the rest of his life in prison for his role in the murder of three law enforcement officials, Amelia and Dean had been determined to find answers for the countless grieving families who'd suffered at Gifford's hand.

But amidst the ruins, there had been no viable evidence. Not until Zack Anders had sifted through the pile of broken cement and debris that covered nearly half of Gifford's office.

Beneath the rubble, Anders unearthed a file cabinet. The top drawer was caved in by the slab of concrete that had slammed into it, but the bottom two were more or less intact.

Lo and behold, when the crime scene techs had popped the lock on the bottom-most drawer, they'd discovered an unscathed laptop.

Apparently, Gifford had been so preoccupied with chopping up Willow Nowland's body that he'd forgotten to deal with the data on his computer. And when the FBI's tech team had gotten ahold of the laptop, they'd discovered a damn gold mine.

Dating back thirteen years, Gifford had recorded the violent deaths of each of the victims. What had come as a surprise to Amelia and the rest of the agents assigned to the case, Gifford had not admitted to killing any of them himself. Instead, he claimed he kidnapped the victims and held them captive for buyers from all over the world. He used the dark web to communicate with his buyers, who obviously wanted to leave no trace of their transactions.

All the information of Gifford's one-man trafficking ring had been handed over to Cyber Crimes, and so far, five of Gifford's clients had been apprehended. Among them was a Fortune 500 CEO, the son and heir of a billionaire real estate mogul, and a Russian mafia commander named Yuri Antonov. The video evidence Dan had was damning, to say the least. Whatever sick fetish the man had about viewing the brutal assaults had come back to bite him and every one of his clients in the proverbial ass.

Analysis of the trace evidence in Willow Nowland's car was the nail in the coffin for Dan. In the driver's seat of the little Civic, the CSU had lifted samples of glitter. To the layperson, sparkles didn't seem like a noteworthy discovery.

To Amelia, however, the little flecks of silver told a story. When Gifford and his youngest daughter had stopped at the Cedarwood Gas 'N Go, the little girl had been clad in a colorful, sparkly dress courtesy of her recent dance recital.

A microscopic examination confirmed that the glitter in Nowland's car was a match to Kaitlyn Gifford's dress. Cassandra Halcott and her boss, the U.S. Attorney, had leveraged the digital and physical evidence against Gifford to persuade him to provide the identities of every victim *and* every buyer. They'd also forced him to release the exact locations of each burial site so the victims' families could have some closure, not that Dan cared about that. What mattered to him was the number of years they'd take away from his sentence in exchange for the information.

Gifford had complied, and he'd pled no-contest to a laundry list of crimes.

Jocelyn Boeldt, whose skull the forensic archaeologist had recovered from the Fox Creek dig site, was Gifford's first victim, according to the video records and Dan's taped confession. Amelia suspected that Gifford had killed before Jocelyn, but they'd likely never know for sure.

The man whose femur had been recovered was Nick Durant. Nick had been a medical student at the University of Wisconsin when he'd crossed paths with Dan Gifford. Though Nick wasn't the only male who Gifford had abducted for his twisted clients, the majority of the victims were female, young, and pretty.

In the end, the tally came to thirty-nine victims and seventeen different perpetrators. Even though the FBI was in the midst of a potentially lengthy ongoing investigation, Dan Gifford was a household name across the state of Illinois.

Law enforcement agencies had tried to minimize his media exposure for fear of retaliation by one of his clients, but they'd not had much success. Natalie Gifford—now Natalie Newham—and her daughters had been under near-constant surveillance for their own protection, and Dan Gifford had spent the duration of his prison stay under protective custody.

News circles merely referred to Gifford as The Fox Creek Butcher, and due to the investigation's ongoing status, few details had been released.

Amelia blinked away the split-second recollection of the past seventeen days.

After spending a week and a half mired in nothing but death, Amelia and Zane had decided to use Gifford's official sentencing as an excuse for a sliver of positivity. That morning, they'd settled on pizza, possibly a drink or two, and a superhero movie marathon.

A gift exchange hadn't been on the menu.

Amelia's palms grew damp as she struggled to recall whether or not she'd missed an important date. She and Zane had finally rid themselves of the bizarre cloud that had shadowed their friendship for the better part of a month. The last thing Amelia wanted was to return to the dark ages because she'd spaced on a crucial piece of information.

Were we supposed to trade Christmas presents early? Was there a gift exchange at work that I forgot about? Shit...when is Zane's birthday?

She shifted her weight from one foot to another, desperately racking her brain for an answer.

March. His birthday wasn't until March.

The Organized Crime Division of their office *had* set up a Secret Santa, but Amelia had elected not to participate. With her luck, she'd have drawn Joseph's name.

Her sister-in-law, Joanna, had told her recently—as she was applying the newest balayage to Amelia's hair—about a website that would send literal shit to a person of the buyer's choosing.

As she buzzed Zane into the secured building, she ran through one last desperate attempt to ensure she hadn't forgotten anything. Her mind had been so consumed with the follow-up work on the Gifford case that she would've been liable to forget what month it was if there weren't decorations strung throughout the entire city.

Turning the deadbolt, she cracked open the door. The light *pat-pat* of paws followed almost immediately, and she stuck out her leg to block Hup from trying to squeeze through the opening.

I need to get his nails trimmed.

She gave the cat a gentle shove with her stocking foot. "No. You're not going out there."

Plopping down on her haunches, Hup meowed in response.

Zane's gaze shifted to the long-haired calico as he slid through the narrow opening in the door. "You don't want to go out there, Hup. Trust me, it's cold and windy."

Flashing the cat a matter-of-fact glance, Amelia pushed the door closed behind Zane. She waited for her friend to discard his black coat and shoes before she ushered him out of the foyer.

Now came the moment of truth. After all her anxious worry, she'd find out what in the hell she'd forgotten. "What's with the box?"

A smile crept to his face as he set the square box on the granite bar. Resting a hand over the top of the white cardboard, he turned to her. "In a second. Business first, okay?"

Amelia didn't know what in the hell the cryptic remark meant, but she nodded anyway.

As soon as Zane's good humor had appeared, the look vanished. "I finally had a chance to talk to Spencer today, a little bit after you left the office."

Amelia's anxiety returned in a rush. Shit. She'd tried like hell to forget about the conversation she'd overheard between Joseph Larson and his girlfriend two weeks earlier. She swallowed past the tightness in her throat. "What'd he say?"

Blowing out a sigh, Zane leaned heavily on the breakfast bar. "Said he's stepping down. SAC Keaton will be announcing it within the next week. I guess the leadership role and the office politics just weren't working for him. The role was stressful in ways he hadn't expected. He misses being in the trenches with us and plans to rejoin us once they've found his replacement."

Amelia's heart dropped down into her stomach. "Does he have any thoughts on who the frontrunner is for the position?"

Zane merely clenched his jaw, but the silence was all the answer Amelia needed.

"It's Larson, isn't it?"

He rubbed his temple, his gray eyes clouded with worry. "Yeah. That's what he's thinking."

Suddenly deflated, Amelia fought the urge to crawl over to the sectional couch and curl into a ball. "I've been thinking about transferring to Violent Crimes…but still." She tugged on a piece of blonde-tipped hair and bit her lip to keep her voice steady. "It still won't get me away from him. And if he's an SSA…"

Zane's touch was cool against her flushed cheek. "If you want to move to VC, then do it. I know you're sick of being shot at by the mob, right?"

His gentle tone and the sarcastic observation lifted a little of the impending doom from her shoulders. "I am. And serial killers are…interesting. They're so much different than hitmen and drug traffickers, you know?"

He grinned. "*Interesting* isn't quite the word I'd have picked. More like 'fucking disturbing,' but, to each their own."

Laughter bubbled from Amelia's lips. "You're not wrong. But two things can be true."

He pulled back his hand and tipped an invisible hat to her, and Amelia realized she lamented the absence of his touch. She knew the increased physical contact wasn't all in her imagination. Though she wanted to know where all these sweet gestures were headed, she didn't want to risk opening her mouth and ruining it.

"Are you going to tell me what's in the box now?"

He flashed her another show-stopping smile. "I'm glad

you asked. You remember that café we went to for lunch a few weeks ago? The one with the bakery that sold cupcakes with cat ears?"

Her eyes nearly rolled back in her head at the memory. She'd never tasted anything so good. "I remember how I ate one of them and then went back to buy three more, yes."

With a flick of his wrist, Zane opened the top of the box to reveal the coconut and caramel frosting of a German chocolate cake. "I know I'm over a month late, but happy birthday. Being late by so much meant one or even *four* cupcakes would never suffice."

Amelia opened her mouth to reply, but he pressed a finger to her lips.

"And just so you know." His eyes locked onto hers, and her heart pounded in her chest. "I am fully prepared to let you eat the entire cake."

Despite her jitters, Amelia didn't miss a beat. "That was exactly what I was about to ask you."

Chuckling, he pulled out his phone and set the device on the counter. "There was one other thing too. I thought about just surprising you with it, but I figured that might be weird, considering all the planning we'd have to do."

Amelia's curiosity was piqued. "What's that?"

He tapped his index finger against the granite beside his phone. Zane didn't have many tells, but the tapping was one. "You're always so…nice, and attentive when I'm yammering on about snowboarding and skiing trips I've taken with my family and my friends. And I also know you've never done any of that, so…" He shoved a hand through his sandy hair. "I thought maybe, since it's almost officially winter, that might be something we could do. A thirtieth birthday present, you know? Other than the cake."

"Like…a vacation?" She mentally berated herself for the stupid question. Of course that's what he meant.

He held up both hands. "Unless you don't want to. If that's not your thing, we can do something else. Or I can get you an oil change, or…something."

Biting her tongue to keep from laughing, she did her best to feign pensiveness. "Hmm…an oil change, or a skiing vacation? That's a tough choice."

"Hey, you drive a BMW, and those things can be a pain in the ass to maintain, okay?" He took a step back. "But, really, if that's too much, or if it's too…I don't know, too *intimate*, then we don't have to. I can buy you a subscription to the cake-of-the-month club instead."

Awash in a wave of contentment, Amelia stepped forward and threw her arms around his shoulders. His offer was generous, but more than anything, the proposed gift was heartfelt. Hell, he'd even remembered her favorite type of cake—no small feat considering how often she professed her love for desserts.

He circled an arm around her waist and pulled her body flush with his.

Every nerve in her body hummed with anticipation. This wasn't a platonic hug. She could feel the rapid cadence of his heartbeat through his hooded sweatshirt, and she loved it.

Inch by inch, she tilted her head back to peer into his eyes. As much as she wanted to give voice to the litany of thoughts whipping through her mind, she doubted she was capable of forming a coherent sentence.

Rather than stumble over her words, Amelia's eyelids drooped, and she leaned in to press her lips against his. As he combed his fingers through her hair, the outside world fell away, leaving only them. Only this moment.

At least until Zane's phone buzzed against the granite. His body immediately tensed. He pulled away from the drawn-out kiss, his rush of breath warm on her cheek. "I can ignore it."

Yes.

She dismissed her knee-jerk response. Resting both hands on his shoulders, she pulled away and offered him a smile. "It's okay. It might be work. Besides, this is my apartment. I'm not going anywhere."

He chuckled slowly, not missing the leer in her voice, stepped back, and scooped up his cell before it could vibrate a third time. "Palmer."

A tinny voice responded, and Zane's countenance fell.

He raked his fingers through his hair. "Where?"

Amelia tried to decipher the response, but she only made out a couple words—one she thought might have been *Michigan*, and the other was *carved*.

"Okay. Storm and I will be there as soon as we can." With a sigh, he pulled the phone from his ear and pressed the screen to end the call.

"Work?"

"Yeah. That was Spencer. The CPD just fished a body out of Lake Michigan. The homicide detective on the scene said the vic's throat was slit so deep he could see the spine."

A sickening chill invaded Amelia's scalp, her sudden rush of desire all but forgotten. She dreaded the answer to her next question, but she had to know. "What landed it in our jurisdiction?"

Zane rubbed his face. "The victim was an informant of Fiona's. Lars Poteracki. And since she transferred to the Portland office a few months ago…"

Special Agent Fiona Donahue had been working undercover when her cover was blown and she was captured and nearly killed, suffering a concussion and numerous broken bones. She took some time off to heal, and after the case was resolved, she transferred to a field office on the other side of the country.

Amelia completed Zane's sentence. "Spencer called you.

Shit. I remember the case. That guy helped us put away a drug trafficker who'd been pushing heroin for the cartels and the Leónes."

"Right. And they haven't gotten a close look yet, but they believe there's a message carved in his skin."

Is this mob retaliation? Why now? Since when does the mob carve words into their vics?

Amelia looked at the cake with longing before settling her gaze back on the man she longed for even more. They wouldn't get answers standing in her apartment.

"We should go."

He nodded. "Our celebration will have to wait."

They had a killer to catch.

The End
To be continued...

Thank you for reading.
All of the Amelia Storm Series books can be found on Amazon.

ACKNOWLEDGMENTS

How does one properly thank everyone involved in taking a dream and making it a reality? Here goes.

In addition to our families, whose unending support provided the foundation for us to find the time and energy to put these thoughts on paper, we want to thank the editors who polished our words and made them shine.

Many thanks to our publisher for risking taking on two newbies and giving us the confidence to become bona fide authors.

More than anyone, we want to thank you, our readers, for clicking on a couple of nobodies and sharing your most important asset, your time, with this book. We hope with all our hearts we made it worthwhile.

Much love,
Mary & Amy

ABOUT THE AUTHOR

Mary Stone lives among the majestic Blue Ridge Mountains of East Tennessee with her two dogs, four cats, a couple of energetic boys, and a very patient husband.

As a young girl, she would go to bed every night, wondering what type of creature might be lurking underneath. It wasn't until she was older that she learned that the creatures she needed to most fear were human.

Today, she creates vivid stories with courageous, strong heroines and dastardly villains. She invites you to enter her world of serial killers, FBI agents but never damsels in distress. Her female characters can handle themselves, going toe-to-toe with any male character, protagonist or antagonist.

Discover more about Mary Stone on her website.
www.authormarystone.com

Amy Wilson

Having spent her adult life in the heart of Atlanta, her upbringing near the Great Lakes always seems to slip into her writing. After several years as a vet tech, she has dreams of going back to school to be a veterinarian but it seems another dream of hers has come true first. Writing a novel.

Animals and books have always been her favorite things, in addition to her husband, who wanted her to have it all. He's the reason she has time to write. Their two teenage boys fill the rest of her time and help her take care of the mini zoo that now fills their home with laughter...and yes, the occasional poop.

Connect with Mary Online

- facebook.com/authormarystone
- goodreads.com/AuthorMaryStone
- bookbub.com/profile/3378576590
- pinterest.com/MaryStoneAuthor
- instagram.com/marystone_author